Love Beyond Repair

Love Beyond Repair

Lyn Ellerbe

Acknowledgements

To all the youth and leaders that serve their communities through service and repair projects—thank you.

To my family, thanks for the patience, for the humor, and for your willingness to serve others in need.

1

"You should be thankful."

The late afternoon sun gave the quiet landscape a surreal look. Eva Conley would normally appreciate the beauty but today her focus was on the directions coming from her navigation system. She took a deep breath as she strained to pick out street signs in the waning light. The keys to her new home were awaiting her final signature on the deed papers at the property management office.

Flashing headlights and a honking horn interrupted her concentration. A late model truck was inches from her back bumper. Eva could see the man in her rear-view mirror, his gestures letting her know he questioned her driving abilities.

"Someone's in a hurry," Eva muttered softly.

As they reached the outskirts of the town, a passing lane appeared and the truck swerved into the oncoming lane. The driver, who was so impatient seconds before, slowed long enough to glare at Eva as he passed.

Imagining red glowing eyes behind the mirrored glasses, Eva saluted him with her best fake smile. His frown deepened before he whipped in front of her and sped off. She laughed and waved in response. A glance into the back seat confirmed that her passenger was still snoozing, so she didn't have to explain her childishness.

Ten minutes later, Eva pulled into the strip mall that housed the management company. Although it was past closing time, an older woman waved from the window as Eva parked her car. The realtor gave her a 'thumbs up' sign when Eva pointed to her sleeping passenger. Across the parking lot, a red vehicle caught her eye.

Great. Mr. Impatient is here.

Using the hood of her car as a temporary desk, she signed the papers and received the keys within a few minutes.

"Welcome to the community!" The realtor's distinctive British accent hinted at her Jamaican roots. With true Southern charm, the realtor gave Eva a hug. A slamming car door interrupted the introduction.

"Now, learn how to drive." The voice behind her needed no introduction.

Eva lowered her sunglasses to cover her eyes before turning to face the rude man. Thoughts raced through her mind. The box in the back seat hid her passenger from view and she hoped he was still asleep. Any interaction between the two males was not what she needed right now.

"Excuse me?" Making no effort to hide her false sweetness, she smiled into the mirrored eyes. Her own eyes, and much of her features, were covered by her oversized shades—a present from her favorite four-year-old. "Are you part of the Unwelcome Committee?" The realtor quickly squelched a laugh.

"You should be thankful that your lollygagging didn't prevent me from getting my bid in on time." The man waved papers under Eva's nose. "If I had lost this property because you drive like a senior citizen, you most certainly would've been 'welcomed' by me."

"I'm sorry." Sarcasm dripped sweetly from her lips.

Eva's chin rose, as did a slim eyebrow above her dark sunglasses. "I didn't realize a lack of time management on your part meant a necessity for speed on mine."

She resisted the urge to slam her door and instead slipped into her car after thanking the realtor who was now laughing outright.

2

"How old are you?"

Air compressors and hammers invaded Eva's semi-conscious dreams at six in the morning. She groaned as she glanced at the clock and pulled the covers over her head. The movement evoked a squeak from the air mattress that was serving as her temporary bed.

When the noise outside didn't recede, Eva sighed and rolled out of bed. She lifted one corner of the extra set of sheets that were serving as makeshift curtains and saw a crew of workers already busy at work.

Glancing up the oak-lined street, Eva saw neglected houses alongside newly renovated properties. The older central Florida neighborhood was part of the targeted renewal in the community. Local governments had responded to the influx in the area by offering incentives to builders. She knew the house next door was under renovation, but she hadn't expected work would begin so early—or so loudly.

As she slipped on sweatpants and a t-shirt, Eva listened for the sounds from the kitchen. Jonah should've been up by now, considering the amount of time he had slept on the trip. It was unusual that he hadn't bounded into her room as he usually did each morning. When she walked into the kitchen to make coffee, she found four-year old Jonah, standing on a box at the front window intent on the activity next door.

"Mommy! There's a truck in our yard! It's red!"

Eva joined her son. She recognized the truck in her driveway. *Either God has a sense of humor or there was a sale on red trucks and every male in the community has one,* she thought. Hoping for the latter, she stifled a groan.

Most of her possessions were arriving later today with her parents so she'd been able to park her car in the garage last night. The workers most likely thought the house was still unoccupied. She decided to address the imposition later, after a cup of coffee.

"Come eat breakfast, Jonah." Eva poured a cup of orange juice and set out his favorite cereal. For herself she settled on a banana and a piece of wheat toast.

"Can we go say hello to those guys?" Jonah asked between sloppy spoonfuls of cereal.

"Well, we'll need to find one of them to move the pretty red truck for us if we're going to go to the store this afternoon." Eva had planned to work in their small backyard this morning, knowing it would be easier to keep her active son occupied outside. Now she was wondering how much work she'd get done while trying to keep Jonah away from the temptations next door.

"I'll go ask them!" Jonah wiggled off the stool.

"Oh, no you won't!" Eva grabbed him before he could head out the front door. "After you unpack your boxes we're going to work in the yard, remember? Grandma and Grandpa will be here this afternoon. If the red truck is still there, I'll let you ask them to move it so we can go out to lunch before they get here. Sound like a plan?"

Jonah's grandmother has wisely suggested that his toys be one of the few items Eva brought with her. Unpacking his toys and putting them on the built-in shelves under his window occupied the active four-year-old for over an hour. By nine o'clock mother and son were in the backyard, cleaning out the neglected flowerbeds. Eva knew her new home was a recent renovation but the investment company that bought it from the builder hadn't maintained the backyard or bothered to do any landscaping in the front.

Even though it was mid-January, the weatherman said the temperature would be above normal today, reaching the mid-seventies by noon. Eva was glad she would be able to get the yard work out of the way early. Of course, she hadn't intended it to be this early. By ten o'clock, she was ready for a break. A pile of bricks in the corner of the yard claimed Jonah's attention for most of the morning and Eva stopped to admire the magnificent structure that resembled a rocket ship. Leaving him to his creation, she carried the yard tools to the side yard to wash them off.

"Are your parents home?" The man jumped out of the way as a startled Eva turned with hose still in hand. "Hey! It was just a simple question. No need to soak me!"

"Sorry. You surprised me." Eva dropped the hose and turned off the spigot. "What was the question?"

"Are your parents home?" The dark-haired man shielded his eyes from the sun as he took a step closer.

She recognized him immediately, even without the mirrored sunglasses, but wasn't surprised that he didn't realize who she was. Yesterday she'd been dressed like an adult, wearing stylish ankle boots, a jean skirt, and flattering floral blouse. Today her outfit made her look like a middle school girl. Having her hair pulled into a ponytail only added to the illusion.

"My parents?" Eva frowned up at him in confusion. His question wasn't the only thing that confused her. *No man has a right to have such beautiful eyes,* she thought.

As the man stepped into the shadow of her house, his light blue eyes widened. Eva saw the dawning recognition.

"You!"

"Yes, me," she said, hoping her voice didn't reflect the fog his proximity had caused.

"How old are you?" Just under average height, Eva's slender frame, along with her freckles, made her look younger than her years. Eva knew she wasn't a striking beauty, but his calm head-to-toe perusal of her was irritating. True, he was good-looking, but why did all handsome men have to be so arrogant? Deciding to return the favor, she let her eyes trail up his frame, keeping one slender eyebrow raised in the process. Dark jeans were paired with a striped buttoned-down shirt. He was just above average height but seemed taller or more authoritative somehow.

"Did you skip school a lot, or just that one class?" Eva crossed her arms as she faced her interrogator.

"What?" He blinked at her.

"You seemed to have missed an important class and I was wondering if your delinquency was habitual or just a one-time thing."

"Class? What the heck are you talking about?"

"The class on etiquette. The one where they teach men not to ask a woman her age."

He was still speechless, so Eva decided to address his earlier misconception in hopes that he would leave her alone.

"As far as my parents being home, no, they're on their way here, not that it's any of your business. Now if you'll excuse me, I need to get these tools cleaned up so I can go to the store." She started to walk away but caught sight of the red vehicle that had haunted her nightmares but had fascinated her son. "By the way, could you get your truck out of my driveway so I can get out of my garage? I'm sure you have somewhere to be—in a hurry."

Had she waited before heading inside, she would have

seen a montage of responses cross the face of her blue-eyed interrogator. Reid Jackson, owner of a well-respected construction company, was chagrined at her daring to return his perusal, shocked at being dismissed so rudely, and angry again at her antics of last evening. It was obvious that Reid's anger won the fight as he spun away. It was only at the prompting of his foreman that he did move his truck.

An hour later Eva checked the driveway. The red truck was gone. Glad that she could avoid facing the unpleasant intruder again, she backed the car out of the driveway. *Too bad good looks didn't automatically translate into good manners*, she thought. The man's dark, close-cropped hair was reminiscent of the military styles she was familiar with from growing up near an Air Force base. Thinking of his icy blue eyes and how they had raked her form when she confronted his rudeness caused her to blush. *How dare he!* Good looking or not, he was rude.

After their trip to the hardware megastore, Eva and Jonah grabbed burgers and fries at a take-out window. Her parents would be arriving soon with her meager belongings that had fit into the smallest of the available rental vans. She was hopeful they could get everything unloaded before nightfall.

Back at home, Jonah paced the front porch until he spotted the yellow van.

"They're here!" He darted for the door, waving wildly. Eva followed at a saner pace. She noticed the site next door was empty now and smiled to herself. Being able to introduce Mr. Arrogant to her parents would've been priceless.

After Jonah led her parents on a tour of the house, the unloading of the van commenced. Eva's brother and sister-in-law had purchased a new sofa as a house-warming gift. Delivery was scheduled for late afternoon, so the three adults worked to get the other large pieces in place first.

8

The recliner handed down from a family friend was the most difficult, since the bed frames were in separate pieces, and the mattresses weren't heavy. Jonah had inherited her chest of drawers and Eva hoped to find an inexpensive dresser at a thrift store to round out her bedroom furnishings. For now, her clothes would have to stay in boxes and suitcases.

After the sofa arrived and the van was empty, Eva and her mom unpacked the kitchen boxes while Jonah accompanied Grandpa to pick up pizza for dinner.

"Are you going to be okay if your father and I leave after church tomorrow?" Mrs. Conley asked as she placed the last of the cups on the freshly lined kitchen cabinet shelf.

Christine Conley had retired last spring from thirty years of teaching elementary school. Eva's dad was a software consultant, himself semi-retired and able to work from home almost exclusively. Their relatively free schedule meant they could travel at will. After they left Eva's they planned to stop at home for a couple of nights before heading north to see their son Derek.

Derek Conley was several years older than Eva but the siblings were very close. He had been disappointed that he couldn't help with her move, but Eva assured him that staying home with his pregnant wife Mariella was more important. The couple was expecting their second child and doctors had put the young Mrs. Conley on a restricted schedule due to minor complications.

"I think so," Eva said. "Although I'm glad I have a couple days before my job starts so Jonah and I can get settled in." The assistant librarian position at the local university was her dream job. A great benefits package, including onsite childcare for Jonah and a kindergarten program he could join next fall, made the decision easy. "Hopefully Jonah will make some friends at school and church."

"And you, too," her mother added.

"Subtle, Mom." Eva knew her parents were concerned about her single state, but for now Eva chose to concentrate on raising Jonah. The image of steely blue eyes flashed through her mind, challenging her concentration.

3

"Can we be friends?"

Waking the next morning in a new home was disconcerting but getting an energetic four-year-old ready for church kept her mind occupied. Eva knew tomorrow would be even more surreal since her parents wouldn't be five minutes away at a local hotel.

The pastor at her home church had recommended the small suburban church they would visit today. Eva had been impressed with the number of activities listed on their website, especially those aimed at single parents and children.

Midway through the service, the pastor dismissed the children to their Children's Church classes. Jonah tugged his mom along, following the trail of kids out of the sanctuary. Her son being a new student meant Eva needed to sign him in and let the teachers know of any allergies or other issues.

"I'm Shelley Andrews." The class teacher introduced herself to Eva after first greeting Jonah and filling out a nametag for him. "Is this your first visit?"

"Yes," Eva said. *It might be our last, though.* The sight of Mr. Unwelcome Wagon and his red truck leaving the church parking lot this morning had been disappointing.

11

"We just moved to town. On Friday." Eva smiled at the friendly young woman who appeared to be close to her own age. Seeing that Jonah had already joined a group playing with a set of cars and blocks on the area rug, she added, "Thankfully my son Jonah isn't shy or afraid of new situations."

After church, Shelley helped Eva gather Jonah's papers—a difficult task since he was intent on explaining the entire lesson and all his activities while saying goodbye to his new friends.

"My son, Bryce, is the same age and they got along well today." She pointed to the young dark-haired boy in the corner. "We should get them together sometime."

"It will be a few days before we get settled in." Eva decided to leave her answer as vague as possible, thinking again of looking for a second church option. Preferably one without a red truck in the parking lot. "Thank you, though."

Unlike Jonah, Eva wasn't as anxious to make friends. Eva's hesitation was well founded. After graduate school Eva spent a couple of years at a large city library before returning to her small hometown—with a son and no wedding ring. The whispered questions and poorly hidden judgment that followed her and Jonah around town had made the last couple of years frustrating. Choosing to move away from her parents had been difficult, but Eva felt it would ultimately be best for both herself and her son.

Excitement for the new chapter in her life was tempered by having to explain—or as she chose to operate, to *not* explain—Jonah's presence. *Either they accept us or they don't. End of story.*

Later that afternoon Eva planted flowers while Jonah explored their yard. Landscaping was high on her priority list, knowing it would increase the curb appeal, since so many properties on the street were under construction or in bad need of repair.

Her parents had left right after lunch and now she wished she had the additional backup. Keeping Jonah off the chain link fence and out of the yard next door was going to be a chore. He discovered all sorts of treasures in the backyard and kept up a steady commentary.

"Where's the red truck? Where are the guys? When will they be back? Can we be friends?" The barrage of questions came as Jonah dragged a branch along the fence separating the two properties. Knowing he didn't expect an answer to each question, Eva let her thoughts wander to her encounters with Blue Eyes. *I really need to find out his name,* she thought. *Then again, why would I? It's not like I'm going to see him all the time.*

That evening, the exhausting day was over at last, and Jonah was finally winding down.

"So how was your day, sweetheart?" Eva asked her tired son as she tucked him in. "Did you have fun?"

"I liked Bryce." His new friend from church had obviously made a positive impression. "He said I can come over and play sometime."

"We'll see," Eva said, then steered the conversation to a different topic. "Should we go pick out some more flowers and plants for the yard tomorrow?"

"Flowers are for girls." The sleepy comment came as Jonah's heavy eyelids shut, offering Eva the day's first minutes of peace and quiet. She offered up a prayer as she readied herself for bed.

Father, thank you for an easy day in our new home. Please guide me as I make decisions and protect us as we meet new people. After meeting my neighbor yesterday, I am thankful we met for Shelley and Bryce. Help me be less pessimistic about our welcome here and help me be willing to make friends so that I don't hold my son back from making friends.

Monday dawned cold but sunny. Empty boxes occupied Jonah, so Eva was able to get the rest of her possessions put away. Internet and television would be connected today, hopefully before noon as promised.

The red truck was next door when the last of the installers left. Eva wanted to finish her landscaping but didn't want to risk another confrontation. Seeing that it was creeping towards late afternoon she decided to be brave. Avoiding Mr. Rudeness was easy. Resisting the urge to glance next door was not.

An hour later, the departure of the red truck interrupted her productivity. Its driver nodded curtly to Eva as he pulled away. She ignored him but Jonah did not. Eva frowned as the contractor grinned and returned her son's exuberant wave.

Her son was still chattering about his new friend as Eva faced her greatest challenge of the day. Jonah's day had consisted of covering himself head to toe in dirt, so two baths were required to remove the grime. The four-year-old was quite proud of the dirt ring around the tub after the first round of bathing.

At dinnertime Eva set Jonah on a stool at the kitchen island with bowls of chopped peppers, tomatoes, and olives. The eager helper carefully poured the contents of each small bowl into the large bowl of cooked pasta. She stirred the creation while Jonah squeezed in the Italian dressing. After retrieving the garlic bread from under the broiler, she joined him at the island.

"Yummy, right?" Jonah asked around a mouthful of salad.

"Yes, dear."

"Can we go outside tomorrow?" Jonah asked when she tucked him in later. "I want to finish my fort." The brick structure begun earlier, which she thought was a spaceship, apparently had a new design. "Maybe those guys next door will be back. They can help me build my fort."

The thought of 'those guys next door' was not as

exciting to Eva as it was for her son.

Fortunately for Eva, Tuesday's weather provided a reprieve. Steady rain meant a day indoors, and it also kept the workers next door away. Jonah's disappointment evaporated when Eva uncovered a box that contained his train set. The quiet day gave her the chance to reflect a bit after the whirlwind of the last few days. The prospect of being on her own had been exciting and still was for the most part. But as she settled in for the night, a red truck and arrogant grin invaded her thoughts, making her realize how unnerving parts of this adventure were going to be.

4

"You're so clever."

Wednesday proved to be sunny but not as warm. Eva made Jonah wait until late morning before heading outside. At least most of the puddles would be dry she hoped. Trimming the overgrown bushes at the back of the yard meant she ended up quite muddy herself by lunchtime. She made sure to keep her back to the house so she would lessen the chance of Sir Rudesby startling her. The fact that she had already given two different nicknames to a man she hadn't officially met, was one she pushed to the denial file in her mind.

"Hola, Señora." An older man approached her from the worksite next door. He pulled off his work gloves and extended his hand. "I am Javier Menendez. Welcome to the neighborhood."

"Gracias, Javier." Eva smiled at the kind greeting, not bothering to correct his assumption of her marital status. "I'm Eva, and the little boy covered in mud in the back yard is Jonah."

"Mr. Reid wanted me to tell you that if you need anything, just ask and I will do what I can to help." Javier helped her wash off the last of her tools as he made his offer.

"Mr. Reid?" Eva asked, but knew instinctively that Javier was talking about her nemesis. "Is that the man who drives the red truck?"

"Yes, and he will apologize for parking in your driveway, too. I hope," Javier said. "We did not know that you had moved in already."

"I appreciate the offer, Javier," Eva said, "although I'm sure Mr. Reid said no such thing. He and I have already met. You are kind to cover for him." Javier's grin confirmed her statement.

"Mommy, mommy, mommy!" Jonah came around the corner with a treasure in need of sharing. It was an earthworm, about six inches long, wiggling desperately to be set free. "I found a worm! It's humongous!"

"Lovely." Eva bent down and observed her son's offering. "He is quite outstanding, but I'm thinking we should let him scoot back underground."

"Aw, you're no fun." Jonah's disappointment brought a smile to Javier's face.

"Actually, Mr. Jonah, I'm sure your mom is right. I'll bet your worm's family is wondering where he went flying off to." Javier had bent down to Jonah's level and was admiring the wiggling creature. "Of course, he'll have a wonderful story to tell them when he gets back."

"You really think so?" He turned to his new friend, eyes wide. The thought of the worm's family and flying adventure stories were novel ideas to the youngster.

"Yes, I do," Javier said. "My name is Javier. But you can call me Javy. All my friends do."

"Javy? I like that name. I'm Jonah. Like the Bible story. But I like worms better than whales."

"Let's go put your worm friend back close to his home, okay?" Javy followed Jonah to the brick structure, which was now apparently a castle.

After she put the garden tools away, she joined them in

time to hear Jonah's explanation of his grand plans for the moat that would surround the castle.

"If my mom'll let me." It was clear Jonah wasn't optimistic that his mother would agree to his scheme.

"I'm sure Javy wants to get back to work, Jonah," Eva said. "Thank him for helping you with your worm, and then we need to try to find your skin under the mud you seem to have rolled around in."

"Thank you, Javy," Jonah said obediently. "Can you come over tomorrow and play?"

"You get to start school tomorrow, Jonah, remember?" Eva tried to rescue the older man from the obligation to entertain her son. "I'm sure we'll see him again." She walked with Javier back toward his worksite.

"Your son is delightful," Javy said. "Reid and I are serious about the offer. Please let me know if you need anything."

"Thank you, I will," Eva said, touched by his sincerity.

Another bath time adventure kept Eva busy for an hour. After setting her still damp son on the front porch with a peanut butter and jelly sandwich so he could watch the workers next door, Eva poured herself a diet soda and joined him. *Maybe this won't be so bad after all. At least I can deal with Javy and not Mr. Reid Whatever-his-name-is.*

Returning indoors to answer a phone call from her parents, she missed the arrival of the red truck. From her vantage point in the living room, she could keep an eye on her son's auburn head, so she knew he was still where she left him. Feeling confident in his staying put she refilled her drink before returning to the porch. When she saw a man on the porch with her son, she almost dropped the drink she had just poured.

"May I help you?" Eva hoped her voice conveyed authority and not the nervousness she felt facing Javier's Mr. Reid.

"The mail carrier put your mail in the wrong box. I'm guessing this is you." The blue eyes glanced at the stack of mail, shuffling through it. "Eva Marie Conley?"

"Yes, that's me. Thank you for *my* mail." Eva placed a slight emphasis on the pronoun, wanting him to know she didn't appreciate his interference.

"Ah, E.M.C. Like Einstein." Reid handed her the stack. "Interesting."

"Oh my." Eva responded, placing a hand over her mouth in mock surprise. "I've never heard that one before. You're so clever. Shall I call you Sherlock? Or Captain?"

"Captain?"

"Yes." She smiled. "Captain Obvious."

"Touché." He nodded, and then offered his hand to Jonah. "My name is Reid. You must be Jonah. It's nice to finally meet you. Javy told me about your castle."

"Do you want to see it?" Jonah hopped off his chair and grabbed his new friend's hand.

"Sure! Lead on, oh Captain!" He shot a broad grin toward Eva. "If it's okay with your mom, that is."

Eva leveled a look at the man, who had yet to introduce himself to her. *That is underhanded, using my son's affections against me.*

"You've had your bath already, so don't get muddy again young man." Eva directed her words toward Jonah, but held Reid's gaze as she spoke, raised eyebrows expressing her warning.

"Yes, ma'am." Reid saluted. As he passed her, following Jonah through the house, he added in a whisper. "But I haven't actually had my bath yet."

She heard him laugh at her as the pair trudged across the yard. *Hopefully he won't be around here all the time.*

5

"Calm down."

The university was a ten-minute drive from the house. Eva and her dad had timed it out weeks ago when they had come to town to look for homes. Even with morning traffic, it would take less than fifteen minutes to get to work since most commuters would be headed in the opposite direction. Still, anxious to be on time for her first day, Eva was handing Jonah his new lunch box a full hour before she needed to be on campus.

I'll sit in the parking lot if we're too early. Eva's friends and family wouldn't be surprised that she was over-prepared this morning. Control freak would be a mild description for her attention to detail. The thought of being late to an important appointment could send her into panic mode.

"Are you ready, buddy?" Eva opened the door from the laundry room into the garage, balancing Jonah's backpack in one hand and her satchel in the other. She used her shoulder to hit the garage door button, and as sunlight streamed into the dimness, Jonah caught sight of the red vehicle at the end of the driveway.

"Reid's here!" Jonah's level of excitement matched Eva's level of annoyance. She had given up getting her son to call him 'Mr. Reid.' The stubborn man had insisted 'Mr. Reid' wasn't what his friends called him.

20

"You've got to be kidding!" After tossing her bag into the front seat, she handed Jonah his backpack. "Stay right there." She pointed to the back of the car when she realized he had followed her as she stormed out of the garage.

Considering her heels, she glanced at the still damp yard and chose the sidewalk path as she marched on the enemy. Reid was standing with Javy on the porch next door.

"Really? Can you please not block my driveway?" She stood at the end of the walkway, pointing to the offending vehicle.

Reid turned toward her, one dark eyebrow raised. He turned slowly back to Javy.

"*La Señora está enojada. Tal vez sea el pelo rojo.*" Reid handed the clipboard to his foreman. Eva saw Javier glance around Reid's lean form. She dropped a stoic mask into place, deciding it was better for neither of the men to know she understood the insult.

Yes, I'm mad, and no it has nothing to do with my red hair and everything to do with your red truck, she wanted to yell, but resisted.

"Good morning, Einstein." Reid strolled down the walkway. "In a hurry today are we?" Instead of heading to his truck, he joined Jonah who was waiting patiently for his mom.

"Reid! I got a new backpack and a Superman lunchbox!" Jonah offered his treasures for Reid to admire.

"Nice! I'm jealous," Reid said as he lifted the small boy up to his eye level. "Have fun today, okay?" Jonah was grinning from ear to ear. Eva watched in stunned silence as the man strapped her son into his car seat, completely ignoring her request to remove his truck.

"Are you going to move your truck or can I just bump it out of the way?" Eva found her voice as she leaned into the car to check the straps on the car seat.

"Calm down," Reid closed the car door when she

finished her inspection. "I didn't realize you'd be leaving so early and I didn't expect to be here more than a few minutes. I humbly apologize for the inconvenience." He bowed. Eva resisted stomping her foot and instead simply walked around to the driver's side.

Forcing herself to pull out of the driveway in control of her emotions, she waved at Javy as they drove away. As she glanced back, she saw the older man shaking his head at his boss's grin.

Despite the day's initial trauma, Eva's first day at work went smoothly. The college semester had begun several weeks earlier, and many students were now busy with their first research papers. Paperwork and familiarizing herself with the office protocols occupied most of her day. At lunch, she walked across campus to check on Jonah. He waved at her from the picnic table where he was busy with some new friends.

"He's doing fine." The day care teacher assured her that Jonah had jumped right into the activities and had already made some friends. "He's a delightful little boy."

At five o'clock, Eva and her delightful son were pulling out of the university's library parking lot. Jonah had talked nonstop since she had picked him up. The boundless energy of childhood still amazed her at times. Her feet, shoulders and back were sore, and her brain hurt, but his genuine joy managed to cheer her up as they drove home.

Turning into their new neighborhood, the thought of facing Mr. Reid—whatever his name is—again made her spirits sink. She planned to pull all the way into the garage and not offer Jonah the chance to visit his new friends next door.

That Jonah was also on the lookout for Reid was evident as they turned the corner.

"Reid's not here." His sigh was so forlorn, Eva was torn between relief and feeling sad for her son.

"I'm sure Mr. Reid has lots of important things to do. We probably won't see him every day," she said. *Thank goodness.*

An hour later, the pair was enjoying a simple dinner of spaghetti and meatballs. Eva had meals planned for two weeks in advance, and many were already prepared and in the freezer. It would mean one less thing she had to worry about every afternoon.

They were discussing Jonah's day and his new friends at preschool when the doorbell rang. Jonah scrambled down from the swivel stool before Eva could stop him.

"It's Javy!" The trusting child opened the door to reveal the smiling face of the older Latino man. It was a welcome sight for Eva.

"Come in, Javier," she said.

"No, Miss Eva," he said. "My shoes are too dirty. I was just checking to see how your day went."

Eva and Jonah joined him on the front porch. She invited the older man to join her on the swing her dad had installed before he left. The boy was now nestled between them.

"It was fine, despite the rough start. I hope I wasn't too much of a shrew this morning. I just panicked at the thought of being late on my first day. I suppose I should apologize to your boss."

"No, Mr. Reid Jackson should apologize to you and I told him so," Javy said as he let Jonah play with his all-in-one tool, keeping a close eye on the boy's attempts to open it. "What he said was rude, but I think you know that."

"Yes, I did understand what he said." She smiled. "Does he know that I know?"

Javy laughed. "No, I did not feel it was my place to tell him. He is a good man, but his tongue will get him in trouble as I have warned him many times."

"Will he be here a lot?" She tried to sound nonchalant.

"I need to know if I should park on the street." She knew Javy wasn't the culprit here, so she grinned and added, "Or perhaps I should park in your driveway?"

"As entertaining as that would be, I think Reid will remember not to block your driveway anymore," Javy said as he stood. "He has several other properties right now, so I don't expect him here a lot. We have things under control."

"He's a very busy man, it seems. I hope our moving in hasn't made his life more difficult. Please assure him we'll stay out of his way."

"Yes, he is busy. Too busy, I think," Javy said as he opened the screen door. "Mrs. Michelle agrees with me, I'm sure." He slipped the fascinating tool back into his shirt pocket and ruffled Jonah's dark red curls. "You two are a welcome addition to our life here. Perhaps this weekend you can come over and meet the rest of the crew."

Mr. Reid is married. Poor woman, Eva thought.

6

"I don't need another one."

Friday afternoon Javier invited them over to meet the rest of the crew. Jonah was an instant celebrity, getting to check out all the work inside and out. Eva followed her son, making sure he didn't disturb any of the work in progress. The house's layout was a mirror image of hers, but the design choices gave it a completely different look. Her kitchen cabinets and countertops were light oak and taupe gray granite. Darker wood floors in this house matched the darker palette of the kitchen. Javy saw her perusal and answered her unspoken question.

"Knowing most of these houses are the same layout Reid is choosing colors that are different than what the other builders are using. It may mean he won't be able to sell this house as fast, but he wanted to take the risk."

"Mommy, mommy, mommy!" Jonah started to interrupt their conversation but fell silent when Eva lifted one finger.

"Yes, Jonah?" Eva turned to her son who was struggling to contain his excitement.

"Manuel says I can help them paint tomorrow!" Her son was tugging the hand of a younger man as he came back into the kitchen after a trip outside.

"That sounds like a marvelous plan," Eva said. "And by

25

marvelous plan, I mean not a good idea at all."

"Aw, Mommy. Please?" Jonah threw his arms around her knees. Eva's resolve wavered.

"Miss Eva, we're just priming the *back* of the shed tomorrow," Manuel assured her. "Jonah won't be in the way at all and will be a big help."

"Are you sure?" Eva glanced from the younger man to Javy. The foreman's nod and wide grin assured her. The width of his smile was outdone by Jonah's as the boy realized his mom had agreed to his plans.

Instead of sleeping in on Saturday, as she had planned, Eva was up by seven, having promised her son to get him up as soon as the workers arrived next door. The cool evenings meant leaving the windows open at night was an option, so she heard them pull in at six thirty.

Except for an occasional check in on her son next door, Eva had the morning to herself. By noon she had finished her to do list and decided to make cookies for the crew next door.

As she rounded the corner with her tray of goodies, a terrifying sight greeted her. Perched on the edge of the roof next door, flanked by Reid and Manuel, was her four-year-old son.

"Jonah!" Eva dropped the cookies and scrambled up the ladder. When she reached the top, she was shaking. Furious eyes turned on Reid. "What were you thinking?"

"Relax, woman." Reid waved her down a step and swung Jonah onto the top rung. He held onto the boy until she had him safely within reach of the ground. The ranch style house had a roofline that was lower than a typical home, so her saner side knew her son wasn't in real danger. That fact did not calm her fury.

"Go inside, Jonah." Her tone made her son scramble toward their house. Eva spun back to Reid, who had now joined her on the ground. "Relax? Are you crazy?"

"He was in no danger. You're overreacting." His ridicule angered her even more.

"Overreacting? I am not overreacting. You're arrogant, patronizing, and have no idea how to deal with a child. Stay out of our lives."

"Gladly. I don't need a boss. Or another mom."

"Good, since I've got my hands full with my own four-year-old. I don't need another one!"

She found Jonah face down on his bed, his small form wracked with sobs.

"Jonah, sweetie, I'm not mad at you." She rubbed his back. "Come here, buddy. I've got some cookies in the kitchen." *The rest are on the ground outside, of course.*

Jonah snuggled into her lap, his tears finally quieting. "You were yelling. You were mad."

"I know I was, but I was mad at Reid, not you. It was very dangerous for you to be up on the roof, and he shouldn't have taken you up there without asking me."

"He said you'd be mad. I guess he was right." Jonah wiped his tears and, typical of a child's recovery abilities, turned his attention to cookies. His exit from the bedroom left Eva alone to contemplate dealing with Mr. Reid Jackson. *I probably should cool down first.*

An hour later, her time to cool down ran out when the doorbell rang. Jonah was in his room, building a fort with the empty moving boxes, so Eva dropped the dishtowel on the countertop. Seeing Reid through the front window, she steeled her nerves as she opened the door.

"I've come to return your tray and thank you for the cookies. They miraculously survived their precipitous tumble and all managed to land on the tray. They were delicious."

"You're welcome." Eva took the tray from him and started to close the door.

"I need to apologize." His hand prevented its closing.

"Go ahead." She folded her arms across the tray, which was now acting as a shield. She saw his jaw clench.

"I shouldn't have taken Jonah onto the roof without telling you first."

"Telling me? Don't you mean without *asking* me?" She tossed the tray onto an end table and reached once again to close the door. "If that's your idea of an apology, I guess it will have to suffice. Good day, Mr. Jackson."

"Wait." A booted foot stopped the slamming door. "I just wanted to make sure Jonah wasn't being punished. Will he be sent to his room without dinner or have you devised something more treacherous?"

"You think this is funny?" Eva pushed against Reid's chest as he stepped inside. "I know you think I'm overreacting but Jonah is *my* son. Not anyone else's." Watching him feign surprise confirmed what she had suspected for a few days. "Don't pretend you don't know I'm a single mom. I know Jonah told you he doesn't have a Daddy."

Up to this point their heated words were quiet enough not to disturb Jonah. Eva no longer cared.

"I see the hamster wheel turning in your head." She shoved past him and opened the door he had just closed. "As endearing as your curiosity is, I would suggest you don't ask questions you don't want the answer to. Knowing my history, which could be as tainted as you imagine, might only confirm your rationalization for disliking me. As you said earlier, you don't need another mom. For myself, I don't need another judge."

"Don't presume you know what I'm thinking, Ms. Conley," Reid said, his voice holding a small warning.

"Don't presume I care what you think, Mr. Jackson," Eva said as she slammed the door.

7

"I plead the fifth."

A quiet two weeks followed as Reid avoided the worksite and Eva only let Jonah outside if the infamous truck was not in sight. Exhausted from the week at work dealing with procrastinating college students facing midterm paper deadlines, meant Eva was looking forward to takeout pizza and a silly movie. Today had been a half day at work, so she and Jonah were going to unwind at the park in the middle of their small town before picking up dinner. Her car tire had other plans.

The animosity towards Mr. Reid Jackson that had started to wane—mainly due to his absence—resurfaced in an instant. Taking a flat tire off for the third time in two weeks meant she had the routine down to a choreographed dance. Jonah, kicking his small soccer ball against the side of the house, was the first to spot Reid.

"Reid!" Jonah kicked the ball toward his favorite contractor. "Our tire is flat again!"

Eva came out of the garage to glare at her least favorite contractor.

"Is there a problem?" Reid followed her into the garage.

Although she hadn't spoken to him since the ladder incident, the memory of his half-hearted apology still rankled. She didn't bother to hide her annoyance.

"No, not at all." Eva wiped off her hands after leaning the offending tire against the car. She grabbed the pile of roofing nails she had on the tool table and held them out to him. "Would you like these back? Only three have come out of my tires, the others Jonah found in the street."

"You know how to plug a tire?" Reid put the nails back on the table and grabbed the tire.

"Yes, don't you?" Eva's frustration made it difficult for her to control her tongue. "I don't need your help."

"Come help me, Jonah." Reid ignored her as he let the boy roll the tire out to the driveway. Jonah followed the man's instructions without question.

Arms crossed, Eva watched from the shadows as the two males plugged the hole in less time than it would have taken her to gather the supplies. *Not that I'd ever admit that*, she thought.

"Thank you." Eva handed Reid a towel to wipe his hands. "Jonah, go inside and wash your hands so we can go to the park."

"You don't like me very much, do you?" Reid's forthright question brought a blush to Eva's cheeks.

"No. I don't." She was embarrassed that she hadn't hidden her opinion of him very well, especially in front of her son, and the realization made her defensive.

"Well, don't worry your pretty little red head. The feeling is mutual."

Eva stepped back, bumping into the back of her car.

"You're ornery, and border on being a waspish shrew. Your hair belies your temperament," he said. "Which is why I prefer brunettes."

"How dare you!" She gasped.

"Me? You've done nothing but attack me since you moved in, but I guess it was to be expected." He shrugged. "You know what they say about gingers." His reference,

30

from a lowbrow animated show that was popular but extremely crude, was familiar to her.

"Somehow your taste, or lack of it, in television viewing doesn't surprise me." She turned away, muttering under her breath. "Typical."

"Don't assume that's what I was talking about. You know what they say about assuming," Reid said, not bothering to hide a smirk. "Perhaps I was referring to the idea that *'those with red hair find it easier to be bad than good.'*"

His words stopped her angry retreat. Surprise and disbelief registered on her face. Redheads, especially those who liked to read, knew most famous literary quotes that referenced their fiery hair.

"What?" Reid took a step toward her but stopped when she put up her hands in defense. He tossed the towel onto the bench behind her. "I see you're familiar with Miss Anne and the famous Green Gables. Because I choose to work with my hands for a living, did you think I was too dumb to know any classic literature?"

"Those are your words, not mine." Anger made her voice stronger.

"You think I'm an idiot?" His arms crossed but he didn't advance any closer.

"I plead the fifth."

"I see we've changed subjects. Is that your attempt to confuse me? So, you also think I'm not smart enough to know the Constitution?"

"It's the Bill of Rights, not the Constitution." Her chin rose. "Now that we've covered genetics, literature, and political science, did you want to move on to Calculus? Or perhaps Psychology?"

The sound of the door behind her cut short their conversation. The two adults stood in silent standoff until the four-year-old intervened. Jonah scooted inbetween them, his clean hands held up for inspection.

"I got all the dirt off, Mommy. I'm all done!"

"So am I," Reid said. "See you later, Jonah."

***

Whether it was guilt or just physical fatigue, Reid was late getting to church on Sunday morning. He didn't make it to the early service so opted to slip into the back of the later one. When the youngsters headed to their classes, he decided to check on his sister who had teaching duties today. He had wrestled with regret all weekend, knowing his words to the neighborhood newcomer had been ruthless. Self-reflection had done nothing to reveal why he reacted to Ms. Eva Marie Conley so strongly. As he turned the corner in the children's wing, he had to face his guilt—literally.

"You!" His thoughts had taken human form.

"Me, yes." Eva stared at him. "Please tell me you're just visiting today. Jonah really likes his class and his teacher. I'd hate to have to find another church so soon."

"I'm sorry." Reid reached for her hand as she pushed past him, and then smiled in surprise when she didn't try to pull away. "I was a boor and said some very terrible, untrue things. I'll understand if you don't forgive me, but please don't change churches on my account. I normally come to the early service, but my bad behavior kept me from a good night's sleep for several days and I didn't get up in time."

"I'm confused. Do you want forgiveness or are you blaming me for your lack of sleep?"

She's not a shrew but she sure is uptight, he thought.

"Again, I'm sorry," he said. "Whether you forgive me or not, I'll sleep better tonight."

Down the hallway, Shelley Andrews had been watching the interchange, and her interest grew when she saw Reid's dejected stance after Eva walked away. Her curiosity about any and all of his relationships wasn't new.

"What was that about? How do you know Eva?" Shelley

asked when Reid finally made it to the classroom door.

"None of your business, Sis," Reid said, tweaking her nose. Deciding to listen to the sermon on the radio from his car instead of risking seeing Eva again this morning, he waved to Jonah and Bryce.

8

"She should be in time out."

Having a fully accredited and award-winning Early Elementary Education program necessitated an extensive children's book section in the college's library. Jonah's class had visited today and their teacher allowed them all to check out two books. Her son insisted on carrying his selections to the car instead of putting them in his backpack. Eva had a large bag full of her own choices. She had waited to get her first couple of weeks behind her before checking out any books for her own personal reading.

It had been a typical Friday, except for the preschool visit. Thinking that by the end of her second week she would've gotten used to the aching feet, Eva was disappointed that her legs were screaming their complaints. High heels were not her normal choice for footwear, but she had decided today to try out the fancy pair her mom had talked her into buying. The salesman's insistence that they were "as comfortable as wearing slippers," was a wild exaggeration. She had spent the day trying to not trip or twist an ankle.

As they pulled into the cul-de-sac, a red truck taunted her.

"Reid's here!" His mom did not share Jonah's excitement. Gathering his discarded book bag, her own bag full of reading material and her purse, Eva walked around the car to undo Jonah's straps. Seconds later, she was sprawled on her driveway. The humiliation was more devastating than the injury, or so she thought until she tried to get up.

"So, Grace, are you trying out for the university's gymnastics team?" Reid's humor only added to her distress.

I'll never hear the end of it if he sees me crying, she thought, and bit her lip to hide her pain.

Reid knelt beside her and straightened out her leg. Warm hands ran down her calf before he unstrapped the offending footwear.

"I'm fine." She batted his hands away. "If you will just move, I'll get up."

"I don't think so, Princess. You twisted that ankle pretty well." He pressed the tender area with unexpected gentleness. "Does this hurt?"

"No." She grimaced.

"Liar." He moved the bags out of the way. "Hey, Jonah. Are you doing all right there, buddy? Your mom was practicing her circus tricks out here, so I'm going to take her inside first, okay?"

Jonah had recently moved to a larger car seat and could get out of the safety device himself. Javy joined them as Reid unceremoniously lifted Eva into his arms.

"Put me down!" Eva's frantic whisper only made Reid grin wider as he carried her to the house. He set her down on the patio chair and took her purse from Javy. Rifling through it to find her keys earned him more admonishment. "Smart men don't go through women's purses."

"I never claimed to be smart," he said as he located the keys and unlocked the door. "Why are you so prickly?"

"Why do you care?" She started to push out of the chair,

but immediately sank back down as the pain shot through her ankle.

"Sit down, silly woman. It's bad enough that you wear these gosh-awful creations," he said as he held up the fancy pump, "but please don't disappoint me. I thought you were smart enough to know not to try to walk on a sprained ankle."

"Do you really think it's sprained?" Now safely inside, Eva fought panic as Reid carefully tested her ankle's range of motion.

"Well, either you have an unbelievable tolerance for pain, or it isn't sprained." He put a pillow on the coffee table and gently settled her foot it. Javy had helped Jonah fill a plastic storage bag with ice and Reid laid it on Eva's ankle.

"Thank you," she said, trying to hide a shiver.

"Do you have an ace bandage?" Reid bent and took off her other shoe and tossed it onto the couch next to its mate. He grabbed the throw blanket from the basket behind her recliner and laid it over her legs.

"No." She spread out the light afghan and pulled it up over her arms. The makeshift ice pack was necessary, but Eva found it hard to stop shaking.

"Jonah, go get your mom another blanket please," Reid said, tucking the current one in around her, and then turned to his foreman. "Javy, can you get the first aid kit out of my truck?"

"On it, boss."

Reid moved the stack of coloring books off the coffee table and sat down. He lifted Eva's unharmed leg up next to him and covered it with the corner of the blanket. Jonah arrived, dragging the largest, heaviest quilt in the house. Reid winked at her when he heard her groan at the covering her son had chosen.

"Perfect, Jonah." Reid took the boy's contribution and

handed him the smaller one. "Let's switch it out with this wimpy one." Once again, Reid tucked her in, being careful not to jostle her foot.

"Is Mommy going to be able to walk? Will she need crutches? Will you sign her cast?" The four-year-old's active imagination was in full gear.

"Your mom is not going to need a cast or crutches, and yes, she'll be able to walk." Reid set the boy next to Eva on the couch. "She should be put in time out for her foolishness, but she'll be able to walk."

"You're so kind," Eva said with only a slight hint of sarcasm, not wanting Jonah to think she was ungrateful. She continued to shiver, more now from the drama than the ice. Reid apparently noticed.

Javy returned with the kit and Reid located the wrap. Uncovering her foot and lifting off the ice pack, he checked the ankle again.

"It hasn't started swelling, which is good." He expertly wrapped the bandage around her foot. "I'm going to make you a cup of coffee before I go, okay?"

Eva agreed, relieved that he had finished his examination.

"Where exactly do you work? Javy said he thought it was somewhere at the university." Reid asked as he opened and closed cabinets looking for the coffee supplies.

"In the library." Eva nodded as he pointed to the correct cabinet. "They had an unexpected mid-year opening for an Assistant Librarian. Being fulltime means Jonah can attend the kindergarten there, too. It's been a blessing."

"Doesn't that require a Masters degree?"

"I see you doubt my intelligence. Shocking. But to satisfy your curiosity, it was a special five-year program. I finished with my Bachelors one May and my Masters the following August." Eva knew he was fishing for her age again, but didn't offer any more information.

"Well, I'm glad it worked out for you." Reid leaned casually against the doorway between the kitchen and living room. "I guess you understand all those silly numbers on the books in the library. Dopey or Dooley something, isn't it?"

"I assume you mean the Dewey Decimal System." Eva rolled her eyes at his pretense. "Yes. I understand it. As do many people who have actually darkened the doors of a library before."

"You wound me!" Reid placed a hand over his heart in mock distress. "How do you like your coffee, Dewey?"

***

"Thank you, again, Reid," Eva said a few minutes later as she sipped the warm drink. "Although I'm sure I would've been fine if you hadn't been here."

"This is like your worst nightmare, isn't it?" Reid had helped himself to a cup and settled into her recliner. Jonah was in his room, playing with his blocks, if the sounds emanating from down the hall were any indication.

"What?" She frowned slightly over the rim of her mug.

"Needing help." Reid stretched his legs out and met her gaze with a grin. "Especially from me."

"Don't you have somewhere to be?" Eva asked. "Home? Your wife? Like I said, I'll be fine."

Reid's coffee spilled as he choked.

"Wife? What on earth are you talking about?" He asked when he returned from the kitchen, wiping the stain from his shirt.

"Javy mentioned a Mrs. Michelle," Eva said.

"*Michelle*," Reid said, "also known as *Shelley*, is my *sister*."

"Shelley is your sister?" Eva's red face was evidence of her embarrassment.

"Yes ma'am." Reid grinned. "All my life." He added a dramatic shudder. "I am definitely *not* married, nor do I want to be!"

"The women of the world thank you, I'm sure." Embarrassment spawned Eva's petulance.

"Tsk, tsk, young lady," Reid said as he finished the rest of his coffee and stood. "No need to be mean. Next time I may just watch you suffer instead of coming to your rescue."

"Sorry." Eva had the grace to blush slightly. "Thank you. I apologize for being so much trouble. I'm sure you'll be glad when the house is done and you no longer have to put up with me."

"Whatever you say, my lady." Reid bowed before calling his goodbye to Jonah.

9

"We'll be rich overnight."

Mr. Reid Jackson, contractor extraordinaire, was in high demand. Some days he spent more time in his truck than at sites, since he was currently renovating seven properties. Only Javier Menendez dared mention that his boss spent an inordinate amount of time at the cul-de-sac worksite.

"How long have I worked for you?" Javy asked early one Wednesday morning, the third morning in a row that Reid had checked on their progress.

"Ten years," Reid said. "Why? You're not thinking of leaving me, are you?"

"No, just wondering why you no longer trust me."

"What?" Javier's words finally drew his full attention. Up to that point, Reid had continued to glance over his shoulder at the house next door.

"You keep showing up here, even though I have the work here under control." Javy's relationship with his boss was at times, part employee and part mentoring. "When are you going to admit what is really going on?"

"Get back to work, old man." Reid maintained his state of denial as he drove away.

Javier refrained from teasing his friend when Reid arrived again late in the afternoon. It was clear something

40

was troubling him as he climbed out of his truck, phone to his ear in the midst of an animated conversation.

"Is she home yet?" Reid ended the call, but didn't seem pleased.

"Just pulled in," Javy said. "What's up?"

"Sand." Reid's cryptic response made sense to the foreman.

Eva had heard Reid's truck pull up next door. So did Jonah.

"Reid!" Her son's excited voice warned Eva that her archenemy was on his way over. She had seen him on the phone as he arrived and was observant enough to know he wasn't in a great mood. Not wanting to admit curiosity, she busied herself unloading the dishwasher, letting Jonah answer the knock at the door.

"Hey, buddy! Is your mom here?"

No, I'm by myself, as usual. She's off having fun somewhere and told me to not to burn the house down. Eva thought it would be worth a lot of money to see Reid's reaction if Jonah had launched this as his answer to Reid's ridiculous question.

"Mommy! Reid needs you!" *Interesting choice of words, Son,* Eva thought.

"How may I help you, Mr. Jackson?" Eva dried her hands as she joined them at the front door.

"I have a problem," Reid said.

"Just one?" Eva couldn't resist the dig, regretting it immediately. Normally her comment would have garnered a response, but Reid was rubbing the back of his neck.

"Will you be here this weekend?" Reid ignored her rudeness, a sure sign his frustration didn't involve her.

"Yes," she said. "What do you need?"

"A delivery that was supposed to come on Friday morning is now arriving on Saturday instead." He pulled a piece of paper off his clipboard. "I have Reserve duty this weekend and Javy has family commitments. I know it's a lot to ask, but could you sign for it? They won't deliver it without a signature."

"That's all I have to do? Sign for the delivery?" Eva glanced at the receipt. "It's a load of sand?"

"The bricklayers will be here next week, and we need some for a couple other projects as well." Reid tapped the clipboard with his pencil. "I'd owe you big time, neighbor."

"I'm guessing 'neighbor' isn't another of your many nicknames for me, but in fact is an attempt to guilt me into agreeing." Eva handed the receipt back to him. "I can do it. What time should they be here?"

"Not before nine, they've assured me." Reid circled the phone number on the delivery notice and described where they should drop the load of sand. "This is a new supplier so they asked for payment up front. You won't have to handle any money."

"Not that you'd trust me with your money, anyway." Eva's teasing succeeded in earning a smile from Reid. "You're in the Reserves?"

She put the delivery notice on the end table closest to the door and then pulled her bouncy son off the sofa.

"Yes. Active-duty Army for two years and now I'm in the last couple years of my enlistment." Reid knelt, turning his attention to the patiently waiting young man. "Can this guy come help me check out the progress next door?"

"I don't see why not." Eva called after the two as Reid swung Jonah up onto his shoulders. "Behave!"

"Me? Or Jonah?" Reid turned back to ask.

"Yes," Eva said.

***

"What in the world is that sound?" Strange noises woke Eva on Saturday morning. The telltale back-up signal, typical of a delivery truck, invaded her dreams. She groaned and fumbled for the clock, then buried her head in her pillow. *Seven fifteen.* Knowing she had made a promise to Reid was the only thing that forced her out of bed.

By the time she threw on a pair of jeans and a t-shirt and headed out the door, the truck was leaving.

So much for having to sign anything, Eva thought. *I could've stayed in bed.*

As she came around the corner of her house, she froze at the sight that met her eyes. The large pile of sand had already been delivered. Unfortunately, it had been delivered to the wrong address. By noon, Eva had given up trying to keep her son off the magical pile of goodness that had suddenly appeared in his back yard.

On Sunday afternoon, Eva checked the driveway every few minutes, finally forcing herself to grab a book and sit on the back porch. Jonah had created an elaborate traffic pattern on the sand pile. Every one of his toy cars and miscellaneous household items comprised his imaginary cityscape. By early afternoon, she thought Reid was waiting until the morning to check in, but at five o'clock, she heard the doorbell.

"Hello, Einstein. It seems we have a problem." Reid leaned casually against the doorjamb. The cliché was true, Eva realized as she opened the door. There was something splendid about a man in a uniform.

"How astute of you, Captain Jackson." Having spent her teenage years near an Army base meant she recognized his rank immediately.

"Yes, my dear." Reid held the door open, inviting her to join him outside. As they rounded the corner of the house, Reid gestured to the mountain in her backyard. "There are little boy footprints and some sort of major traffic pattern all over my pile of sand."

"Excuse me?" Her reaction was born of the two days of worry. "You're unbelievable! When you invent a magic formula to keep an active four-year-old boy off a sand pile that magically appears in his back yard, let me know. I'll invest all my money in your project—we'll be rich overnight!" She marched back toward her front door.

"Whoa, there, Princess." Reid grabbed the tail of her loose flannel shirt. "No need to be so testy. I was joking."

"Let go!"

Reid complied with no further comment and joined his young friend in the backyard.

"We'll begin the removal process in the morning," Reid said as he delivered her sand covered son to her back door an hour later. "Of course, it may take you that long to find Jonah under this second skin he's acquired."

10

"Your words, not mine."

Eva volunteered for overtime the next day, hoping to avoid any chance of confrontation. Her plan was unsuccessful. Reid had supervised the sand transfer himself when he saw that it was going to be a bigger job than originally expected.

Concerned that her son's adoration was bordering on hero worship, Eva didn't allow him to leave the porch while the backhoe worked to move the monstrous pile from one yard to the other. When Reid asked if Jonah could join him on the rented piece of heavy equipment, Eva had adamantly refused.

"Don't wrap him in bubble wrap, Supermom." Reid's unsolicited advice didn't aid in creating less tension between them.

Reprieve came in the form of several days of rain, and on most of the other days the crew next door had already cleared out by the time Eva and Jonah arrived home.

One Saturday, a couple of weeks after the sand fiasco, Eva planned to pour a small patch of concrete under the gate leading to the back yard. The weekend would ensure avoiding Reid since it wasn't likely that any of the crew would be at the house today. She realized her mistake as Javier and Manuel greeted her when she finished setting the frame in place. She waved at them, and glanced casually toward the cul-de-sac. At least she didn't hear Reid's voice, or see his truck.

She mixed the quick-setting concrete in her new wheelbarrow and armed Jonah with kid-sized waterproof gloves. Checking that the wooden frame was level one last time, Eva carefully poured the batter-like mixture into the space. Jonah used a small trowel to smooth out the pile. Eva joined him, kneeling to spread out the rest of the concrete.

"When can I put my hands in?" Jonah was looking forward to leaving his handprints in the slab.

"It'll have to dry for a couple minutes first. Let's get the wheelbarrow cleaned out while we wait." They wheeled it to the corner of back of the yard, where Eva had already pulled the hose. She cleaned Jonah's arms and legs off too, making sure to get any concrete off his skin, knowing it could cause a rash.

Jonah donned new kid-sized rubber gloves and then giggled in delight as Eva helped him push his hands into the quickly hardening slab. After she checked him to make sure his skin was still clear of concrete, she sent him to the back porch to play. She used a screwdriver to etch his name next to his handprints then spent the next half hour cleaning up the tools. As she washed off the quickly drying concrete from the shovel, her preoccupation meant she didn't hear Reid's truck arrive.

"Nice concrete." His voice startled her. "If you ever lose your job, I could use another mason." He dodged the spray of water inadvertently aimed at him as she jumped in surprise.

"I'll keep that in mind." Eva tried to ignore the man, but he seemed bent on admiring her handiwork. That or he was analyzing it for flaws.

"You put gloves on Jonah, didn't you?"

"No, I'm an idiot, remember?"

"Your words, not mine." He leaned against the large tree that straddled the two properties as he watched her finish winding up the hose.

"Jonah's on the back porch if you want to say hello," she said, not adding how much her son had missed him. If she heard, *"When can I see Reid again?"* one more time she was going to scream.

"He can wait." Reid pushed away from the tree. "So, have I been forgiven yet?"

"For which offense?" Eva continued to put away the tools, traipsing past him twice to the shed. On her last trip, she was rubbing the skin above her wrist.

"Stop." Reid stepped in front of her, blocking her movement. "Give me your arm." The tone of authority made her obey without question. *"Esto no es bueno."* He muttered as he looked at her wrist. In the process of ensuring Jonah was free of concrete dust, Eva had missed an area on her own arm.

"Well, Princess, looks like you've done it now." Reid hauled her through the back yard and into her kitchen. "How long have you had this on your skin?"

"Ow!" She complained as he stretched her arm under the faucet. "I don't know. Half an hour, maybe."

Despite his harsh tone, his hands were gentle as he rinsed off the area under a stream of cold water. With his foot, he pulled the stool over to the counter and motioned for Jonah to climb up.

"Be careful." Eva watched as Jonah climbed on the stool and located the vinegar under Reid's direction. After pouring the entire bottle on the affected area, Reid patted the area dry under Jonah's watchful eyes. The four-year-old was assisting the surgeon, who was now referring to himself as Dr. Reid.

"Do you have any bandages or gauze?" Reid asked. She

sent Jonah to find the 'white stuff we use for our mummy wrap.' At Reid's raised eyebrows, she explained.

"We did a History Camp at our last church and used gauze to wrap dolls as part of one of the activities."

"Inventive."

"Not as fun as the race at the closing ceremony. We divided the kids into teams and they wrapped the teachers in toilet paper." Eva smiled as she remembered the hilarity of the event, the memories helping her ignore the painful spot on her wrist—and the proximity of her handsome but annoying medic.

Jonah returned with the first aid kit and helped Dr. Reid wrap her arm.

"There," Reid tucked in the tail end of the gauze and handed the rest of the roll to his assistant. "If I ever need an assistant in surgery again, Jonah, you're hired."

The four-year-old giggled as Reid chased him from the kitchen.

"Thank you, Reid." Eva examined his handiwork. "I didn't realize I had gotten it on my arms."

"No problem." He glanced at his watch. "I've got to go, but please keep an eye on that spot, okay Einstein? It'd be a shame to have to change your nickname."

The brief moments of camaraderie evaporated.

11

"I'll add it to your tab."

Sunday morning Reid waited for her outside of Jonah's classroom. He was hauling her into the classroom before she could respond. Ignoring Shelley and the curious youngsters, he pulled Eva into the small bathroom.

As he unwrapped the bandage, what he saw confirmed his fears.

"Let's go," he said and he re-wrapped the bandage.

"Go? What do you mean? I'm fine." She struggled against his hold, which was firm but not painful.

"I beg to differ," he said. "You are far from fine."

"Beg all you want, it doesn't make it true."

"What is true is that your wrist is infected. We're going to the doctor." Reid gathered her purse and sweater from where she had dropped it as he dragged her across the classroom.

"But Jonah," she protested.

"Will be fine with Michelle." He nodded to his sister whose response could have been scripted by Reid himself.

"I'll take him home with us if you're not back by the time church lets out," Shelley said before turning to the wide-eyed little boys. "How does that sound to you two?"

"Great!" Eva's traitorous son responded with glee.

49

"Thanks, Sis." Reid closed the classroom door behind him, still holding Eva's hand. Remembering Eva's mistaken assumption of his marital state, he teased her. "You did hear that, right?"

Since the day she fell in her driveway, Reid had continued to tease her about her mistaken assumption of his marital state. He even questioned her lack of observation skills since he didn't wear a wedding ring. She had in turn promptly retaliated with the reminder that many men, especially those working with their hands, chose to go without one for safety reasons.

"Yes, I know she's your sister, but thanks for the reminder. The more I thought about it, the idea of you being married was ludicrous. I don't know why I was ever confused."

"I see your injury hasn't damaged your tongue," he said, still laughing at her. "You should be glad I'm so forgiving, otherwise I'd let you suffer the consequences of your foolishness."

"Sorry," she mumbled. "I think I could handle my own medical care, though."

"Yes, you probably *could*," Reid said. "*Would* you? Probably not."

Their bantering stopped as he drove the short distance to the walk-in clinic. The waiting room was empty when they arrived. Reid insisted on checking her in and filling in the information form. She squirmed visibly as he asked the health history questions. When he reached the more personal ones, he relented.

"Thank you." She yanked the clipboard out of his hands as he held it out to her.

"Afraid I'll find out how old you are?"

"Seems like we've been through this conversation before," she said. "You're not a very quick learner, are you?"

"It will just be a few minutes." The nurse at the reception desk smiled as Eva handed in the form. "The doctors just arrived and are getting settled in."

Two doctors were talking quietly behind the nurse's station. The younger of the two caught Eva's eye and smiled. The tall, dark-haired doctor's smile faltered as the nurse asked Eva about Reid.

"Do you want your boyfriend to go back with you?"

"Boyfriend?" Eva blinked at the woman. Realizing the woman was referring to Reid, she sputtered. Shaking her head vehemently, and added a shudder for effect. "Reid? No, ma'am. He's not my boyfriend. Not at all."

The young doctor's smile returned.

"What was that all about?" Reid asked when she returned to her seat.

"Nothing." Eva opened the closest magazine, not realizing it was *Men's Health*. She tossed it back on the rack when she saw the ads for swimsuit calendars.

"Didn't look like nothing." Reid nodded toward the receptionist's desk. "Dr. Adonis seemed to be very interested in whatever you were discussing. Should I go ask him?"

"Stop it." Eva grabbed his arm as he started to stand. She winced as the movement reminded her why they were here. "They thought you were my boyfriend. Don't worry, though. I set them straight."

"Good." His response was quick.

The older doctor examined her wound and confirmed Reid's assessment. A younger nurse came in, applied an antibiotic, and rewrapped her arm. As Eva left the examination room, she saw Reid at the front desk, slipping his credit card back into his wallet.

"What are you doing?" She took the prescription he held out to her.

"Paying. The doctor said to use this consistently for ten

days. If the rash doesn't improve in three or four days, we'll be coming back."

"I can pay for this, you know." She let him open the car door for her. When he slid behind the wheel she added, "I'll pay you back."

"I'll add it to your tab." Reid pulled out of the parking lot and turned the opposite direction from the church.

"Where are you going?"

"Pharmacy, then lunch." He turned to her as the light turned red. "I don't trust you to not fill the prescription, and Shelley texted saying she and the boys will meet us at Burger Barn."

They rode in silence to the drug store. Reid let her pay for the prescription, but insisted on buying a new roll of gauze and a bottle of vinegar to replace the one he had used.

"Spoils of war," he said. "So, were you terribly disappointed that Dr. Dreamy wasn't chosen to treat you?"

"No." Wondering why he was so interested, she couldn't resist the urge to annoy him. "In fact, it was a good thing. Isn't there some rule about not dating your physician?"

"He asked you out?" Reid swerved to miss the curb he came dangerously close to hitting.

"Pay attention to the road, please. I don't relish a second trip to the emergency room." Knowing they weren't in any real danger, she laughed at his frown, but added a sigh to tease him. "Unless of course, Dr. Dreamy is still on call."

"You're hilarious." Reid pulled into the hamburger restaurant. "Are you sure they didn't give you anything stronger than aspirin back there?"

"No. Sorry. This is all me."

"Speaking of back there, you didn't tell them that we're not exactly friendly, did you?"

"Why?"

"That would only lead to complications."

52

"Like what?"

"Like he may think I hurt you."

"Oh." Eva stopped short. "I can see that."

The pair paused at the doorway of the restaurant. Reid glanced down at her and realized she was serious.

"That I'd hurt you," he asked, "or that he might think that?"

"I don't know." She held his gaze for a moment and then turned away, waiting for him to open the door.

"Eva, I know I'm certainly not your favorite person, but I'd never physically hurt you." He fell silent, until he noticed her blink rapidly, trying to hide the threatening tears.

"Are those tears from pain, embarrassment, or frustration?" He pulled her around to face him.

"Maybe a little bit of all three." Eva shrugged, and then forced a smile. "Are we going to ever go in? I'm starving."

12

"He leads with his mouth."

Shelley and the kids arrived a few minutes later. Jonah and Bryce held the door as Reid's sister navigated through with a diaper bag and her daughter.

"Thank you, gentlemen." Reid took the toddler from her and scooted the boys to the table.

"What did the doctor say?" Shelley asked as she settled into the booth.

"Which one?" Reid asked, one dark eyebrow shooting up as he glanced at Eva.

"Do tell," Shelley said as she watched her new friend's sudden interest in the menu.

"There's nothing to tell." Eva concentrated on finding her wallet in her purse. "I'm buying lunch. What do you guys want?"

Half an hour later, still fuming from the quiet battle she had fought with Reid over the bill, Eva sipped the last of her soda. She and Shelley were watching the kids play in the brightly decorated play area. Reid had volunteered to supervise.

"Look, he's pouting. I think he's just mad that he's too tall to play on it," Shelley said. "So, tell me about the doctor. Was he good looking?"

"Not really. I'd say he was pushing sixty, actually." Eva took another sip.

"C'mon, Eva," Shelley said. "Spill it. I know my brother and his little comment meant there's more to the story."

Eva relented and described Dr. Dreamy. Michelle was genuinely curious about the whole incident and somehow Eva found herself pouring out her history with Reid that had culminated in his heavy-handed supervision of her medical care.

"He's got a vicious tongue, doesn't he?" Shelley waved at her brother who was now the boys' chosen climbing wall. "He leads with his mouth, for sure."

"What do you mean?" Eva tried to keep her voice indifferent.

"He spends an inordinate amount of time apologizing for things he says. It'd be a lot easier for him if he'd just keep quiet and let his actions speak for him." Shelley sighed as she turned back to Eva. "He really is a nice guy. I don't know what we'd do without him."

Eva had learned that Michelle's husband, Troy, was a junior officer in the Navy. His ship was due back in several weeks. Shelley was hoping this was his last deployment and that his final year of enlistment would be stateside.

"Reid lives with you?" Eva asked.

"Actually, we live with him," Shelley said. "He kept one of the first houses he renovated. He lives in the mother-in-law bungalow out back and the kids and I are in the 'big house' as he calls it."

Eva watched the boys and little girl march around Reid in the play area. Apparently, he was now their captive.

"So, Eva," Shelley said, recapturing her attention. "Reid has trouble with his tact, or lack of it, actually, but he would tell you that I have insatiable curiosity. I know you and Jonah have a story, but any curiosity I show is just that—curiosity—not judgment. I know what it's like to be in a new place with no support system. If you ever need to talk, just let me know."

"Thank you, Shelley." Tears threatened again as the genuine offer took Eva by surprise. "I do have a hard time trusting people. The treatment I received when Jonah came into my life, even from my church family, was tough. It's a shame that the church is one of the few places that single moms still suffer criticism."

"Although I'm curious about what really happened, I understand why you don't tell people. You'd get pity, prejudice, or patronizing, wouldn't you?"

"I would," Eva said, "and I have. I know it may be prideful on my part, but I'd rather have people wonder than have them know. At least that way I get a genuine reaction from them."

Shelley's frown concerned Eva. She decided honesty was better than thinking she had a new friend when she didn't.

"It would be nice to be accepted and loved unconditionally." Knowing her statement was judgmental, she launched it anyway. "I've received that from God, is it too much to ask to receive it from His people?"

"Wow, I've never thought about it like that." Shelley squeezed her hand. "I'm serious, though, about being here if you need to talk. The boys seem to have hit it off, so I'd love to spend more time with you guys."

Eva stared, unsure of Shelley's sincerity. Still, seeing her son with his new friends was a powerful sight.

"That would be nice," she heard herself say.

"Great!" Shelley's inherent optimism took over. "Come tomorrow night. The young adult Sunday School class meets at my house once a month for an inexpensive night out. It's a good mix of singles and young married couples. Of course, the guys come more for the food than the fellowship, but we do have a good time. Everybody drops the kids at the church and enjoys some adult time for a few hours."

"I'm guessing there are people at the church to watch the kids?" Eva's dry sense of humor sneaked out. Shelley hadn't experienced it yet. "Or do we use this as a time to teach them survival skills?"

"What's so funny?" Reid asked as he rejoined them, dragging one boy on each leg and balancing a two-year-old girl on his back.

"Eva," his sister answered. "She's hilarious! You should have warned me."

"No way," Reid said. "The surprise is half the fun."

Reid insisted on taking Eva back to the church to retrieve her car. She had hoped Michelle would overrule her brother.

"I've got to protect my investment," he said. "How do I know you won't convince her to stop on the way and let you roll around in concrete?"

As they pulled into the parking lot, Eva noticed Jonah was nodding off in the back seat, so she asked Reid the question that one of his many quips had raised. "What did you mean about not warning Shelley? You said something about wanting her to be surprised."

Reid lifted the sleeping boy out of his truck while Eva unlocked her car. He strapped Jonah in and then turned to answer her.

"She was surprised at how hilarious you are. Personally, I think you should come with a warning label," he said. "The packaging is false advertising."

"Packaging?" Eva squinted up at him, the sun making it hard to read his expression. She heard him take a deep breath.

"You know—the package." He looked her up and down. "The hair, the cute freckles, wide brown eyes. They all portray innocence. Fooled me completely."

"Fooled you?"

"Yup," he said as he held open her door, "until you opened your mouth. Not everyone is adept at dodging your verbal arrows."

She blinked up at him, but not because of the brightness of the afternoon sun. Honest with herself, she knew blaming the tears that threatened again on the pain medication the doctor had given her would be a lie. It had been a long time since words had hurt her, having built up a tough skin over the last two years.

"Wow." She finally found her voice. "I'm sorry. I'll strive to refrain from speaking to you anymore." She closed her door, barely waiting for him to move his hand. "Please tell your sister I appreciate the invitation to the gathering tomorrow night, but since her assessment of you was correct, I'll be unable to attend."

Eva watched the clock expectantly, not surprised that it took less than ten minutes before her phone rang. She successfully ignored the first two calls. Thinking he would be helpful, Jonah answered the third one.

"Mommy, it's Bryce's mom." He handed her the phone. "I guess you didn't hear the phone ring."

Thanks so much, son, Eva thought.

"No, Shelley, I won't change my mind." She decided not to pretend she didn't know the reason for the call.

"He won't be here," Shelley said. "I bought him a ticket to Siberia."

"One way, I hope," Eva said without hesitation.

"I'm so sorry, Eva." Reid's sister spent the next few minutes making apologies for her brother. "I did tell you he has a mouth problem. It's not quite big enough for his two feet. If it's any comfort, he feels terrible."

"Honestly, Shelley, he's not the only one at fault. Not that it's an excuse for my own actions, but I think I should stay far away from him since I can't seem to tame my own tongue when I'm around him."

"Will you come? Please? He's promised to stay in his apartment if you'll agree to come over."

"The apartment's in Siberia, right?" Eva didn't want her relationship with Reid to prevent her from meeting more of the church members, and more importantly didn't want it to keep Jonah from his new friends. Reluctantly, she relented. "I'll come, and I'll even promise to behave if you-know-who wants to show up. Your house is big enough for me to stay out of his way, isn't it?"

Shelley laughed and gave her the details and directions. Eva was nervous but knew it was the right decision, especially when she saw how excited Jonah was about the event.

***

A few miles away, Reid had eavesdropped on the conversation.

"You've been granted a reprieve." Shelley turned to her brother. "It will be brief if you mess up, even a little bit. I like Eva and I know she needs friends. What she doesn't need is to have to duck every time you open your mouth."

Reid nodded mutely.

"You may speak to her when she arrives, but only to offer a simple apology," Shelley said. "After that, steer clear of her. Understood?"

Another nod.

"Are you going to send me to my room with no dinner?" He looked like a child caught with his hand in the cookie jar.

"Maybe." Shelley said. "What is it about her that drives you to be so childish?"

"I don't know," Reid said. "Maybe it's because she acts like I'm torturing her every time I offer to help her."

"Does she really need help?" His sister asked. "Or does it frustrate you that she isn't needy? I thought that type of

59

girl drove you crazy."

"For some reason the fact that she doesn't want help, and my help in particular, is annoying." He shrugged. "I don't know why, but this is different."

I'll say it is, Shelley thought.

13

"Just a friendly warning."

On Monday night, Eva met Shelley at the church. They would leave Eva's car there and she could pick it up when she got Jonah later. Shelley lived only minutes from the church, so they had little time to talk.

"I'm glad you changed your mind," Shelley said. "Reid has promised to stay away from you, except to apologize."

"He doesn't need to do that." Eva's heart began to pound, along with her head.

"He does if he wants to eat dinner." Shelley grinned.

Perfect. Now he'll blame me for his starvation, too, she thought.

"I'm sorry," Reid said as he handed her a cup of soda. "I promise not to say anything else to you tonight, okay?"

Eva only ventured a shrug, not trusting herself to be able to use the words from her nice list. Turning away, she filled a plate from the impressive spread. She had made cookies for her contribution, forgetting that Reid would remember her previous batch. The assistant pastor, Jim Baldwin, and his wife Angie were one of the few people she had already met. The young married couple oversaw the class that included young couples and single professionals. Several of the class members introduced themselves as she moved through the kitchen and dining room. Before she settled into a corner of the living room, Shelley pulled her aside.

"Eva, meet my parents." Shelley introduced Byron and Susanne Jackson. "They belong to Reid, too, but since we're all still mad at him he's been temporarily disowned." Their parents had arrived earlier that day to spend a couple of weeks with their grandkids, giving Michelle a much-needed break. In the craziness of the buffet, Eva was able to blend back into the crowd. She couldn't escape to a corner fast enough. *His parents are here. Lovely,* she thought. *And I'm stuck here without a car.*

Thinking she had hidden herself well enough, Eva was surprised when one of the men asked if the seat next to her was available. Unable to speak since she had just bitten into a piece of pie, she simply smiled over her still-raised fork. Eva quickly took in the blond hair and green eyes, thinking it an unusual combination. Then he smiled. *Dimples.* Her own smile widened.

"Adam Richter." The dimples had a name.

"Eva Conley. Nice to meet you."

"Ah, *Eva.* Perfect," Adam said, still holding the hand she had extended in greeting. "Adam and Eva. Sounds like we're meant to be. Shall we book the church for a big wedding or just elope?" He accompanied his teasing with a wink, so Eva responded in kind.

"Oh, a big wedding, definitely." Eva freed her hand and laughed.

"So, you're new to the area, I hear. How have you found our quaint little community? Pleasant and friendly, I hope."

"For the most part," Eva said, glancing across the room. Reid, sitting between his parents, was frowning. *Surely he can't hear us from way over there.*

Adam kept the conversation moving, telling Eva what he knew of the history of the area and the new growth that had begun in recent years. It was very informative and not surprising when he revealed he was the newest member of the city council. A realtor by trade, he was quite a salesman.

Eva finished her plate of food, having put very little on it at first. Adam offered to refill it for her, but she declined.

"I need to see if there's anything I can help Shelley with anyway." She smiled her thanks when he promised to save her seat, and then made her way to the kitchen.

"You seem awfully cozy with your new friend there." Reid's voice was so close behind her it almost made Eva drop her plate.

"Excuse me?" The closeness of the area between her and the island limited her ability to turn and look at him. "I thought you weren't going to talk to me anymore."

"Just a friendly warning." Reid reached around her and took a sausage ball off her plate. "Are these any good?"

"Do you mind?"

"Not at all. Since you're hogging the counter space, could you fill me a plate?" He handed her his empty dish. "I know you don't believe me, but I'm not joking when I tell you he's not your type."

"I thought you'd appreciate it if I was someone else's problem." Eva handed him a plate of snacks she had made for him, grabbing a celery stick from the edge before he claimed it.

"Gladly." Reid grabbed a can of soda from the counter behind him. "Just not his."

Eva ignored Reid's warning and rejoined Adam. A flurry of activity interrupted their conversation as Shelley pulled out the main entertainment. It was a karaoke machine. Groans alternated with cheers.

Mr. and Mrs. Jackson had insisted on cleaning up the dishes so the group could enjoy their evening without interruption, so they missed the banter as the battle began.

"Do you sing?" Adam asked Eva, just as Shelley was wheeling the machine past them.

"Oh, please say 'yes,' Eva." Shelley clapped her hands. "Reid needs some competition. He's a born ham and we're tired of his showboating!"

"By all means, Miss Conley, please say you'll be a good sport." Reid managed to make his simple request sound like a challenge.

"Certainly." Eva smiled, hoping she sounded sincere.

"Great! I just got a new set of songs," Shelley said. "It's got all the latest movie themes." She and Eva settled on the latest radio hit from a new animated fairy tale. All the parents groaned.

"I hear this song in my sleep." Jim whispered to Reid. "Maybe they'll give it a twist that will make it less excruciating."

"Or more," Reid mumbled and decided to refill his drink during his sister and Eva's performance.

The next group, two married couples and Adam, offered a roaring rendition of an Elvis favorite. Thirsty after her turn, Eva refreshed her drink, and ended up following Reid as he left the kitchen.

"Not bad. Are you going to wow us with another, Al?" His latest nickname for her—another apparent reference to the famous scientist—had appeared only yesterday.

"Only if I find the right song." Eva smiled at his obvious challenge.

"As in?" Reid had grabbed the playlist from his sister's hand.

"*You're So Vain* would be a good choice." Eva raised her glass to hide her smirk, but Reid saw the one elegant eyebrow she lifted. Adam's group had finished their song and she settled back in the chair next to the handsome realtor. Reid strolled across the room and handed her the playlist.

"I'm not sure we have that one, but feel free to choose what you like," he said.

"What about you? I hear you consider yourself an expert."

"True," Reid said. "My pick would be *Cold as Ice*." Intent on the list, Reid missed the warning glances from his sister and Angie, both close enough to have heard their interchange. "I also like number twenty."

Eva paled as she read his choice.

"I surrender to your expertise, Mr. Jackson." She stood, and handed the list to Shelley, careful to avoid contact with Reid who was standing in front of her. She smiled widely at Adam who had just returned to their corner. "I'm going to get another soda. Would you like a refill, Adam?"

She was shaking as she sought refuge in the kitchen, holding her glass of diet cola that she just now realized was already full. Even with her eyes squeezed shut, the song title, *Devil with the Blue Dress On,* would not disappear. Then Eva's safe haven became anything but a refuge. She smiled at Reid's parents.

"Eva, isn't it?" The older Mr. Jackson asked. "Michelle says you're new in the area. It seems that you know Reid, too."

"He's working on the house next to mine." Eva decided to impart as little information as she could.

"Speak of the devil," Mr. Jackson said. Eva almost choked on the older man's choice of words.

"Reid, Eva just told us that you're renovating a house next to hers," Mrs. Jackson said. "How delightful."

"Yes, Mother," Reid said, then turned to Eva. "May I speak to you on the back porch, please?"

"That's not necessary." Eva knew he would try to apologize. She had seen Shelley's pointed look tossed his way.

"I disagree."

"Disagree? With me? I'm so surprised." She paused, the pitcher of iced tea poised mid-air over Adam's glass.

"Please, Dewey," Reid's use of nicknames no longer surprised her. "You have to let me apologize."

"I see it's now my turn to disagree." A tight smile accompanied her volley. "By the way, I should correct your song choice. As you can see, my outfit is decidedly *not* a blue dress." She pointed to her sleeveless top. "This is purple." She then lifted the hem of her short, flowered skirt. "And this is purple, this is yellow, and this is green. Perhaps Jonah needs to review colors with you."

His parents had watched the verbal sparring. Reid shot a pleading look toward his mother as Eva returned to the living room.

"What on earth did you do this time, Reid?" They followed him out to the porch where he described his contentious relationship with Michelle's newest friend.

"You're not going to offer your two cents worth of advice?" He said as he looked at the amused look on his parents' faces.

"My advice would cost much more than that." Byron Jackson said.

"I'm on her side," his mom offered. "What you did was mean."

"I know, and I'm sure it's going to be a trial to get her to let me apologize." Reid said with a bitter laugh. "But I guess that's what I deserve."

***

The rest of the evening included a time of sharing and announcements about the class's plans for the rest of the spring and summer. Jim reminded them that their Sunday School lessons would correspond to the upcoming sermon series topic, "The Importance of Words."

Although Eva had successfully eluded Reid since leaving the kitchen, she couldn't help but smile when she heard Reid choke.

As the group began their mass exodus, Adam offered to take Eva to the church. Jim overheard the offer.

"Angie and I can take her. We have to pick up Kendra."

"We've got to go by the grocery store on the way home, honey." Angie kicked him and he didn't hide his grimace well. Although they had been married less than five years, he got the message—loudly, clearly, and painfully.

"I don't mind," Adam said. As Reid joined the discussion, Adam took a step closer to Eva.

"Shelley or my parents will take her." Reid eyed the taller man. "Thanks for the offer, Richter, but we've got to get Michelle's imps anyway."

"Eva?" Adam touched her arm. "It's your call."

14

"I can agree to be civil."

The men stood in silent battle. Eva glanced from one combatant to the other.

"I wouldn't want to be responsible for any bloodshed." She stepped between them, placing a hand on Reid's arm. "I'll call a cab."

"That's ridiculous and you know it," Reid said without taking his steely gaze off Adam. The brief moments stretched uncomfortably. The handsome realtor yielded.

"Thank you, Adam," Eva said as she walked him to the door. "But it does make more sense for Shelley's parents to take me. You said you lived in the opposite direction, right?"

"Yes," Adam said. He leaned over and asked quietly, "Can I call you?"

His request surprised her and she agreed without thinking. As he smiled and lifted her hand to his lips, Eva glanced over her shoulder. Reid was scowling.

Jim was collecting dishes from the den while Angie said goodbye to Shelley. Eva took a stack from him as he entered the kitchen.

"I think Michelle is going to take you, if your threat to call a taxi was a bluff," he said. "I've been informed by my wife that those were the plans all along."

"I hate to be a bother," she said to Shelley. "I should have just driven my car over."

"Now you're being silly," Shelley said. "We have to go get the kids anyway. Plus, with my parents here, you don't even have to choose between Reid and me. Although we both know who would win in that vote."

Thinking she would have to wait for Shelley to take her to get Jonah, Eva offered to help clean up. Of course, Reid had done the same, still trying to make amends to both his sister and her new friend. Shelley and her parents watched the two curiously.

The two worked side-by-side silently. He handed Eva a tray ready to be dried. She stacked the tray to the side of the counter, not knowing where it belonged in the large kitchen.

Michelle and her parents watched the quiet interaction occurring across the kitchen. "He's in way over his head," her dad said.

"Yes, he is, and he has no idea." Shelley laughed and relieved Reid of his dishwashing duties so he could help his dad stack and store the chairs. "I need to go get the kids, since everyone will have picked up their kids by now." The teens that were babysitting were also in charge of cleaning the rooms, but Shelley was the designated person responsible for locking up the church.

"Your mom and I can go," the elder Mr. Jackson said, then glanced at his wife. He hastily amended his offer. "Or not."

"I'm still wrapping up the desserts," Mrs. Jackson said, then patted Eva's hand that was now gripping the counter. "Reid can take you, dear. Here's a piece of the cake that you liked."

"Thank you, Susanne," Eva forced a smile as she accepted the foil-wrapped plate. "Can you send me the recipe? It was delicious and I'd love to add it to my collection."

"Are you ready to go, Einstein?" Reid came back into the kitchen, trailed by his dad. It was plain to Eva that he was making his offer under duress.

"I'm sorry to be causing a problem." She followed him to his truck after she said her goodbyes.

"Don't be ridiculous." He helped her into the truck, but hesitated at the driver's side before climbing in. "I was going to have to send my keys with Shelley to lock up anyway. This actually makes more sense."

"You have keys to the church?" She didn't hide her surprise.

"Shocked?" Reid frowned as he closed his door. "Unlike you, many people think I', a pretty nice guy."

"Sorry," Eva mumbled. "I can walk if you like. You could just drive really, really slowly and follow me. It would be more pleasant for the both of us." She fell silent as Reid fiddled with his keys.

"Eva, my stupid trick during karaoke was shameful," Reid said before he started the truck. "You somehow manage to bring out the worst in me."

"So now your rudeness is my fault?" Eva's temper flared immediately. His next words, barely audible, confirmed she had hit her mark.

"If you don't want to forgive me, I'll understand."

"I'm not going to pretend it didn't hurt my feelings," Eva finally broke the silence that reigned for several moments, deciding the situation couldn't get any worse. "I realize since we're never going to be friends anyway, I shouldn't let your opinion bother me. I can agree to be civil, for Jonah's sake."

"So, am I officially forgiven?"

"Sure." Eva shrugged/ She ignored his outstretched hand, pretending she didn't see it by staring out the window. "I should ask for your forgiveness, too, since I threw the first punch tonight. I think I just need to stay away from you. I can't believe I acted so childishly."

"Please look at me." He ventured a touch on her arm, but drew back when he felt her flinch. "Even if you did technically start the collapse of the evening, it doesn't excuse my actions."

"True. It's all your fault. You goaded me and I couldn't help myself." Her resolve faltered as she saw his shoulders slump. "Relax, Reid. I'm just kidding. You don't like me. I don't like you. Nothing will change that. Let's just agree to be cordial."

He stared at her as he started the car, and shook his head to get rid of the thought that had suddenly popped into his brain. *What if I don't want to just be cordial?*

Reid's parents and sister weren't surprised that Reid went straight to his apartment when he returned. They spent almost an hour discussing the intriguing evening in general and Reid's reactions to Eva in particular.

"His penchant for nicknames has returned, I see," Byron Jackson said. "I heard him call her Dewey, Al, and I think Princess one time, too. I understand the Dewey, but not the Einstein."

Shelley explained the reasons behind the names she had heard so far, and laughed as they all realized his use of Princess was an unconscious indication of his true opinion of Miss Eva Conley.

Shelley ventured a call to Eva the next evening.

"Did you forgive him?" Shelley asked Eva. "Even if you do, I don't have to. I'm going to stay mad at him for a while. I can't believe he's being so childish."

"Like I told him, we're not destined to be best friends, so I'm going to have to develop a tougher skin around him," Eva said. "I'm as much to blame. I can't seem to guard my tongue around your irritating brother."

Shelley put her phone in speaker mode while she prepared a salad for dinner. The two moms talked about the class party, including Shelley's offer for Eva to perform the Heimlich maneuver on Reid when Jim told them about the upcoming series of studies.

"He seemed more concerned about the remedy than the ailment." Shelley laughed, then got to the original reason she had called. "Since a truce has been declared, does this mean I can plan a play date for the boys?"

"That would be fun," Eva said. "Jonah's birthday is in a couple of weeks. Since he hasn't had a chance to make many friends, it would be nice to do something special. My parents are planning to come down, but he's disappointed that his cousin Ricky, uncle, and aunt can't be here. He's not quite old enough to understand the reasons Aunt Mariella can't travel."

The two ladies brainstormed about parties and activities appropriate for four-year-olds, and settled on trying out the new activity center. Built in one of the new shopping centers, Kids Castle boasted a large bouncy-ball room, age-appropriate craft activities, and pizza. They were laughing over Shelley's description of her son's disastrous first birthday when Reid walked into his sister's kitchen.

"Ask Reid. He just walked in with the pizzas. Mom and Dad are entertaining the kids out back." Shelley pointed to the phone on the kitchen counter. "I was telling Eva about Bryce's first birthday party."

"I remember it well," Reid said. "Mrs. Andrews here was so convinced that we needed to have the perfect first birthday party that she turned into Mommyzilla."

"Yup, and I forgot to be Mommy," Shelley said as she swatted Reid's hand away from the salad bowl. "Bryce missed his nap so he was whiny, I was concentrating on looking like Supermom in front of all the other moms, and it got worse from there."

"We call it the birthday from you-know-where. Are you planning round two? Kids Castle is a great idea. I know it's not Bryce or Vickie's birthday, so it must be Jonah's." He leaned over his sister's shoulder. "Or Eva's."

"Mine, of course." Eva laughed. "That is my idea of a perfect birthday. Pizza, video games, obnoxious kiddie songs, and a roomful of four-year-olds."

"So, we've got yours all planned, what are you planning for Jonah?" Reid asked as he nabbed a cherry tomato and popped it into his mouth before his sister stopped him.

"I thought I'd crack open a bag of concrete and let them play in it." Eva launched a salvo just as Reid started to swallow. "Or let them play on your ladders."

Shelley pounded Reid's back as he choked. "I'll call you later. I have to revive my brother."

***

"That's the wrong weekend," Reid informed Eva the next Sunday. He was sitting in Shelley's classroom while she gathered the craft supplies from down the hall.

"I'm pretty sure I know my son's birthday," Eva said.

"I meant that's not going to work for me."

"I'm so sorry, but since a much higher authority was in control of the timing, you'll have to take your complaint to Him."

"That's my guard duty weekend," he said, disappointment evident in his tone. Reid sat quietly, obviously struggling with having to change his expectations.

"Oh," Eva said. "Jonah will be disappointed." She busied herself signing Jonah in on the classroom roll, trying to deny the disappointment she also felt.

"You'll let me make it up to him?" His question sounded more like a command, but Eva squelched her initial bristle and merely nodded.

Her parents came in on Thursday afternoon for the

birthday weekend, and insisted that Eva treat herself to a night out. Angie and Shelley joined Eva and her mom when Reid and Jim offered to watch all the kids, inviting Eva's dad to join them. Reid was insistent since it was his only chance to hang out with the birthday boy. They all met at Shelley's house since it was the largest and most centrally located.

Manicures, window-shopping, and milkshakes followed an early dinner. The four ladies were laughing at their own silliness as they greeted the exhausted trio of brave men.

"It's unanimous," Jim said. "We have a new appreciation for all you ladies do. We surrender!"

While Eva said her goodbyes, Reid helped Jonah buckle into his seatbelt.

"I'm sorry I won't be here for your party, big guy."

"That's okay," Jonah said. "Uncle Derek can't be here, either, 'cuz Aunt Mari is having a baby soon."

"I'm sure they wish they could be here, too," Reid said.

"Mommy said you have to go be a soldier this weekend and the Army needs you 'cuz you're so important and that's why they wouldn't let you skip out, even for my party which is important too, only not as important as soldiering stuff."

"You're the best, Jonah." Reid shook his hand formally. "Have a great birthday."

Eva had joined them in time to hear her son's soliloquy and Reid's genuine response.

"Thank you, Mr. Jackson. We hope you have a fun and safe weekend, doing your soldiering stuff."

"Your wish is my command, Princess." Reid offered a stately bow before saying his goodbyes to Eva's parents.

"What a nice young man," Christine Conley said as they drove away.

"Whatever you say, Mom." Eva stared at the passing landscape.

20

"He's not going to hurt me."

The college's spring break meant Eva had several days off the following week. Having inherited her grandmother's green thumb, she was planning a small vegetable garden in the back yard. Since the household was only the two of them, Eva planned a small four-foot square plot. Anything larger would mean she would have to spend too much money on soil, defeating the goal of savings on produce purchases.

Growing up with a handy man as a father meant Eva knew how to handle all sorts of power tools. However, since her father had refused to give up his prized collection, a circular saw was going to be Eva's first splurge purchase after her first full paycheck.

In the meantime, Eva decided to count on the friendship of Javy and his crew. She was cutting boards that would provide the structure for the raised bed. Jonah watched patiently from the stool far enough away from danger but close enough for observation. Eva noticed that Javy and several of the crew lingered in the garage, too. *Probably because they're afraid I'll hurt myself or worse yet, hurt Reid's tools.*

She smiled at the looks of surprise as she expertly cut

the first board. As she finished, Manuel was standing with the rest of the boards, ready to help haul them back next door. The noise of the saw meant Eva missed the new arrival.

"Are you distracting my workers again?" Reid was leaning against the garage door, arms folded.

"No, just amazing them with my carpentry skills," Eva answered as she dusted off her jeans and t-shirt. "I have talents you can't imagine." She had turned away so she missed Reid's look.

"Talents?" He squeaked out.

"Yes, I understand the Dewey Decimal system, can bake a cake, cut a two-by-four, and walk in high heels." She unplugged the saw and handed the cord to Javy before facing Reid defiantly. "I can even chew gum and ride a bike—at the same time!"

Reid watched her lead Manuel and Jonah back to her yard, then glowered at his workers as they laughed at him. He avoided her the rest of the afternoon.

Jonah enthusiastically joined the spreading of the bags of garden soil, although Eva suspected once again, that he was wearing more than he distributed. As evening approached, a tired little boy was winding down. While they were washing up, Jonah held the hose for his mom to wash her legs and arms. She was careful as she rinsed the tender spot on her arm that was still a reminder of her foolish cement event.

The youngster giggled. Eva saw his grin, but she was too late.

"Don't do it, Jonah," she said, laughing as she wagged her finger at her son. He giggled as he squirted her with the hose, then dropped it and ran. Picking up the weapon, she chased him with a stream of water. His squeals of delight rang through the yard.

"Hey! Keep it down! We're trying to work over here!" Reid leaned into their yard, elbows resting on the open gate.

Eva pretended to ignore him as she turned slightly toward Jonah and whispered. She calmly filled up the sand pail he had been using to spread the soil, then handed her son the hose. As she hoped, Reid moved closer. *I'm sure he's not used to being ignored.*

"I'm going to count to three," she whispered to her son. "You spray him and I'll get him with the pail, okay? One, two, three..."

When they turned, Reid had indeed advanced on their position. He received the full brunt of the pail of water, right in the chest.

"Oh, I'm sorry. Did we get you wet?" Eva smiled sweetly. A chase ensued.

"You're in trouble now, woman!" Reid growled as he grabbed the hose from Jonah. His tone and dogged pursuit of Eva confused Jonah.

"Don't hurt my mommy!" Jonah ran after them and grabbed the leg of his mom's attacker. Reid immediately dropped the hose, the little boy's tears of confusion stopping the flirtation almost before it began.

"It's okay, honey. Reid and I were just playing." Eva knelt next to her son, trying to reassure him. "He's not going to hurt me."

"But I heard you tell Grandma that Reid doesn't like you and he's always mean to you. I thought he was mad at you for throwing water on him." Jonah choked out his words between frightened sobs. Reid turned on his heel and marched away.

An hour later, Jonah was napping peacefully. Eva stepped out onto the front porch, hoping to catch Reid before he left. The squeaky screen door, normally an irritant, served to alert Reid. She motioned him over and met him on the edge of her driveway.

"Is he asleep?" Reid asked.

"Yes, I wore him out sufficiently," she said. "I'm sorry

about squirting you."

"The soaking isn't the issue and you know it." His defensive tone sounded more like an attack. "Why would you tell him that I was mean and would want to hurt you?" His defensive attack shouldn't have surprised her, but it did.

"I did no such thing." She ignored the audience that had stopped its work when they heard the raised voices. "Yes, I did tell my mom that you didn't like me, but as far as the meanness goes, you've managed that all on your own."

"What?" Reid stopped her as she delivered her guilty verdict and turned to leave.

"Jonah has overheard your high-handed attitude." She jerked her arm away from Reid's grasp. "You berate me, call me names, and point out what I'm doing wrong. He's even asked why I can't be your friend like he is."

"And what did you tell him?"

"What could I tell him?" Eva shrugged. "That we're enemies?" She turned to go back inside. "I thought we had crossed that off our list, but I guess not. Besides, I don't need a friend that only sees what I do wrong."

Javier had joined Reid as Eva let the screen door slam closed behind her. He had heard her last words. Reid relayed Jonah's accusations to the foreman.

"Why would Jonah think I felt that way?" Reid's question was rhetorical, but his foreman wisely assessed the situation.

"Out of the mouth of babes, *mi amigo,*" Javier offered.

***

Reid spent an inordinate amount of time cleaning up the worksite. It hadn't looked this organized since before he purchased the foreclosure.

"Putting it off doesn't make it go away." Javy closed the toolbox on the back of his truck.

"Do you ever tire of telling me what to do?" After

cooling down in the hose behind the house, Reid grabbed a clean shirt from his back seat. "How do I look?"

"You should be more concerned about how you sound, boss." The wise Latino pointed to the patch of wildflowers at the back of the property. "Flowers wouldn't hurt."

"I'm apologizing, not proposing," Reid muttered. As he came around from behind his truck, he saw a teenager from church walking up Eva's driveway. The teen's presence could only mean one thing. *She has a date tonight. Perfect.* Wondering if it was Dr. Dreamy, Reid headed to her front door.

"Reid!" Jonah spotted him first. "Mommy's got a date!" The boy shared the news with his favorite friend. In his excitement, he missed the frown his comment generated.

"Did you need something, Reid?" Eva joined them at the front door. Carly, the babysitter, trailed close behind.

"Just begging your forgiveness, and making sure Jonah and I are still friends." Reid was now kneeling next to the bouncing young man, trying to ignore the sight of Eva in a short, gathered skirt and sleeveless summer sweater. Used to seeing her in a t-shirt and shorts, or in her dressier Sunday clothes, he found the sight disconcerting. "I'm assuming our earlier misunderstanding has been cleared up?"

"Yes. Feel free to schedule an all-out water fight in the next few days. He is ready and willing." Eva bent down to speak to her son. "Jonah, go with Carly. She'll get your dinner for you."

"See you, Reid!" Jonah gave Reid high fives and fist bumps in an elaborate ceremony the two had apparently practiced before.

"Thank you," Reid said, "for whatever you told him to fix my mess."

"No problem." Eva let Reid follow her inside while she gathered her purse and light sweater. "I thought it was unfair to let our mutual animosity interfere with Jonah and his best friend."

"Best friend?" Reid helped her slip on the wrap. "Jonah says I'm his best friend?"

Eva stepped away from Reid and adjusted the already straightened sleeves.

"Yes," she said, turning back to face him. "He doesn't know many people yet and you have so much in common."

"As in?"

"Level of maturity." Eva smiled sweetly up at him. "Was there anything else, Mr. Jackson?" Reid laughed in agreement, and then returned to his interrogation.

"Who's the lucky guy? Dr. Not-in-your-wildest Dreams?"

"No."

"Who is it?"

"You're awfully nosey tonight, Mr. Jackson," Eva said. "It may surprise you to know that I do have a life outside of this two-house radius. In fact, I leave every morning and stay away for nine hours. I hope I haven't shocked you too much."

One dark eyebrow rose. "Is sarcasm your only talent?"

"No, it's my special gift just for you." Eva slipped her phone into her purse as the sound of the revving engine reached them. Reid frowned as he recognized the vehicle.

"Richter!" Reid turned to her, eyes blazing. "You've got to be kidding!"

"Is that a problem? Did I forget to fill out the permission slip correctly? Perhaps I needed my mommy's signature." Eva crossed her arms. "Do you expect me to screen all my relationships through my dad and older brother, too?" The moss green sweater made her brown eyes glow and the current fashion flattered her slender form. Reid considered retreat in the face of her confident defense, but decided on a less direct attack.

"Here." Reid pulled out his wallet and handed her a business card. "I'm not confident Richter will act the gentleman for the entire evening. Use this in an emergency. The second number is my personal cell phone."

"Are you warning me? Again?"

"Not specifically. I don't know Adam very well, but let's just say it's a vibe."

She was staring at the card in her hand when Adam knocked on the frame of the open front door.

"Are you ready, Eva?" He extended his hand to Reid. "Jackson."

"Richter." Reid's terse response earned him a glare from Eva, and he reluctantly shook Adam's hand.

"Reid was just telling Jonah goodbye," Eva said, justifying the other man's presence. Adam nodded but his smile did not reach his eyes.

"Miss Eva?" Carly stood at the edge of the kitchen and glanced from one combatant to the other. Her interruption broke the growing discomfort created by the quiet standoff. "Can Jonah have ice cream before bedtime?"

"Yes, but only a little bit." Eva turned her back to the men and slipped the card into her purse. Reid saw her and gloated in victory when she glanced over her shoulder. She rolled her eyes, causing him to grin wider.

"Have a good time, you two." A more serious look—aimed toward Adam—replaced Reid's grin. Unable to resist stirring the conflict, he added. "I'll see you tomorrow, Eva."

21

"Once or twice."

Curious about her date, the next afternoon Reid knocked on Eva's door, using the excuse of delivering a gift to Jonah.

"I ordered this kid-sized tool belt for Bryce, but the company sent two by mistake."

"Are you stretching the truth?"

"Widely," he admitted. "I knew you wouldn't let me buy one for Jonah outright."

"I'm not a bad mother, Reid."

"I know." Reid reached for the box and took a step back. "Let's start over. Knock, knock."

"You're a goofball." Eva laughed as she pretended to open the door again. "Oh, a gift! For me?"

"No, for Jonah," Reid said, playing his role perfectly. "Is he here?"

After the ceremonial ripping open of the package, Reid helped Jonah strap on the kid-sized tool belt. Jonah retrieved his small hammer from the back porch and modeled his new look for his mom.

"Javy said he wanted to see it," Reid said, "so ask your mom if you can go next door and show him."

Eva nodded her permission and smiled as her son bolted

out the door. "Thank you, Reid."

"No problem. I did buy one for Bryce and knowing they may become good friends, thought it'd be a good idea for Jonah to have one, too."

"Was there something else?" Eva noticed he seemed hesitant to leave.

"How was your date?" He plopped down on her sofa and stretched out with his feet on Jonah's kid-sized recliner.

"Fine." She lifted his feet and kicked an ottoman under them, rescuing Jonah's chair.

"Eva, I know I'm not on your list of favorite people," he said.

"Nor am I on yours," she said before he could continue.

"You may think that if you like, but I do care enough to warn you about Adam Richter."

"We've had this conversation before, Reid. He didn't misbehave on our date and besides, he seems nice enough to me." She decided not to reveal that the date hadn't gone well and she wouldn't be going out with Adam again.

"Guys know guys. Trust me, his 'nice' guy act is just that—an act."

"Funny. He implied the same about you."

"Did he? How did you respond?"

"I told him I had yet to see your 'nice guy' act."

"Ouch." Reid clutched his chest, but laughed off the insult.

"I call it as I see it," Eva said. "Now, was there anything else?"

"Something smells delicious," Reid said, leaning forward, elbows on his knees. "Unless it's your pastry-scented perfume, you must be baking. Can I have some?"

"Your boldness knows no bounds, does it? From anyone else I would consider that rude, but somehow from you, it doesn't surprise me."

"C'mon, Eva." He stood and made his way to the

kitchen. "I'm starving. Have mercy."

Jonah's class was having a bake sale, planning to take advantage of the ever-hungry college students. Cookies covered several cooling racks on the counter. One batch had just come out of the oven.

"They're not cool yet." Eva warned him as he picked up a double chocolate chip cookie.

"That looks familiar." Reid pointed to the cake wrapped decoratively on the counter. He tossed the hot cookie from one hand to the other. "Is that my mom's cake?"

"Yes, I got the nicest letter from her," she said. "It was odd."

"Why was that odd? I heard her say she was going to send you the recipe." He took a tentative bite of the warm cookie, and then finished the rest in one mouthful.

"Didn't you hear me? I said I received a *nice* letter from your mom. It was pleasant, kind, and gracious."

"And?" He took another cookie and she swatted his hand.

"It was confusing, that's all." She moved the cooling rack out of his reach. "Were you switched at birth?"

"You're hilarious." Reid reached around her and swiped another cookie.

"That's enough. I won't have enough for tomorrow." Eva opened the fridge and handed the milk to the man-sized kid who was searching her cabinets for a glass. "Here, little boy."

"Are you attempting to beguile a special guy with your baking skills?" Reid's bold question was unexpected.

"Excuse me?" Eva turned, a spatula poised midair.

"Just curious." He drained his glass of milk. "You went out with Adam, against my advice, so I was just wondering. Have you been dating a lot?"

"How is that any of your business?"

"I was just asking." Reid shrugged. "If you don't want to

84

tell me, that's fine."

Deciding that painting a true picture was better than letting his imagination run wild, Eva caved in.

"Once or twice," she said.

"Which is it? Once?" He put his glass in the dishwasher. "Or twice?"

"What about you, Mr. Nosey Pants?" Eva counted the cookies before putting another batch in the oven. "I'm sure you have an active dating life, right?"

"If you say so." Reid pulled out a stool, settling in while she continued to work.

"Who's the lucky girl?" Eva set the timer and began returning baking ingredients to the pantry. "And by lucky, I mean patience-of-Job, slightly deranged, and blind-as-a-bat."

"Ouch!" Reid stacked the empty mixing bowls in front of him. "You're a regular walking thesaurus. Why don't you tell me how you really feel?"

"Are you sure?" Eva laughed.

"No. Not sure my ego will survive." Reid leaned back and crossed his arms. He didn't respond to her laughter in kind, and Eva paused.

"Sorry. I guess that was a little mean."

"No, really. If I can't take it, I won't be allowed to dish it out and that'd be too much to give up," he said. "But nice attempt to change the subject. You still haven't answered my question."

"Why I am answering your questions, I don't know, but it seems to be the only way to get you to leave," Eva said. "If I must suffer through an interrogation, you have to help me wrap these cookies."

Reid carefully held the plastic bags as Eva placed two cookies in each.

"For your information, I've had one other date. It was with a new adjunct professor at the university." Eva tied a bright ribbon around the bag and stacked it the box Jonah had decorated.

"How did that go?" Reid filled a couple more bags, setting up a makeshift assembly line.

"Not well. He asked me flat out if Jonah was due to indiscretion on my part. Basically, he wanted to know if I was 'one of those' girls in college."

"Wow! I kind of feel sorry for the guy." Reid's laugh was unexpected, but managed to bring a smile to Eva's face. "What did you do? It made for a short date, I'm sure."

"I wielded my sword." Eva continued to tie the ribbons as Reid filled them.

"Sword?"

"I pulled out every scripture verse I could think of. He couldn't back pedal fast enough. It was the highlight of the evening. He was calling for the check, trying to interrupt, and I just kept quoting. I think I threw in some Shakespeare, Confucius, and even a Jane Austen quote or two."

"Oh, that's rich!" When Reid's laughter waned, Eva's smile fell. She could see his hesitation. She braced for his next questions.

"He was way off base though. Wasn't he?" Reid watched her intently.

Should I trust him? Eva thought.

"Yes, he was." Her simple response didn't answer the obvious question still on Reid's mind. "Thank you for helping with the cookies. Please send Jonah home."

22

"Are you being fair?"

Eva's parents had encouraged her to find someone in the church she could trust with the truth of her story.

"You need to give up this idea of righteous indignation and let people know what really happened." Her dad had given up on subtle hints.

"So they can stop judging me? Or stop pitying me?"

Only the inner circle of her family knew the whole story. The circumstances around Jonah's birth were not as personally devastating as many wanted to believe. How she came to be his mom was more through divine intervention than by any human action.

Her months in the new environment had softened Eva's attitude. The exhaustion of answering questions—or *not* answering questions—in her hometown had faded. Still, it was infuriating that people masked prejudice and curiosity behind false offers of support and care.

When the Baldwins invited her and Jonah to dinner, she gladly accepted. They had a five-year-old girl, and although Jonah wasn't excited about spending the evening with "a yucky girl," Eva knew it would be good for him to expand his base of friends. She needed to do the same. The water fight fiasco made it clear that Shelley Andrews could not be her only friend. Running into Reid frequently wouldn't be healthy for either of them.

After a delicious dinner, the couple and Eva moved to the living room while the two kids built a fairy castle—or a fort, depending on which one you asked—on the dining room table.

The small talk that had characterized the dinner conversation, gave way to a more serious topic almost immediately. Eva had prepared herself for the questions, spending time in prayer this morning.

Lord, I know I'm being prideful and judgmental myself. Please help me be willing to be vulnerable and open up to Jim and Angie tonight. I could use the support. This yoke is not as easy to bear as I'd like people to believe.

Now sitting with sympathetic listeners, warmed by a good meal and even better coffee, she welcomed the questions.

"Eva, we know you haven't shared your story with many people, if any, outside of your family, but we care about you. Our Heavenly Father didn't mean for us to face this life alone, you know."

"Your unwillingness to be honest comes from where?" Jim asked.

"I want people to judge me for who I am, not for what I may or may not have done. They treat me differently depending on what they think they know of my story." She took a sip of coffee, then placed it carefully on the table in front of her. "I've gotten good at ducking the first stones; it's harder to resist lobbing them back."

"Eva, it's not your place to judge them any more than it's theirs to judge you." Jim's pointed words weren't anything she hadn't already considered.

"Eva, I'm not sure you're being fair." His wife added. "Not everyone is going to judge you harshly. You have to give them a chance to care."

"I know, but the questions all come with preconceptions and that makes me angry. Admitting that my anger is just as bad as other people's prejudice isn't easy."

"Can we make it easier for you?" Jim asked. "I can say out loud what we all know everyone is thinking or you can do it. Maybe it will help you release some of the anger."

"True." Eva held up one finger. "So, scenario number one. I was a wild college student who got pregnant, but decided to keep the baby."

"Check," Jim said. "He looks too much like you to make that one not the obvious first choice."

"Yes. That one brings out the judgmental ones pretty quickly." Eva raised a second finger. "Number two. This one gets the most pity: young bride, tragic loss. My husband died in a car wreck, was a soldier, or left me without a word. Pick your favorite."

"That one is usually dismissed, though," Angie said, "since no one would understand why you wouldn't want anyone to know that."

"True. Number three." Eva added a raised finger. "This one is the most tragic, mainly because it demeans those that have really faced this. In this scenario, I play the victim. I suffered a vicious attack, got pregnant, but nobly decided to keep the baby."

"Why does that one make you the angriest?" Jim asked. Eva realized her body language communicated her frustration.

"Because, obviously, they say, I shouldn't have been wherever it was I was when I was attacked. Or, I shouldn't have been wearing whatever it was I was wearing."

"It sounds like you faced some of these very questions. I bet that was tough."

"Yes, it was." Eva drank the rest of her coffee before she continued. "Even worse were the people that couldn't believe I would keep the baby."

"The real story is an adoption, right?" Angie broke the silence. "A family member? He does look like you, Eva."

"A second cousin." Eva spoke the truth for the first time to people outside her family. "She made some bad choices in college. The family wanted to keep the baby, but her parents had some health issues. My brother was a newlywed, and expecting his first child, so my parents were the next logical choice."

"I sense an 'and,' am I right?" Jim asked.

"How astute of you Rev. Baldwin." Eva allowed herself to relax. "I had a very bad relationship experience in college and had sworn off men completely. I even contemplated the mission field—albeit for all the wrong reasons. When Jonah's grandparents could no longer keep him, I had just graduated from college. My parents and I spent several weeks praying specifically and seeking wise council."

"How did you decide to adopt him yourself?" Angie asked from the window separating the living room from the kitchen. She was brewing more coffee and had provided the busy kids in the dining room with more milk and cookies.

Eva took the tray with the rest of the cookies from Angie and passed it to Jim. The break gave her a chance to gather her thoughts.

"I'm such a control addict that I resist change of any kind. Making plans, long range ones, short-term projects, to do lists, and even lists of lists I need to make, was a habit I didn't want to break. Then Jonah happened. To say my reaction to him was unexpected would be a major understatement. All my well-laid plans no longer mattered. It seemed so natural to think about being his mom. It was the first, and biggest, leap of faith I've ever taken."

"Spoken with a parent's heart." Jim kissed the top of his wife's curls as she snuggled against him. Eva watched the young couple's easy affection with a twinge of jealousy. Giving in to loneliness wasn't an option, so she shook off the malaise.

"How much does Jonah know or understand?" Angie's question didn't surprise Eva. It was one she often asked herself.

Being in a classroom setting now meant Jonah had come home talking about different dads and moms. Since her cousin had been unable, and unwilling, to narrow down the biological dad, Eva had been careful about explaining their unique family make up to Jonah.

"He understands that some babies come in mommy's tummies, but that he came in a special way. So far that seems to have sufficed," Eva said. "There have been some complications with the adoption. Since it isn't final yet and may not be for another year at least, I haven't even mentioned it. Letting people think he's mine helps. His questions about daddies, though, get tougher each time it comes up."

Eva intercepted a familiar look between the couple.

"Don't even think about it, you two." Not willing to admit she had already been out once with Adam Richter, she verbalized her new resolve. The date with Adam had been nearly unbearable. "I'm not interested in a relationship, nor do I think Jonah needs a daddy right now, so don't try to set me up with anyone, okay?"

"She's psychic," Angie said.

"I promise," Jim said with a hand over his heart, "but I don't promise I'll be able to control my wife." Angie threw a dishtowel at him.

23

"What's a prude?"

Rainy season was upon them. The official start of hurricane season wasn't for a few weeks, but several downpours in recent days had replaced the typical springtime showers. Eva was glad for the garden's sake, but it made for a restless preschooler.

On Thursday night, the meteorologists were already predicting a ninety percent chance of rain for Friday night and Saturday. Thinking that entertaining two restless little boys couldn't be any more difficult than dealing with one, Eva called Shelley.

"Can Bryce come over and spend the night? I'm going to let Jonah turn the dining room into a fort. Tomorrow is my monthly half-day, so I'll be home early. I can swing by and pick him up around two."

"What a great idea!" Shelley agreed immediately. Troy was returning in a couple of weeks and she had a long to do list still ahead of her. "That'll give me time to get some cleaning and shopping done. Vickie is so much easier to handle and seems to enjoy shopping. Not sure that bodes well for us when she's a teenager, bur for now it's nice."

Eva gathered sheets, blankets, and pillows from both bedrooms. Arming her young helpers with one pillow each, so they could claim to have helped build the fort, she piled the supplies on the dining room floor. Then she let them help her put a couple of chairs on top of the table. Standing on the other chair, she draped Jonah's spare superhero sheets over one side. The fort's prospective occupants didn't appreciate the lavender flowers and green ivy on her spare set until she explained that the girly pattern would confuse any enemies that dared approach their lair.

While the boys gathered the rest of their supplies that included every toy in his toy box, if the sounds coming from Jonah's closet were any indication, Eva balanced a broom to give the tent a proper entryway. Reid's voice at the front door interrupted her construction efforts. Belatedly, Eva remembered she had left the main door open, leaving only the screen door for protection from intruders.

"Anybody home?" He ignored convention and took the open door as an invitation to make his way into the living room.

"Come in, Reid." Eva's sarcasm was lost in the melee that ensued as the two boys heard Reid's voice.

"Hey, you rug rats. I see you're constructing some sort of monstrosity." A hand on each boy's head, he shooed them back toward their castle. "Back to work. I need to check out Eva's bedroom."

"My bedroom?" Eva gulped.

"The drywall. The cinderblock along that outer wall had some issues before the renovations. I want to make sure it's up to the rain we're likely to get tonight."

"Renovations?" Her one-word questions were all she could manage.

"Yes. Didn't you realize this was one of my masterpieces?" Reid leaned closer, the teasing smile Eva had come to expect making its routine appearance. "I'm quite familiar with your bedroom, actually."

As hard as she tried, she couldn't prevent the flame that spread across her face. Reid watched intently.

"Is that modesty genuine or are you just that much of a prude?" His smile tempered his words, letting her know he was joking. His joking didn't stop her concerns about the little ears only a few feet away. It was a valid fear.

"What's a prude Mommy?"

"I think Mr. Reid said *prune* dear." Eva refused to meet Reid's smirk.

"What's a prune?" Bryce asked.

"It's like a big raisin." Eva turned her attention to balancing the sheet over the broom handle. Reid's grin turned to outright laughter.

"Why did he call you a big raisin?" The inquisition continued from inside their fort, the curiosity of two boys not satisfied with the adult's overly simple answers.

"Lack of imagination, I suppose," Eva said, then frowned at Reid as he fought to catch his breath. "You're no help."

"Please continue," he said as he helped her adjust the entry to the boy's fort. "This is fascinating."

"Don't you have something you need to do?" Eva's reminder only made his grin widen.

"Right. Your bedroom. Don't worry." He winked as he dropped the lavender flowered sheet into place. "I remember."

"I'll leave you to your business, then," Eva said, letting him go alone to her bedroom. The inner battle that the intimacy of the situation created raged only briefly. Pride won over modesty. The sparseness of her furnishings was more embarrassing than being alone with him.

When Reid finished ensuring the moisture problem hadn't returned Eva and the boys were hiding in their newly finished fortress. Despite her best efforts, Eva was sure Reid had heard the boys excited whispers.

"Knock, knock." On all fours, Reid lifted one edge of the sheet covering the door of the cave. As he stuck his head through the opening, he came nose to nose with Eva.

"You smell good." Eva's involuntary declaration shocked her more than it did Reid. Closing her eyes against the sight of his mocking, she hoped the words had only been in her head. She was not so lucky.

"Why thank you, Princess Einstein. It's not chocolate cake scent, but the ladies seem to like it." He crawled his way into the lair, grinning as he squeezed past her. "But if you think that overt flattery will make up for months of verbal abuse—you're absolutely right."

The fort's primary landlords were thrilled with their first official visitor.

"Uncle Reid! This is our fort! We're gonna sleep here tonight. Are you going to stay too?" His deep laughter followed Eva as she scrambled out from the suddenly very small quarters.

A few minutes later, he emerged from the man den. Eva was taking a load of laundry out of the dryer. Knowing the storm may knock out power at some point this weekend, she had done her weekly load of whites early. Meeting Reid's smirking form comfortably leaning against the kitchen island with arms folded, brought another blush. *If he thinks my blushes are fake, he must think I'm an expert actress by now,* she thought. As she ducked her head to hide the red cheeks, she realized her laundry basket was full of the most intimate of her apparel. She glanced up to see that he had indeed noticed, too.

"Did my bedroom pass inspection?" As the words left her mouth, she realized her mistake. Laughter replaced Reid's grin as he nodded.

"You're priceless." His enigmatic comment went unheard as Eva hurried to the newly approved room. She dumped the load of underclothes on her bed, not realizing

Reid had followed her.

"Everything's fine." He came around the bed and motioned for her to join him. Pulling out the moisture meter once more, he ran it along the wall under her window. "Looks like whoever made the repairs did a fantastic job."

"I hear he's quite humble, too." Eva recovered her sense of humor, but moved quickly to vacate the closeness of the room.

"Humble, talented, good-looking, smart." Reid followed her back down the hall listing all his attributes, real or imagined. "Even smells good."

"Will there be anything else, Mr. Jackson?" Eva stopped her retreat and turned to face him. Girding herself with the stance she usually took when confronting Reid, she crossed her arms across her chest. "I have a lair full of ferociously hungry boys and I need to prepare their feast."

"Very well, milady, and as tempting as my nephew's offer was, I won't be able to stay. Unfortunately," Reid winked. "I'll be back in a few minutes, though. I have a couple of flashlights that will work nicely for the 'den of danger' if the power goes out tonight."

"Thank you." When he returned a few minutes later, Eva met him on the front porch. She didn't want to risk his coming inside again.

"You're welcome." He bowed, but ruined the formality of his response with a crooked smile and a wink. "It's been a delightful afternoon."

Eva closed the door, a little more forcefully than necessary. The barrier didn't prevent the sound of his laughter as he walked away.

24

"I'll try to behave."

The worship director welcomed the new members with enthusiasm. During their dinner evening, Angie Baldwin had discovered that Eva had been a longtime member of her former church's choir.

"We need another soprano on Sunday mornings. The guys have been drowning us out the last few months." Angie had said, telling Eva about the practices and asking permission to give the director her phone number. He had called the next day.

As Eva settled into the choir pews, she glanced through the stack of music set aside for Sunday. Familiar with all of them, she felt some of the tension leave her shoulders. It had been a difficult day at work, and as if to confirm the cliché *"When it rains it pours,"* Jonah had been sent to time out for an incident with a classmate. Receiving the never welcome call had only added to Eva's already unpleasant day. Dealing with a pouting five-year-old made Eva consider backing out of this new commitment. Now that she was enjoying the blending of voices among her new church family, she was glad she had come. Of course, the reprieve of Jonah being in a class with his peers, learning Bible verses, and making crafts, was an added bonus.

The voice behind her sent a shiver down her spine. *It can't be.* Without even turning, Eva knew it was Reid. *Why, oh, why did I agree to this?*

"Have you taken up stalking?" Reid asked as they took a break midway through the practice. "Perhaps you need a hobby."

"Or perhaps you do." She handed him a cup of coffee. "I'm shocked you have time to fit this in your busy schedule—what with constantly checking up on me and all."

"I take issue with that statement." He added a heaping spoonful of sugar to his cup. "I was here first, you know."

"Not tonight, you weren't."

"Was too," he said.

"No, you weren't." Eva blew across the lip of her coffee cup, trying to cool down the steaming liquid.

"My dad can beat up your dad."

"Him and what army?"

"Children, do I need to separate you two?" Jim's voice interrupted their banter.

"No sir," Reid and Eva answered in unison.

"She started it." Reid pointed at her.

"Did not." Eva rolled her eyes.

Jim laughed as he moved away. When the choir director gave them the five-minute warning, Eva drank the last sip of coffee, which had finally cooled down. Eva raised an eyebrow over the edge of her cup as Reid approached her.

"If I make you uncomfortable, I can drop out." Reid's earlier humor seemed to have disappeared.

"We were joking, weren't we?" Eva's smile faltered. "I was, at least. If anybody should drop out, it should be me. I'll let the director know right away.

"No, stay." Reid stopped her retreat with a light touch on her arm. "I'll try to behave."

"I wouldn't want you to strain yourself."

Eva waited for the humor to return to his eyes. When it didn't, she added, "I'm just kidding, Reid. I'll try to keep my mouth shut, except when I'm singing. Will that work?"

"I think we've shown we can be in the same room without World War breaking out." He shrugged, holding her gaze. "I'm willing if you are."

Eva nodded silently before he walked away. She remembered very little of the rest of the practice, except for a growing dread in her stomach and the rich baritone voice over her shoulder. Deciding avoidance was the best weapon, she chose a side door as she left the sanctuary.

"Mommy, do I still have to go straight to bed tonight?" Jonah remembered his punishment for the incident at school. The teacher had told her Jonah and another boy had strongly disagreed over whose turn it was to play with one of the building sets.

"Yes, dear." Eva grabbed his hand and tugged him quickly out the side door. "You cannot call someone a mean name and not be punished."

"Yes, ma'am." The little boy hung his head as they walked across the parking lot. "Can I draw a picture to show him I'm sorry?"

"That would be lovely, dear." Eva ruffled his hair. Neither of them saw the man at the front entrance who had heard the last bit of their conversation.

***

Reid slumped at his sister's dining room table. Shelley was making cookie batter to freeze, a trick their mom had perfected in their childhood. It meant a warm batch of cookies was only minutes away whenever the need arose.

"Why can't I just keep my mouth shut around her? It's like she has some magical ability to turn me into an ogre." Head in hands, Reid waited for his sister's scolding.

"You call her Princess, so the metaphor is appropriate."

"You're supposed to be helping me."

"You and Eva have had verbal battles before, what was different about tonight?"

Reid described the epiphany he experienced as he heard the dejected little boy in the church parking lot. "That should have been me."

"What do you mean?"

"Jonah's dejection over being mean. He seemed genuinely sorry for the offense, not just for the punishment. I, on the other hand, seem to relish being mean and judgmental toward Miss Eva Conley." Reid's head sank back into his hands. "Here she is, a single mom in a new town, and all she gets from me is judgment and ridicule."

Reid glanced up at his sister who had fallen silent. Shelley advanced on him, wooden spoon in hand.

"Are you telling me you looked at her situation and *judged* her? You assume you know her history, assume that it's sordid, and you've set yourself up as judge and jury?"

"Whoa, Sis!" The look of anger was so unexpected Reid put up his hands in defense. "That's not true at all. You know my past. I'm no angel and I'd never put myself in a place of judgment." Reid's college years had been filled with rebellion and regret. It had taken a lot of love and prayer for his family to convince him that God could forgive his mistakes.

"Explain yourself, then, Brother." Shelley stopped her attack in midstride. "Please tell me you don't view her differently because of Jonah. Do you?"

"What? No!" Reid's vehement response satisfied Shelley, but confused Reid himself.

"Don't you realize how much prejudice, gossip, and callousness she probably faces?"

"Not from me, Michelle." Reid stared at the coffee mug his sister had handed him when he arrived at her door, despondent over the evening's events.

Shelley poured herself a cup of coffee and joined her brother. "Have you ever thought about why you've never wondered about how she became Jonah's mom?"

"I never said I haven't wondered." He drained the last of his now lukewarm drink. "I have. Somehow, it doesn't seem to matter. Jonah stole my heart the first time I laid eyes on him."

"He did, did he?" She smiled behind the mug she raised to her lips. Reid didn't catch the obvious implication in his sister's words and tone. "What are you going to do about your motor mouth? I have a suggestion."

"Give it to me. I'm desperate." Reid took his mug to the sink. Leaning against the counter, he waited for her wisdom.

"You know those collars that send a small shock to the dogs so they learn not to bark? We need to get someone to modify one of those for you. Every time you say something mean, it will shock you."

"That'd be a death sentence for me, and you know it." Reid's grimace made his sister laugh.

25

"Once again, I'm kidding."

The head librarian waved Eva over to the main desk, a wide smile on her face. Eva recognized the handsome male leaning casually on the expensive oak structure, obviously flirting outrageously with the older woman.

Reid had kept his distance for several days. In a case of 'absence makes you less annoying,' the sight of him was not as irritating as it once would have been.

"This nice young man was asking for you." The older lady patted Reid's arm. *Another conquest, I see.* Eva mentally rolled her eyes.

Eva had just finished stacking several large tomes that had finally been located in the fiction section. An inept intern, or perhaps a mischievous student, had shelved them incorrectly. Either way, it had taken her most of the morning.

"Mr. Jackson," she said, "how can I help you? Perhaps a book on manners or were you more interested in Ancient Chinese literature?" Eva knew the library allowed the community members to check out materials with the purchase of a yearly library card.

"Cute," Reid said. "No, I'm here to meet with one of the staff. I just thought I'd stop by to make sure you're behaving. I know it's difficult for you."

"How kind." Eva led him to a couch in the adjoining reference section, away from the prying ears of her co-worker. "So why are you really here?"

"Honest." Reid threw up his hands in defense. "I simply wanted to thank you for recommending me. It means a lot that you respect my work, even if you don't like me."

"You're welcome." Eva looked at her watch and realized it was close to time for her afternoon break. "Would you like a tour or do you have to be somewhere right now?"

"I'd love one," he said. "I allowed myself plenty of time, since I'm not as familiar with the campus as I should be." He stood and waited for her to let the desk know where she would be. When she returned to his side, he was frowning.

"What's wrong?"

"Your shoes. You're an idiot." His harsh words didn't offend her. She grinned instead.

"I'm not an idiot. I've been practicing." She strolled down the row of encyclopedias and performed a runway model turn before sashaying back to his side. Reid's eyes widened as her skirt swirled above her knees as she strutted past him. Eva missed his reaction.

"Aren't you impressed?" Now standing back in front of him, she pulled him to his feet.

"Not even remotely." He took her arm as they headed for the stairs. "You'd better hold on. I don't want to have to carry you again."

"Once again, your kindness astounds me," she said. Deciding he needed another lesson, she pretended to stumble as they reached the top step. In a split second, she found herself hauled against his chest, one strong arm around her waist.

"See?" His breath was warm against her cheek. "I told you those shoes were stupid." He set her down quickly when she giggled, realizing she had pretended to stumble.

"That was too easy!" She smoothed her skirt back into place before seeing his angry glare. "I was joking, Reid. Lighten up."

"That wasn't funny, Grace."

"It was a little funny, and you know it," Eva said, "and you say I'm the one with no sense of humor." Hearing her own breathless voice, she realized the brief embrace had surprised her. She stepped back, hoping a little distance between them would cool his temper, and allow her to regain her balance—both literally and emotionally.

They moved through the shelves filled with popular releases, classics, and modern fiction, before heading back to the first floor to look at the children's literature area.

"Why are you so dressed up?" he asked.

"Trawling for men." She grinned over her shoulder. "Since pimply-faced, nineteen-year-old frat guys are what I'm looking for in a father for Jonah. Why else would I bother to dress up, put on makeup, and wear these gosh-awful shoes?"

"You'd best be joking now, Dewey." Reid recaptured her arm, forcing her to stop mid-stride.

"Surely you didn't think it was simply to appear to be a little more professional and a little less matronly? How silly that would be!"

"So, you're *not* looking for a father for Jonah?"

"Reid Jackson!" Eva whispered her reprimand as she wagged her finger under his nose. "We started out so well this afternoon and now you've messed it all up. What I have planned for my personal life is none of your business. I think you're just afraid someone will replace you in Jonah's life."

"Of course," Reid said and fell silent.

"Wow, you're in a mood today. Once again, I'm kidding," she said. Thankfully, Reid didn't seem to notice her slight hesitation. She didn't want to face the inevitable interrogation that would come if he knew the whole truth.

"Sorry," he said. "I was just wondering why you're allowed to dress that way."

For some reason, his discontent didn't annoy her today. She responded with more light-hearted teasing.

"It helps the boys pay attention," she said.

"You're clueless if you think that outfit is going to help them concentrate." Reid's muttered response put Eva's good humor in danger.

"Listen, Officer Jackson of the Dress Police, you're starting to annoy me. I was serious. How would you have liked it if a sour-faced old bitty ripped apart the masterpiece you had just created for your freshman level English class? Wouldn't it be better to have someone who at least tried to look nice deliver the brutal news that you weren't going to be the next Ernest Hemingway?" Eva had punctuated each sentence with a finger poked into Reid's chest. He backed up, blinking in surprise.

"Men! You're all crazy!" When he didn't respond, she turned away with a mocking huff.

"Wait, Einstein." Reid grabbed her arm before she fled. The return of her original nickname let her know he was realizing his mistake. "You edit papers for the students, too? Is there anything you can't do?"

"Haven't found one yet." She realized he was attempting to deflect her anger as he latched onto this latest piece of information in his growing knowledge of her. Deciding now wasn't the time to reveal that she had double-minored in Spanish and English Composition, she simply grinned and shook her head.

"Can I add Chaucer to your nicknames?" Reid finally relaxed and smiled. "Or would you prefer Oscar? Wilde? How about Shakespeare?"

Her informative tour coaxed him the rest of the way out of his mood, and let her cool down. He was impressed with

105

the library's collections, and she teased him over his excitement about the children's section.

"You're just a big kid, aren't you?"

"Who's a big kid?" The silky voice accompanied the distinct scent of expensive perfume.

"Daphne." Eva turned to the tall blonde that had come out from behind the section's information desk. "I've just been showing my son's friend Reid the library."

"Reid Jackson, I'm working on the house next door to Eva." His handshake lasted longer than normal as Daphne Winters hesitated to release him.

"Daphne's in charge of the inter-library loan department. She's filling in for the Children's Section Librarian who's on vacation this week." Eva refrained from adding that the temporary post didn't fit Daphne's skill set. The elegant Ms. Winters was not very kid-friendly.

"Nice to meet you, Reid." The stunning woman turned to Eva. "Why haven't you introduced me to him before? Hiding him for yourself?"

The blatant invitation didn't surprise Eva, but she watched Reid try to hide his shock.

"Absolutely not!" Eva didn't resist teasing Reid. It had become a favorite past time. "He's all yours. Right, Reid?"

He blinked, whether in awe of Daphne's gorgeousness, or Eva's nerve, it was hard to tell.

"Oh, Eva, he's adorable!" Daphne laughed at Reid's mild panic attack, but that she was an expert at flirtation was obvious as she rested her well-manicured hand on his arm. "I'm teasing, Reid. Enjoy the rest of your tour, and feel free to come back. *Any time.*"

"That was hilarious." Eva choked back laughter as she wiped the tears from her eyes after Reid sped them out of the area.

"Glad I'm so entertaining," Reid grumbled. "I'll be here all week. Don't forget to tip your waitress."

***

Eva had shared the scene with Shelley at church the next Sunday, while Reid tried to interject his own take on the situation.

"I did not look like a deer in headlights, Al. Daphne's behavior was just in such stark contrast to how you treat me, that I was surprised. That's all."

"Nice try," his sister said. Reid left in a mock huff, their laughter trailing him down the hall.

"Were we too brutal?" Eva asked. "He does date, doesn't he?"

"That's a long story," Shelley said. The two ladies were cleaning the preschool classroom while their two boys and Vickie played quietly in the corner. Shelley waved Eva to a chair.

"Reid was in a serious relationship a couple years ago, the first one since he got serious about his faith. We were stationed overseas at the time, so I never met her and only know the story from his side." Her recollections over the next few minutes gave Eva a new insight into the mystery of Reid Jackson.

Reid had been studying for his first contractor's exam for months. He was a natural at his trade, so everyone assumed he would pass easily. Unfortunately, the state had changed the test format—significantly—and he missed the grade by less than a point. Very few others passed it.

"He was devastated. Instead of support, he got backhanded disapproval." Shelley finished organizing the crayons and stood to put them in their spot on the shelf. "Instead of telling him that she was proud of him, she told him that he needed to work on his confidence. Her 'encouragement' was more like criticism."

"Someone needed to explain the male ego to her," Eva offered.

"True." Shelley picked up her daughter and handed her to Eva. "Javy helped, though, according to Reid." She finished her story, describing a major problem that Reid had handled with expertise the following week. Javy had praised him and Reid said it was like his Heavenly Father was reminding him, '*You are mine, you are gifted, everything will be fine.*'

Shelley started the boys on the task of putting their blocks away. "Reid broke up with the woman the next day, and he hasn't dated since then."

"At all?" Eva put the coloring books away and helped the boys finish their job.

"Part of the problem is that it all happened right before the kids and I moved here when Troy was deployed. I've encouraged him to get out and there are plenty of willing women, but he always responds that he's too busy or doesn't want to be bothered." Shelley locked the classroom door behind them. "The worst one, though, is when he says, 'No thank you. Not interested.' He's infuriating."

26

"Is this a last fling?"

Troy was due home in two days. Shelley had called to invite Eva and Jonah to see the latest animated children's movie, claiming it would be her last night of freedom. Eva hadn't been out since her date with Adam, and Jonah had been clamoring to see the movie, so she agreed.

Shelley hired a babysitter for Vickie and the foursome enjoyed a fast-food meal before the movie. Thankfully for the adults, the feature was one of the rare G-rated movies that weren't torture for the parents. Both Eva and Shelley laughed as much as the boys.

Eva volunteered to wait for the boys while Shelley visited the ladies room. Minutes later, they switched roles and now the boys dragged Shelley across the lobby toward the arcade area. The moms had promised the boys they could each play a game before they left.

"Reid!" Jonah spotted his friend at the ticket kiosk. Shelley released the boys who promptly besieged her brother. She hesitated as she saw Reid wasn't alone. Shelley glanced over her shoulder, but saw that Eva hadn't emerged from the powder room.

"Daphne, this is my sister, Michelle Andrews. These two monkeys are my nephew, Bryce, and Eva's son Jonah." Reid placed a hand on each boy's head, trying to stay balanced, a task made more difficult with one boy tugging on each arm.

"Boys, say hello to Miss Winters," Reid said.

The stunning blonde offered the tips of her fingers to the enthusiastic young men. Jonah and Bryce each politely shook Daphne's hand. The boys were oblivious as she removed a small bottle of hand sanitizer from her designer purse, but Reid's frown was proof that he understood the insult. A quick glance at his sister's squinting eyes let him know she was seconds away from making a scene. As Daphne finished cleaning her well-manicured hands, the confrontation was averted.

"Mommy, Reid's here!" Jonah spotted his mom, who was now weaving her way through the patrons to join them.

Reid untangled himself from the grasp Daphne had reclaimed on his light blazer as soon as the boys had released him.

"Eva, darling!" Daphne hugged Eva, her exuberance implying more familiarity than was true. "What a cute outfit!"

Daphne's low cut floral top, paired with stylishly tight designer jeans, made her look like she had stepped out of a fashion magazine. Eva's simple peasant skirt and short-sleeved peach top did flatter her coloring, but the style had been at its height of popularity well over three years ago.

"Thank you." Eva suspected the compliment wasn't sincere as she took in the sight of Reid through lowered lashes. The dark jeans and light blue button-down shirt perfectly matched his eyes. He and Daphne made a striking couple.

"I'll take the boys to the arcade." Without waiting for permission, Eva led the young men away.

"What movie did you guys see?" Daphne asked Shelley without waiting for an answer. "Reid and I are going to see the one about that silly couple that can't seem to make up their minds about staying married or dating or something like that. It's supposed to be hilarious and it has that gorgeous actor in it too!"

As Daphne continued her monologue, Shelley watched her brother stare after the retreating trio. As his date took a breath, he finally spoke.

"Is this a last fling before Troy comes home? The boys seemed to have enjoyed the movie. How about you and Eva?" He glanced across the lobby again. "Was it bearable?"

"Yes, it was very good," she said. "I only hope yours is just as wholesome."

"Not likely," he said quietly as Daphne was busy reapplying her shiny lip gloss. "I did try to change her mind."

Eva and the boys returned from the arcade area in time to hear Daphne describing their expensive dinner to Shelley. Reid's sister saw Eva blush as her co-worker pressed against Reid, gushing her appreciation.

"Are you guys ready to go?" Shelley asked. "I told the sitter we'd be home by nine."

"Well, we'll let you guys go, then." Reid pried himself out of Daphne's grip once more. "Goodnight, Miss Conley."

"Buy me some popcorn, sweetie?" Daphne thwarted any chance Eva had to reply.

Leaving Shelley behind, Eva quickly led the boys out of the lobby. As Reid leaned over and kissed his sister on the cheek, Shelley grabbed his blazer lapels and whispered in his ear.

"How much would you give me to switch places, brother?"

Reid reached for his wallet as soon as he straightened up. Flipping it open, he held it out to his sister who simply shook her head as she headed out of the lobby.

Eva had looked back over her shoulder before she stepped out into the cool night air. Reid waited until Shelley waved from the doorway, before he and Daphne joined the refreshment stand line, the blonde again holding tightly to his arm. He nodded as he saw Eva glance back, but she turned away without acknowledging the gesture.

As they pulled into Eva's driveway, Shelley turned to her friend.

"You haven't said a word since we left the theater," she said. "Are you so upset?"

"Just surprised." Eva shrugged. "I didn't think Daphne was his type."

"Surprised?" Shelley asked. "Or disappointed?"

"A little of both," Eva said, not admitting the entirety of what was bothering her. "His love life is none of my business."

"Are you sure?"

"Absolutely." Eva opened the car's back door for her son. "Except as it pertains to his sanity and the influence he has with my son." The sound of Shelley's laughter as she got Jonah hooked into his booster seat did nothing to lighten Eva's mood.

27

"He was a perfect gentleman."

Eva avoided Reid on Sunday morning, but Monday afternoon he was next door when she and Jonah arrived home. As usual, Jonah was thrilled to see his friend. Figuring it would give her a reprieve from having to face Reid herself, Eva let her son join the crew as they cleaned up.

Thinking that Reid would simply send Jonah home on his own, she left the front door open.

"Delivery, ma'am," a male voice reached the kitchen. "Do you want to sign for it or should I just drop it here on the couch?" Jonah's giggles followed as Reid dumped him carefully on the sofa.

"Jonah, go wash your hands. Dinner is almost ready." Eva took a deep breath before facing the bogus deliveryman. "Thank you for the delivery. I hope he wasn't bothering you."

"Never." Reid followed her back into the kitchen. "Have you talked to Shelley today? Troy got in late last night."

"Well, then I'm sure she wouldn't have appreciated the interruption." Eva stirred the pot of pasta that was bubbling on the stove. "Was there anything else?"

113

Reid's hand gripped the back of a barstool. They stared at each other across the kitchen island.

"Are you upset with me for some reason?"

"Why would I be upset?" Eva turned away and took two plates from the cabinet. Walking past him, she set them on the dining room table, then returned and collected the silverware and glasses.

"I have no idea, but you *are* upset," Reid said as he took the glasses from her hand and filled them with ice. "I'm not leaving until you tell me. Either set another place for me— dinner smells delicious, by the way—or you can walk me to my truck and tell me on the way."

"Then let me walk you to your car, Mr. Jackson." Eva tossed the oven mitts, which she had donned to remove the garlic bread from the oven, onto the counter. She called to her son as she followed Reid out the door. "Jonah, I'll be right back. Don't touch anything in the kitchen."

"Did you enjoy your date?" She couldn't hide her sneer. Having replayed the scene at the movie theater for two days now, she was beyond pretending that his behavior was acceptable.

"Not at all, but thank you for asking." Reid stopped abruptly. They had reached the end of her driveway. She knew he sensed a brewing battle when he crossed his arms. "I didn't realize I had hidden my level of discomfort so well that night. I was miserable."

Doubt whispered in Eva's mind, but she ignored it. Years of practice hiding her feelings meant Reid didn't sense her confusion.

"It seemed to me that you were anxious for us to leave you two alone." Eva matched his stance, her own arms now crossed, combat ready. "I'd even venture to say you were assuring your sister that you were *prepared* for the rest of the evening."

"What on earth are you talking about?" Reid's brow

furrowed as he took a step toward her. "I peeled Daphne off my arm, left the theater for more popcorn during the gosh-awful bedroom scenes, and regretted greatly not taking my sister up on her offer."

"Her offer?" Eva's confusion was evident.

"She didn't tell you?" Reid took Eva's arm and walked to his truck. "It doesn't really matter now, but you can ask her. I know you saw me pull out my wallet. You'll probably think it's hilarious." He glanced at Eva in time to see her pale.

"Wallet? What did Shelley want with your wallet?" Eva remembered the disappointment she had felt thinking his display had been to assure his sister that he was ready for the evening to progress as far as Daphne would allow. Depressed and saddened that she had so misjudged him, Eva had been miserable all weekend. Now it seemed that misery was unfounded.

Her thoughts raced, but their chaos didn't match the tumult that Reid was experiencing. Picturing the scene through Eva's eyes, he realized how she had interpreted his offering his wallet to his sister. Anger followed dawning understanding.

"You thought I was showing Shelley I was *prepared* in case I wanted to sleep with Daphne. That's rich! You of all people!" He leaned close, his forehead almost touching hers. His quiet tone let Eva know he was angrier than she had ever seen him, but his words stung and the memory of that evening were too fresh.

"What do you mean, 'Me of all people?' Just because I have Jonah, you think I can't be offended by your plans with Daphne?"

"I *mean* that I thought you would've experienced enough judgment over Jonah to know to think twice before making assumptions. How dare you think that I'd have a night of intimacy planned with *any* woman who was not my wife, much less Ms. Daphne Winters. I take my faith more seriously than that. If your analysis of my character wasn't so offensive, it'd be comical. You're a piece of work, ma'am."

"Reid, I..." Eva tried to respond, but he waved off her attempt. He climbed into the cab of his truck.

"Ask Shelley what she told me that night, and if she tells you, know that there's *no way* I'd accept her offer any more. Good night, Miss Conley."

Eva stared as he peeled out of the cul-de-sac without a backward glance. Her conversation with Daphne the next morning only served to increase her guilt.

"So, have you talked to Reid?" Daphne cornered Eva in the break room mid-morning on Tuesday. Eva nearly dropped her cup of coffee. "When I asked him out, I was hoping he'd be a little more exciting. I hated having to tell him it wasn't going to work. I hope I didn't break his heart."

"It looked like your date was going so well when we saw you," Eva said with forced aloofness. "I hope nothing unpleasant happened."

"No, he was a perfect gentleman," Daphne said with a sly smile. "That was the problem—if you know what I mean."

Whether she responded to Daphne or not, Eva later couldn't remember.

At lunchtime, Eva called Shelley. She dreaded the conversation, but knew now that she had made a huge mistake.

"I hate to bother you, Shelley." Knowing she couldn't face Reid without apologizing, and knowing he probably wouldn't want to speak to her, Eva decided to confess her foolishness to his sister.

"As long as you're not backing out of tonight. Troy's looking forward to meeting you and Jonah."

116

"First, even though your brother felt the right to warn me away from Adam Richter, I have no right to interfere in his relationships. But, Shelley, I've done something really stupid." Eva was glad she was alone in the break room as she fought back tears as she poured out the story, her bad assumptions, and her guilt.

"I'm disappointed, Eva," Shelley said quietly when the confession was done. "I know just because a man goes to church, that doesn't always mean he lives a godly life, but I thought you knew Reid better than that. I thought you knew *me* better than that. I would've yanked him out of the theater by his ear if that's what he was showing me." Shelley paused. "I do understand, though, that his animosity and wicked tongue is partly to blame. He does seem bent on making you think the worst of him."

"No, that's not true. This is all on me." Eva sighed. "I won't be coming tonight. I don't think I can face him."

"I think that's exactly what you need to do," Shelley said. "Did he tell you what the wallet thing was really about?"

"No. All he said was that if you wanted to tell me, you could," Eva said. "He also told me that there's no way he would want to take you up on your offer now. Of course, I don't have any idea what he was talking about."

Eva heard Shelley sigh.

"Telling you now would only embarrass both of you, so I'll save it for later," Shelley said. "Please come tonight. Apologize. It will be okay, I promise."

After she hung up, Shelley filled Troy in on all the Reid and Eva drama.

"He's a goner, for sure," Reid's brother-in-law said. "How bad do you think this latest snafu is? Sounds like it's not their first."

"Not likely to be their last, either," Shelley said. "I think Eva had started to tolerate him, and even like him a little bit, so when he showed up with that, uh, *woman*, it really shocked her. I still don't know the story behind her and Jonah, so for all I know her reaction could have something to do with that, too."

"Eva sounds like a perfect match for Reid, if her sense of humor is anything like you've described," Troy said. "Tell Reid why you think she misunderstood the situation. It will make it easier for him to forgive her."

"That's true. I'll tell him, but make sure you don't say anything to them about her being a good match for him! Their relationship is quite humorous, but still has a bite of animosity in it. He's a long way from admitting that he sees her as anything other than an annoyance who happens to be Jonah's mom."

Reid had heard their car. After he sent Jonah around to the backyard where the other kids were playing, he took the opportunity the privacy of the driveway afforded to confront Eva. As she gathered the bouquet of flowers that she had cut from her backyard garden, Reid grabbed the cake carrier. He placed his burden on the hood of her car and took the flowers from her hands, setting them down next to the cake.

"So, Dewey, I hear you want to apologize." He leaned casually against the front of her car.

"Yes," Eva took a deep breath and kept her head down, not wanting to see his response to her confession. "I'm sorry. I knew even when I was doing it that my assumptions were wrong. The only excuse I have is that Daphne is so dazzling, and I was confused." She peeked up at him as she finished.

"Dazzling? No." Reid shuddered. "Dangerous, yes. You're forgiven, but please don't introduce me to another Daphne. Ever. Promise?"

"I promise." Eva laughed. The relief was liberating.

118

28

"Won't this be too dangerous?"

The email went out to the Young Adult's class on Monday morning. There was an unexpected opening on a community service project scheduled for late June. A group of college students and adults were going to work on homes for elderly and disabled residents in northern Mississippi, an area that had been hit by a series of tornados and flooding over the last couple of years. One of the female adult team members had a family emergency, which meant she couldn't make the trip.

"Angie, this is Eva." Before Eva thought through the implications, she made the phone call. During her teen years, her home church had participated in work camps every summer. Some of her most significant spiritual decisions had been made on those trips.

"You've just made my day!" The assistant pastor's wife was thrilled with Eva's offer to take the open slot on the trip. "We have a team meeting before choir practice. I'm so excited!"

Angie's excitement kept coming to mind as Eva began to doubt her hasty decision. A phone call to her parents confirmed their willingness to have their grandson for a week. Time off from work wasn't an issue. The college closed its offices and buildings two weeks in the summer for campus wide repairs. When Jim announced the opening, Eva realized that the trip fell in the middle of the college's shutdown, and let that guide her hasty decision. Hoping the meeting with the team would confirm her choice, Eva and Jonah headed to church early on Wednesday.

As she pulled into the parking lot, her stomach did a flip.

"Reid!" Jonah leapt from the car as soon as Eva opened the door. The contractor swung her son up onto his shoulders.

"What are you feeding this little monster?" Reid asked Eva as they walked into the church building. "He weighs more than an elephant."

Jonah's giggles didn't bring the usual smile to Eva's lips. *No, no, no! How did I not think about the possibility that Reid would be on the trip, too?*

"Please tell me you're not here early for a meeting." Forcing optimism, she ventured a question.

"Sorry, Einstein." Reid swung Jonah down and opened the sanctuary door for Eva. "I could beg the same of you, but that would be rude, now wouldn't it? Looks like you're taking the open spot on our little summer adventure."

"I'm not so sure anymore."

"Backing out before even beginning?" Reid pointed Jonah to the pew where Angie and Kendra were sitting. "Not that I'd be surprised given your sensibility to anything remotely risky."

"Excuse me?"

"C'mon, Princess. You can't deny that you're lean to the cautious side, my dear." Reid mirrored her stance, crossing his arms as he leaned toward her. His face was only inches from hers. "Won't this be a little too dangerous for you?"

"You're ridiculous!" Eva turned and marched up the aisle to join Angie.

A few minutes later fate provided a silver lining. Adam Richter walked in. His grin, framed by those gorgeous dimples, perfectly matched the size of Reid's frown.

"This trip just got a whole lot better," he said, slipping into the spot next to her on the pew.

Although Eva wasn't interested in Adam in any way, she couldn't resist the chance to annoy Reid. She smiled broadly up at the handsome realtor. From where they sat, she could see Reid across the aisle. Somehow, the frown on his face didn't make her as happy as she had hoped.

Jim introduced Eva to the members of the team and handed her the documents she would need to complete to confirm her registration. The finances weren't going to be a problem, since the team member that dropped out had already paid for the spot. Everything was falling into place.

The service project was part of a nationwide ministry that visited several cities each summer. The teams of college students and adults would sleep, dine, and have their meetings at a local university campus. Church teams spread out among several worksites during the day and all four hundred plus workers would meet in the evenings for a time of sharing and worship.

"Do you have any questions, Eva?" Jim asked her as the meeting ended and the others filed out of the sanctuary to their respective Bible studies or children's ministries.

"No," she said. "Sounds like they run their programs just like they did when I was in college."

"You'll have a chance to be part of the worship team, if you want. I know Reid had planned to do that, isn't that correct, Reid?" Jim greeted the man who had strolled up to join them.

"That was my plan." His words hung in the air as he stared at Eva. She could almost hear the added phrase, *until Eva joined the trip.*

"Great!" Jim was either unaware of the tension or was

ignoring it. "I'm sure Reid can fill you in on any details I missed." Eva hated to think the kind young pastor would be intentionally cruel, but his comment seemed purposeful. Her suspicions increased when she saw the high five Angie gave her husband as they left the meeting.

"They've asked me to be one of the lead contractors," Reid said. "Otherwise, I would back out if you asked me to."

"Why would I do that?" Eva gathered her purse and stepped around him, trying to avoid brushing against him. The task was impossible when he refused to move out of her way. The contact was brief but sent a shiver down her back.

"Obviously, you find my presence annoying." Reid seemed to interpret her shudder as disgust. "My offer is serious, but you should let Jim know soon if he needs to find a replacement for me."

"I'm sure you're irreplaceable," Eva said over her shoulder. "Besides, the campus should be big enough to handle both of us." She dismissed the growl she heard as the noise of the sound system warming up.

***

The ten-hour trip to Mississippi meant an early departure time. The removal of the van's back seat accommodated the suitcases and most of the team's tools were stowed in the back of Reid's truck. The extended cab meant the whole team wouldn't have to squeeze into the limited seats in the van. The five adults would take turns driving. Jim had confirmed that Eva was comfortable driving the large van, so she was surprised to see that she was on the rotation for driving Reid's truck instead.

A surprise call from her brother meant that Eva wasn't dreading the trip as much. Derek planned to join the group for lunch since Mariella's mother had arrived from Mexico to help as the new baby's arrival was close.

A recent conversation with their father gave the protective older brother an additional reason for making the two-hour drive to meet up with the convoy.

Reid didn't think anything was unusual as he saw the man leaning casually against a mini-van as they pulled into the restaurant parking lot. The man's wide grin was perplexing, though. As Jim slowed to a stop, Reid saw Eva leap from the van. The embrace was more bear hug than romantic, but Reid's brow furrowed as he watched. As the male wiped apparent tears from Eva's cheeks, Reid decided to intervene—strictly as a friend he told himself.

"Everything okay, Einstein?" He asked as he approached the couple, with forced nonchalance. His concern would've turned to chagrin had he known that Eva's companion has just asked her which man was "the guy Dad told me about."

"Reid, this is my brother, Derek," Eva elbowed her brother as she turned toward the frowning contractor. "Derek, this is Reid Jackson. He's the one that's bumped you out of first place on Jonah's list."

"I see the resemblance now," Reid said. The two men shook hands, but Eva noticed the coolness on Reid's part. Derek followed them back to the van so Eva could retrieve her wallet that she had left in her excitement. By unspoken agreement, Reid joined the siblings at a table away from the others—a choice not lost on Jim and Angie. The restaurant was buffet style and Eva reluctantly left the two men alone while she filled her salad plate.

"So, you and Jonah are best friends I hear," Derek said as he watched Reid watch Eva. "My nephew has very discerning taste, so you must not be a derelict or a criminal." The sarcasm was hereditary.

"Not yet." Reid's barbed response drew a laugh from Eva's brother. When Reid relaxed and smiled in return,

Derek pressed on, intrigued by the praises his parents had for this Mr. Jackson. Derek, almost seven years Eva's senior, was protective to the point of hovering at times. By the time Eva returned to the table, to shoo Reid toward the buffet line, Derek had joined his parents and nephew in the Reid Jackson Fan Club.

Eva launched immediately into questions about Mariella's condition and her nephew Enrique's feelings about the soon-to-arrive baby sister. "Oh, and don't tell Reid that I can speak Spanish. When he finds out Mari is from Mexico, he may put two and two together. It's a skill I want kept secret."

"Eavesdropping on conversations are we, Sis?" Derek asked.

"No, just being able to understand ones that he thinks are veiled."

The rest of the meal was uneventful but informative. Derek left convinced the two shared a bond as unacknowledged as it was undeniable.

Eva was sad to say goodbye to her brother so when they switched drivers after lunch, she was glad to find that Angie would be riding shotgun and two of the college girls would join them. Despite enjoying the company, Eva was exhausted when they eventually arrived at the campus. Her shoulders were sore and a tension headache was in full force.

Reid noticed her discomfort as she tried to work out the kinks while the students unloaded the truck.

"Need a massage?" Adam's hands rubbed her shoulders, his thumbs expertly working out the knots. "Why so tense?"

"Richter!" Reid called from the back of the van as he tossed out a duffel bag. "Is this yours?"

"The task master summons me," Adam said. Before he walked away, he turned her around. "Feel better?"

"Yes, thank you. I think I was just tense because I was driving Reid's truck." She stepped away from the closeness Adam had created. "He already doesn't like me. Can you imagine if I had damaged his baby?"

"The look on his face proves your point." Adam's laughter wasn't contagious as Reid scowled at the pair.

Determined that Reid's presence wouldn't dampen her experience, Eva had agreed to be part of the worship team. The free time most of the participants enjoyed before dinner wasn't available to those that were helping with the music or the evening program. Even though she had expected it, seeing Reid join the group of singers made her rethink the wisdom of her volunteering.

As the worship leader led them in prayer, Eva confessed her attitude.

Lord, help me put aside my feelings toward Reid and enjoy this week. I want to see You work through our whole team and I'm struggling with getting out of your way so You can show up in my life. She peeked up as she prayed. She blushed as she saw Reid watching her. He nodded and she squeezed her eyes shut again. *And, Father, please help Reid have a good week, too.*

29

"I do know how to do this."

The next morning her resolve was tested. As she made her way to her group rally point, she saw the red truck that was a recurring part of her nightmares. *Great. We're at the same site.*

Theirs was one of the three worksites and involved a row of four homes in an older part of the small community. Two were new homes, partially started by another national group known for encouraging poverty-stricken neighborhoods in their renewal efforts. The group would be completing the drywall installation and all the finishing touches in the two homes. It would be quite a task. The other two homes were older. One was getting a new roof, repairs to rotting wood, and a complete exterior paint facelift. The last home had a porch that needed some repairs, and then that crew would be constructing a short wheelchair ramp.

As two other men joined their group, both wearing Staff shirts, Eva's hopes rose. At least there was a chance she'd be working with another contractor. Jim, Angie, and Adam were all at other sites, so Eva had to face the day with only two students from church at her site. As the group finished loading their supplies into Reid's truck and a trailer

126

belonging to another church, Reid called everyone together.

He pointed out the three vehicles that would transport the group of thirty or so people to their site. Eva grabbed her tool belt and headed toward one of the vans.

"Where do you think you're going?" Reid intercepted her route.

"To the van." Eva pointed around the form blocking her way.

"Chicken?"

"No, thank you. I'm not hungry." She climbed into the van but turned in time to see his salute and smile.

After unloading their tools at their site, which was less than ten miles from campus, the group introduced themselves to the residents. Eva felt an immediate connection to Miss Edith, the elderly homeowner of the house that would be getting a new wheelchair ramp. Assuring her that she would visit with her later, Eva followed the group to the staging point. Reid was taking charge, of course. *It's going to be a long week,* Eva thought.

Wanting to remain out of his line of sight, she scooted into the shadow of a large oak tree. The adults had received advanced notice of their tasks, so Eva only half listened to the instructions. She knew would be working on Miss Edith's house because of her carpentry experience.

"To make it easier to keep track of where we are, we've named the houses Alpha, Bravo, Charlie, and Delta." He pointed to each house as he assigned them their military tags.

"Oh, please." Eva mumbled mockery caused several of the girls to giggle. Although she was sure the noise wasn't loud enough for him to hear, Reid glanced her way. When he turned back around, she stuck out her tongue. The childish act set off another round of chuckles.

"You find something comical, Einstein?" Reid leveled a look at Eva, one dark eyebrow raised.

127

Trying to hold in her laughter, she merely shook her head and followed the others toward her assigned work spot.

Explaining the project to the crew working with her took up most of her day. Several of the girls were inexperienced, and a couple hadn't handled a hammer before.

One of the best gifts her dad had given her was the working knowledge of tools and cars. From the time she was four or five, he had let her hang out with him in the garage and around the house when he did repairs. The local hardware store also had monthly woodworking projects for kids and Eva had been to every one.

Hoping to pass this skill on to another generation of young ladies, she decided to spend the extra time to teach this attentive trio. The difficult first step was convincing them that holding the hammer further back on the handle was key.

"Don't choke it." As she demonstrated, a movement at the edge of the house caught her eye. Reid was watching her. Thinking the smirk was indicative of his normal patronizing, she challenged him.

"Reid, come here. I want to prove to them that holding the hammer correctly makes all the difference." Eva explained the challenge to the crew. Reid would hold his hammer the way the girls had begun, with his hand next to the head. Eva would grasp hers near the end of the handle.

"Are you sure you want to do this?" Reid asked as he flipped his hammer into the air and caught it as it rotated. "I'd hate to embarrass you in front of your students." The girls giggled in response. Eva ignored him.

"We'll race and you'll see that I'll beat him even though he's stronger and faster than me."

"He'll let you win," one of the girls said.

"No, he won't." Eva laughed. "He doesn't like me, even

a little bit, so there's no way he's going to 'let' me win. Right, Reid?"

The girls turned to Reid, waiting for his answer. He hesitated.

"Right." He finally shrugged. "She disliked me from the moment she laid eyes on me."

"Really? That's your story?" Eva set aside the challenge and placed her hands on her hips. "I'll explain, girls. My dislike stemmed from the fact that he had blocked in my car, in my own driveway, on my first day of work. But suffice it to say, he has made it clear that the animosity is mutual."

The silent standoff stretched past the point of comfort. One of the young ladies finally broke in. "Are you two going to race or not?"

The sound of hammers filled the air for only seconds. Eva won. Reid conceded, perhaps not gracefully, but conceded nonetheless.

At the afternoon break, Eva grabbed her snack and stepped away from the group. "I'm going to call my family," she told one of the girls.

"Tell Jonah I said hello," Reid said when he found her hiding spot.

She shook her head.

"Yes," he said.

"No," she said as she covered the phone. "Go away."

"You're so stubborn." He didn't move.

"So are you," she said, "and sometimes that's a virtue."

"Not when it's out of selfishness, it's not." When he still didn't leave, she sighed and relayed the greeting to her son.

"Reid says 'Hello,' buddy. I have to go now. Behave for Grandma and Grandpa."

As they walked back to join the crew, Reid tugged on the back of her t-shirt. "You're wrong you know," he said.

"Again?" She tugged her shirt out of his grasp. "About

129

what this time? Just tell me so I can get back to work."

"About me not liking you." Reid winked and pulled her ponytail before heading to the house next door.

***

An hour before the end of their workday, Eva's crew was finishing the demolition of the damaged boards on the porch. One of the team warned Miss Edith that it was no longer safe to come out the front door, so she had locked it and put a chair in front of it.

"Sometimes I forget things," she said. Eva decided to take the extra precaution of nailing a temporary board across the outside of the door. When Reid and two other contractors came around the corner of Miss Edith's house, he saw Eva nailing the board while two students held it.

"What are you doing?" His demand startled her and she missed the nail.

"The foxtrot." Her quick comeback earned a chuckle from one of the other contractors, an older man named Fred. Realizing he wasn't alone, she resisted further discord and explained the situation.

"Good thinking." The affirmation from Fred and the other contractor made Eva want to gloat. Instead, she forced herself to simply finish the task and set the students to cleaning up their tools. A few minutes later, she saw a chance for a private conversation with Reid.

"I do know how to do this, you know. If you wouldn't spend so much time checking up on me, you'd probably have a better day." His grumpy mood confused Eva given the teasing he had done earlier. Her admonition didn't help. "I'm sure there are many other helpless females at the other sites that need your 'assistance' more than I do."

"Excuse me?" Reid's raised eyebrows and a sudden grin transformed his face. Eva watched in fascination, thinking again how beautiful his eyes were. Catching herself, she

130

shook away her wayward thoughts.

"I'm sure they would love to have you hover over them. They'd welcome it in fact, judging by the looks you get."

"Sounds like someone's jealous." His smile was now a full smirk.

"Sounds like someone's delusional," she said.

30

"Can we declare a truce?"

That evening, Eva opted for the early dinner. She was almost done with her meal when Jim and Angie joined her. The women's dorms featured suite type rooms. Eva and Angie were rooming together and were sharing a bathroom with three of the college girls from their church. Knowing the girls wouldn't be done quickly, Eva had decided to take the last shower time.

"I'm messy, so you might not want to get too close." As they sat down, Eva noticed Angie had showered. "Did the girls leave you any hot water?"

"Sure did. Shower's free now, too." Angie waved her fork toward the dinner line. "They came in right behind us."

Eva decided to have another cup of coffee and enjoy her dessert with the couple, a decision she regretted when she returned to the table. Reid was now sitting with them.

Escape would be admitting she was uncomfortable in her disheveled state, next to his clean, fresh smell. That wasn't an option. She could just imagine his grin of victory.

"You guys are at the same site, correct?" Angie smiled at Eva, letting her know she understood the awkwardness. Her attempt to spur the conversation wasn't successful, though. "How was your day? Did you get a lot done?"

Reid was busy shoveling in his meal but took time to nod. Eva stayed noticeably quiet.

"Eva? You disagree?" Jim asked.

"I think things could've gone better, but that's probably not an opinion shared by everyone on our site."

"Meaning?" Jim dodged a kick from his wife under the table.

"If some people would trust other people to complete tasks, even if they do it differently from the way those people expect..." Eva shrugged as she let her words trail off. "Well, let me just say, my day would've gone better."

Reid dropped his fork and pushed his meal away—a motion that would have been more dramatic had he not been eating from a paper plate.

"Well, Princess, if *some* people would trust that *other* people know what they're doing and just follow directions instead of arguing, then maybe *my* day would have gone better!"

When Reid's rant ended, silence had descended on the table. He ignored the tension and stacked his dishes on top of Eva's, then pointed to her half-eaten apple pie. "Are you going to finish that?" His question was met with silence.

"I'm going to excuse myself. Hopefully the shower will be open now." Eva pushed away from the table. "Besides, I seem to have lost my appetite."

"You'd better hurry if you're going to make it to music practice." He spoke around the last bite of her apple pie before reaching for his untouched piece.

"I'm not sure I'll be singing tonight." Eva reached for the stack Reid had created. "I don't think my attitude will be appropriate." Eva balanced the tower of plates and dropped them in the trash bin by the door. Reid watched her leave, then hung his head.

"Are you going after her or not?" Angie glared at Reid.

"Trouble in paradise?" Adam Richter had just arrived at the table, having observed Eva's hasty retreat and Reid's morose face.

"Shut up, Richter." Reid trotted after Eva and spied her walking toward the women's hall.

"Einstein, wait!" He called her as she rounded the corner of the long hallway. Once she passed through the double doors past the wide lobby, he would miss her, since the women's hall was off limits to the guys. He saw her slow her pace, but she didn't stop. "I know you heard me."

"What do you want now, Reid?" She kept one hand on the door even though Reid stopped several feet away. "I really do need a shower."

"Can we declare a truce?"

"Truce?" *No apology, of course,* she thought.

"Just for this week?" Reid advanced a half step closer.

Eva searched his face for signs of mockery. He looked as tired as she felt. Giving in, she nodded.

"I'm tired of the drama." She extended her hand in a symbolic offering. "Deal, but I may need to be reminded occasionally."

"Deal. One week truce." He took her hand, surprisingly gently, and raised it to his lips.

Eva jerked her hand away. As if on cue, her phone rang.

"I've got to take this. It's Jonah and my parents." She moved away from the door and moved back into the lobby where phone reception was better.

"Let me say 'hello.' Can you put it on speaker?" Because of the newly declared truce, she complied, only to regret it as Jonah seemed more excited to be talking with Reid than her.

Reid's conversation regressed into commentary that included statements like, "I hope you're obeying your grandma and grandpa. Your mom is having a bit of trouble in that area, but I'm working on her." Eva could hear her parents laughing in the background. After the weekend of Jonah's birthday party, when her parents had met Reid, Eva had spent a couple of days ignoring their glowing praises of Mr. Jackson.

"Good luck with that," her dad called. Eva pulled the phone out of Reid's hand.

"Jonah, Mr. Reid needs to get back to his dessert. I'm sure it's getting cold." Switching the phone off speaker mode, Reid saluted as she waved him away in dismissal.

Just around the corner, Reid remembered that he had intended to ask Mr. Conley about the weather. As he turned back, Eva's next comment reached him.

"He's just as big a bully here as at home. This week's going to be unbearable," Eva said. Reid wheeled on his heel before she saw him. Escaping back to the cafeteria, he missed her clarification.

"I know it's more my issue than his, and God's dealing with me, but I'm not happy about it," Eva said before ending the call. "Hopefully we'll be able to stick to the truce we've declared."

Reid rejoined the others in the cafeteria.

"How did it go? Not so well if your face tells an accurate story," Jim and Angie were waiting expectantly for his return.

"She called me a bully." Reid slumped into his chair.

"To your face?"

"No, she got a call after dinner from her folks and Jonah. She thought I was on my way back here, but I overheard."

"You were eavesdropping?" Angie asked. In defense, Reid explained why he had turned back around.

Jim leaned back in his chair, crossed his arms, and shook his head at his friend. "Reid, why do you think she makes you so mad?" he asked.

"Some weird overriding desire to protect her from

herself, I think." Reid finished his now cold coffee.

"Just from herself?" Jim glanced toward Adam Richter, who had moved to another table where a rousing game of 'Go Fish' was in progress.

"Because of her..." Reid hesitated, "...situation, I think Richter sees her as fair game. One of these days I may have to take away his ability to deliver that leer." Reid dropped his voice after glancing toward Adam who had apparently heard his name. "But my desire to keep her away from him is beside the point. I care about Jonah. The manner in which he arrived in her life makes no difference to me."

"Are you sure?" Angie unsuccessfully hid a smile behind a sip of her coffee.

"Yes, Mrs. Baldwin," Reid said not fooled by Angie's nonchalance. "Our relationship is contentious because of *her*, not because I've judged her *situation*. Miss Eva Conley harps on me every chance she gets. From the very beginning, she's done nothing but rail at me."

"I think you're exaggerating," Jim said. "From what we've seen of Eva, she's not purposefully trying to make your life difficult. Can you honestly say she rails at you *all* the time?"

"Well, almost all the time." Reid remembered their water fight and smiled into his now empty coffee cup, missing the look between the young pastor and his wife.

"From what I remember, you did have her blocked in and almost made her late for work." Angie's reminder earned only a halfhearted concession from Reid.

"True, but she really, really overreacted. You'd have thought I purposely tried to get her fired."

"Let me get this straight," Jim said, describing Reid's actions that Eva faced on her first day of work. "She's a single mom, on her own, in a new town, on her first day of a new job. Some stranger blocks her driveway preventing her from getting out. I'm sure you profusely apologized and moved your truck immediately, right?"

"Well, maybe not." Reid had the grace to look a little embarrassed.

"Do you think her reaction could have been out of fear and not just anger?" Jim leaned back, arms crossed, waiting for Reid's attempt to defend himself. "What would you have done if she *had* lost her job because she was late?"

"Fine!" Reid stood abruptly. "I'm a terrible person. Eva's a saint. Case closed. I'm done."

"Do you think we pushed him too far?" Angie asked her husband as they watched Reid's forlorn journey out of the dining hall.

"Someone needs to," Jim said. "The sooner he figures out what's going on, the better for all of us."

31

"It's amazing you're still single."

Reid was half an hour early for music practice, but he knew he needed to cool down. Taking advantage of the quiet, he prayed for patience and understanding. *Lord I don't understand why I can't keep control of my words when I'm around Eva. Please help me be more of a gentleman and less of a boor.*

After the music team made a quick run-through of the well-known praise choruses, the auditorium doors opened and the seats filled up quickly. Reid saw their group enter, but noticed Eva wasn't with them.

Because tonight's meeting was going to be short, the speaker had asked the vocalists to sit up front so they could return quickly for the ending number. After the opening music, Reid saw Eva settle into the seat Angie had saved for her. The evening speaker's brief message reminded them that they were sharing God's love in a very visible way. Sharing the verses from Matthew's gospel, he reminded the campers that they were honoring their Heavenly Father as they ministered to the residents. Closing the program, he encouraged the participants to get a good night's sleep and thanked them for their hard work. Reid watched in frustration as Eva slipped out before the closing prayer, avoiding him altogether.

Refusing to let the evening end like this, he stopped Fred on his way out of the gym.

"I need to go check with Eva about something," he told the older man. "Can you tell Jim I'll be back in the room in a little while?"

Reid headed to the lobby of the women's dorm. Seeing one of the girls from their worksite, he asked if she could find Eva.

"Just tell her one of the leaders needs to see her." He paced the sitting area while he waited, turning anxiously toward the heavy metal doors every time they opened. Reid was close to giving up when a group of campers scurried through the lobby doors, giggling as they hurried to make curfew. As the young ladies pulled open the hallway doors, he saw Eva heading his way.

"You!" Spotting him, she turned around to head back down the darkened hallway. Some of the building's interior lights were already off, warning the campers of the approaching lights-out time. Only the chaperones were still allowed in the halls.

"C'mon, Eva," he called after her, "give a guy a break." She relented, marching past him through the darkened lobby and out onto the front steps. The cool night air was a welcome reprieve from the heat they had felt most of the day.

"I agreed to your ceasefire," she said as they stood in the shadows of the front walkway. The breeze blew her hair, which she had taken out of her customary ponytail, and she brushed it out of her eyes. "What did I do now?"

"Nothing," he said. "I just wanted to make sure you were okay. When you didn't show up for music practice, I thought you had changed your mind about the truce."

The wind picked up again. Strands of hair blew across her face, and Reid reached out instinctively to tuck them behind her ear.

When she jerked away, the movement put her face in the light from the lamppost.

"What did you do to your face?" Reid exclaimed as he got his first good look at her. The girls in the suite next to hers were having a makeup session. Eva, who normally wore little if any makeup, had relented and let them apply eye shadow, mascara, and blush. She had thought it would lift her spirits. Apparently, their handiwork was not impressive.

"Why all the makeup? Trying to entice someone in particular?" He continued his tirade, forgetting he was supposed to be attempting reconciliation.

"No, not that it'd be any of your business if I were." She crossed her arms against the cool breeze of the evening air

"Why are you so ornery?" Reid took a step closer, stopping inches away as her golden eyes stared up at him.

"I'm amazed that you're still single." She spun away and returned to her room.

***

Reid snapped off his lamp and turned over in a huff. He had spent the last half hour discussing his latest run-in with Eva.

"This isn't funny, Rev. Baldwin. I'm going to sleep before I say something I can't take back."

"To me or to Eva?" Jim's laughter was met with a growl.

"You're so far gone it's funny," Jim said before he turned off his own lamp.

"I haven't gone anywhere." Reid's muffled response came from under the pillow that covered his head.

"You may not have gotten on the train yet, but you've bought the ticket," Jim's penchant for terrible metaphors reared its head. "Now you're just waiting for it to get validated." The young pastor seemed to find his own humor much more entertaining than his roommate did.

Silence lasted only a few minutes when the light of Jim's phone brightened the dorm room.

"What are you doing?" Reid sat up in protest.

"Searching for heavy equipment rentals." Jim's bizarre answer did nothing to help Reid's mood. "Do you think a back hoe or a crane would be better?"

"What on earth for?" Reid swung his legs off the bed and sat up.

"To help you out of the hole you're digging for yourself." Reid's pillow hit Jim in the face. A grand fight—worthy of any middle school sleepover—ensued. The noise drew college boys from neighboring rooms and the pillow fight morphed into a mock wrestling match. The fun lasted until the noise woke Fred. The older contractor, known for his ability to sleep through most anything, broke up the party.

"First a train ticket, then digging a hole," Reid said as he and Jim turned in once more. "You're mixing your metaphors, which have gotten worse over the last few months, by the way. I doubt that the pastor will ever let you preach again if I tell him how awfully you've treated those of us under your care this week."

32

"Nice to know you care."

Tuesday morning came much too early. Adults and college kids alike, unused to much physical exertion, were moving slower than usual. The camp had asked for volunteers to set up the meals and Eva had signed up for Tuesday morning. She was returning to her room, taking the chance to be outside before it heated up. As she came around the corner outside the dorm, she ran into Reid, literally.

Reid had gotten up early for a short run. He didn't consider himself a fitness freak, but after the disintegration of his efforts last night, he needed to clear his head. He was honest enough with himself to admit it was only Miss Eva Conley that he needed to clear out of his head. Running into her, literally, as he was slipping his t-shirt back on, wasn't a welcome event.

Hands she had thrown up in defense now rested on his chest. She froze, unable to pull her gaze away from his chest.

"See something you like?" He asked as he lifted her hands away and pulled his shirt on the rest of the way.

"Not particularly." Recovering her composure, her defiant eyes, sans makeup, met his. She hoped he couldn't see the blush she felt moving up her neck and across her face. "It may be difficult for you men to understand, but not all women find sweaty men attractive."

"I'm flattered you find me attractive."

"That's not what I said." She made a show of wiping her hands on her shorts. "Even moderately intelligent women can differentiate between a man's outward appearance and his inner character. Good character will win over a gorgeous body every time."

"You think I have a gorgeous body?" The raised eyebrow, which she had seen so often accompanied by a smirk. How the expression could be so annoying and attractive at the same time maddened her.

She started to turn away, but his hand on her elbow stopped her. Instead of pulling away, she simply stood still, waiting for him to release her.

"I'm sorry about my stupid comment last night." Reid dropped his hand. "Sometimes I think there's something wrong with the connection between my brain and my mouth." He paused as he saw her try not to smile in agreement. "It was just a surprise to see you with so much make-up on. In the spirit of our truce, I hope you can forgive me."

As he turned to go inside, Eva laid a hand on his forearm, and she could feel his muscles tense under her light touch.

"Thanks, Reid, but I need to apologize, too. I let my opinion of you undermine your leadership on the site yesterday. You're the team leader, and a very good one. I'll try to be supportive and follow your lead more willingly."

"Eva Marie Conley, are you saying you'll *submit* to my authority?" He covered her hand with his free one. The teasing words let her know the tension of the last night was easing.

"I said no such thing." She tugged her hand free. "I'll see you at the site, Reid."

"I'll be there, Princess."

An hour later, Eva poured coffee into her thermos, and grabbed a pastry before driving her crew to the site. She had skipped breakfast, not wanting to face Reid again before arming herself with caffeine. Over her shoulder, Eva saw Angie and several of the church girls come into the cafeteria.

"There's Eva." One of the girls from church waved as she and Angie made their way toward Eva. "She'll know."

"Where's Reid?" Angie asked.

"He's in the tool room." Eva answered without thinking.

"I told you she always knows where he is," the college co-ed giggled. "I think she has ESP."

"Nope," Eva said, hoping they didn't see her blush. "It's a defense mechanism. Forewarned is forearmed."

Angie joined in the laughter as the young ladies left to head to the van, and then turned back toward Eva, watching her stir creamer into her coffee. When Eva glanced up, Angie was grinning.

"What?" Eva asked. "It's true. He's constantly on my case, so why wouldn't I want to know where he is so I can avoid him?"

"Yeah, right. Avoiding him—that's what you're doing." Angie's laugh followed Eva out of the cafeteria.

***

"Are you good without me this morning?" Reid asked her as she set up the tools needed for the porch repairs. She blinked up at him, confused for a moment.

"I suppose I can survive one day." Sarcasm came to her defense. "It's quite a miracle, though, how I've managed for this many years without you."

"Is that so?" Reid took a step toward her as she realized the foolishness of her words.

144

"You know what I meant," she said, backing up until she bumped into the porch support.

"Do I?" He stopped his advance but leaned in. "Do you?"

"Go away." Eva straightened up and pushed him back, forcing herself to not reveal how the feel of his chest beneath her palms—for the second time that morning—affected her. "We'll be fine here. We're cutting the boards and since I now have expert hammer wielders we should be moving on to the ramp by lunchtime."

"Super." Reid seemed to be in a hurry to escape now. "Fred will check on you guys. I have to be on Bravo's roof most of the day."

"Be careful." Her involuntary warning stopped his retreat.

"I will." Reid turned back with a smile. "Nice to know you care."

Quickly covering her mistake, she forced a nonchalant shrug.

"Jonah would never forgive me if you got hurt." It was harder to ignore his chuckle as he moved down the sidewalk.

33

"Listen to me, young lady."

By mid-morning the new porch boards were in place and Eva helped Miss Edith onto the now sturdy structure. The crews took regular water breaks and had a mid-morning snack scheduled, so Eva let the crew join their friends next door.

This morning Miss Edith's grandson Landry was visiting and he joined them for some lemonade and cookies. As if sensing the goodies, Reid appeared within minutes.

"I hear the best cookies on the planet are on this porch." He plopped down next to the young boy. Formally extending his hand, he introduced himself. "My name is Reid. Is Miss Eva behaving?"

The wide-eyed boy shook hands but didn't answer. He glanced between three adults, finally smiling when he heard his grandma's laughter.

"Well, Miss Edith, tell us what you think of this new porch." Reid took a cookie from the plate she offered. Appearing to listen intently to the older lady, he watched Eva's interaction with Landry. The youngster had a yo-yo and she was helping him untangle the long string. After the job was done, Eva refilled their drinks. She felt Reid's hand on her shoulder.

"Are you okay?" He turned her toward him and wiped the lone tear from her cheek.

"I miss Jonah."

He gave her a quick hug. "I do too."

"Who's Jonah?" With the innocent curiosity of most four-year-olds, Landry interrupted their brief contact. They sprang apart. Eva moved back to sit next to Miss Edith letting Reid field the question.

"Jonah is Miss Eva's son. He just turned five and has wonderful taste in friends." His self-serving comment was lost on Landry, but not on his grandmother. The wise woman understood there were untold layers to this situation, but with the boldness of age, she jumped right in.

"He's a big fan of yours, Mr. Reid?" Edith asked. "What does his Daddy think about that?"

"Jonah's dad isn't in the picture." Eva's quiet answer sent Reid into action.

"C'mon, Landry." He stood and extended his hand to his new young admirer. "Let's go check out the other houses. These two are going to talk girl talk."

"Yuck!" Landry responded appropriately.

"No, Reid. Stay." Eva's steady gaze met Reid's over the youngster's head.

"Are you sure?" When Eva nodded, Reid bent to whisper to Landry. Calling to one of the young men next door, he passed off the tour guide duties.

Reid rejoined the two ladies, but pulled his chair off to the side where he could watch Eva but not interrupt her.

"You're very brave," Miss Edith said after Eva summarized her story into just a couple of minutes. She freely admitted her prideful attitude that prevented her from sharing Jonah's story, knowing she should celebrate how much of a blessing it was that she got to be his mom. The sympathy that the older lady offered meant Eva even shared her fears about the adoption issues and what legal

147

steps they may face in the future. Reid saw Eva wiping tears and used that as an excuse to step away.

He grabbed a roll of paper towels out of one of the tool pails.

"I'm going to get everyone back to work. I'll keep them away for a while." Handing the roll to Eva over her shoulder, he leaned down and quietly relayed his plans. Eva, who had kept her eyes tightly shut during her narrative, didn't respond.

Miss Edith had watched Reid during Eva's story and nodded to him as he left. After wiping her tears, Eva shook off the melancholy and smiled at the older lady.

"Thank you, Miss Edith," she said. "I've gotten so used to keeping my secret that I forget how freeing it is to have someone to share it."

"Is that young man truly just Jonah's friend, or is there something more to it?"

"He really is just Jonah's friend." Eva gathered their glasses and stacked them on the now empty cookie tray. "Reid and I barely tolerate each other."

Edith's silence revealed her doubt of that statement, but she let it go without comment.

"I've just recently started dating, but it is hard to find someone who doesn't automatically assume that I'm willing to jump into bed, or who doesn't view Jonah as a liability. I know a lot of people think that Jonah needs a father."

"Listen to me, young lady." The older lady's suddenly more serious tone stopped Eva's nervous movements. "Do not get into a relationship just to get Jonah a daddy. Marriage is about the husband and wife. Children are just icing on the cake."

Eva absorbed the admonition. Years of building her life around her young son had pushed her own needs and desires to the background.

"I know you need to get back to work." Edith let Eva

help her to her feet. "I'm going to leave you with one last piece of counsel. Mind you, I was married for forty-three years, and the best advice I ever received was to major on the marriage and the minors would be fine."

The double meaning of the wordplay wasn't lost on Eva, or on the man who had stopped just around the corner, listening to the last of the conversation.

***

Always one to appreciate irony, Eva smiled as an hour later as the conversation of the students turned to adoption.

Bizarre, was all Reid could think. *Either that, or God wants Eva to have some clarity.* He had finished the tarpaper on the roof and had set the oldest of the college students to work on the shingles. Several of them had roofing experience, including one who worked on a summertime construction crew. After confirming that their work was above par, Reid checked on the other sites, leaving Eva's until last.

"I could never give up my child." One of the younger girls was saying. Reid watched Eva pale.

"Even if you couldn't provide a good life for them?" The young lady's companion countered. "I don't think I could raise someone else's kid, and I don't think I'd want to be a single mom, either."

"Hey, ladies!" Reid delivered the post hole digger they would need to set the posts for the wheel chair ramp in the morning. "Sounds like you're having a serious conversation. I'm a well-known expert on just about every topic. I couldn't help hearing you were talking about adoption."

"One of the girls working on Charlie house is adopted. We were just talking about how hard that would be."

"Well, in my not so humble opinion," Reid said, his playful arrogance tempered his reproach, "adoption is actually the perfect picture of God's love for us. First, you do realize He *gave up* His son for us, right? And secondly,

149

He *adopted* us into His family. He *chose* to love us."

Eva kept her back turned and fought the desire to contribute to the conversation. Realizing commenting would lead to more questions about her situation, she kept quiet.

"Wow, I never thought of it like that," the first girl said.

"Yeah, but I think it would be kind of selfish to give up your kid just because you didn't want to raise it." Her companion seemed unconvinced.

"I think adoption is the most self-*less* act a mom could have." Reid's tone was gentle. "Giving up a child for the good of that child on one hand, and taking in a child that is not your own on the other. Both show a divine sort of love."

Eva escaped the heat of the porch, knocking quietly on Edith's door, not waiting for a response before she ducked inside. Reid followed a few minutes later.

"Are you okay, Dewey?"

"You know Mr. Jackson, comfort and compassion are starkly uncharacteristic of our normally contentious relationship. It's confusing."

"Alliteration? Well done." Reid gently closed her jaw that had dropped open. "Does it surprise you that I know such an unusual literary term?"

"Let me guess, you're either a frustrated writer or an eighth-grade spelling bee champion."

"Neither. Just brilliant." Reid turned away to help Miss Edith with the tray laden with a second round of cookies.

"Your little tidbits of knowledge continue to astound me." Eva followed Miss Edith and her handsome helper toward the front door, glad for the joking that allowed her to recover from the effect of the crew's discussion. "I can't figure out if you're actually that deeply intellectual or if you just know a little bit about a lot of things."

"So, either I'm deeply mysterious or broadly shallow?"

150

Reid blocked her path, leaning down so their noses were inches apart. "Which would you prefer?"

34

"I see the list is growing."

Outside the cafeteria that evening, Eva passed Reid on her way to dinner. He had sought the semi-privacy of one of the office doorways. His back was to the hallway traffic, talking on his phone. Curiosity won over her desire to avoid him, and she stopped to eavesdrop. *It's not as if he hasn't done the same*, she thought.

"You did what?! She's going to kill me." Not knowing *she* had walked up behind him, he turned in surprise as Eva chimed in.

"I see the list is growing."

"What list?" He covered the phone as he turned to her in surprise.

"The list of women who want to do you in." She smiled as he rolled his eyes.

"Yes, it's Eva," he answered the person on the other end of the call. Lowering the phone once more, he added. "Javier says hello."

"Hi, Javier." Eva pulled Reid's arm toward her and laughed when he pulled it away. They looked like two toddlers fighting over a toy.

"Great, now he wants to talk to you." Reid handed her the phone. She gloated over her victory.

"*Hola*, Javy," Eva said. Javier asked her if Reid was behaving. *Of course, he's not,* she thought. Watching Reid closely, she decided to answer the foreman in his native tongue. *"No, por supuesto que no."*

Reid choked on the drink of soda he had just taken. She grinned at him as he wiped the soda splatters off the office door with the tail of his t-shirt. The rest of her conversation with Javy was comprised of simple 'yes' and 'no' responses, but her secret was out.

"That was mean, young lady," Reid said. His tone was teasing, so Eva knew he wasn't mad at the fact that she was conversationally fluent in Spanish and had kept it secret from him.

"I know, but you have to admit it's a little funny," Eva said as she handed him the phone.

Reid finished his conversation with Javy after he waited for her to walk away. Before he ended the call, he remembered to ask, "Did you tell her? No? Coward." His laugh faded as he saw her stop a few feet down the hallway, in the doorway of another office suite.

"Did he tell me what?" Eva asked as Reid reached her side.

"What makes you think I was referring to you?"

"I guess there really is a list, then. Doesn't surprise me." She lifted one slender shoulder.

"Wait." He grabbed her elbow before she could vanish once more. "I'd better tell you so you can get your tantrum out of the way."

"What have you done?" Her accusation was automatic.

"Me? I've been here with you all week!" Hand over his heart, he pretended to be emotionally crushed. "It wasn't me this time."

"Well, that's once." She gestured for him to continue. "Give it to me. I'm a big girl."

"The crew did something that a normal person might

take as a gift, but that you probably won't appreciate."

"Thanks for the vote of confidence." The closeness of their conversation was necessary for any amount of privacy. It made the air in the hallway stifling, so Eva pulled her long hair up into an impromptu ponytail, using the elastic band she kept on her wrist. Her movements seemed to rob Reid of his ability to talk.

"Are you going to tell me or do I have to guess?" She poked him to get him to respond. "It's hot and I want to go back to my air-conditioned room."

"They built Jonah a play set with some left-over supplies." He delivered the news quickly, and then stepped around her.

"They what?" Grabbing his arm before he could flee, she wheeled him back around.

"See? I knew you'd freak out."

She turned and left, not appreciating his attempt at humor. He abandoned the idea of pursuing her as Adam gestured for her to join him in line. Reid funneled his anger into a kick of the office door, followed by a careful inspection to make sure he hadn't left a dent.

Eva took her food back to her room, pleading fatigue. Angie saw the look on Reid's face when he entered and knew Eva's fatigue had more to do with their ongoing emotional battle than physical exertion.

"What did you do?" Jim asked when Reid slumped into the empty chair. "It must have been really bad for her to not want to hang out with me and Angie."

"Don't quit your day job," Reid grumbled, not appreciating Jim's attempt at humor. He described the latest pitfall he had stumbled into. "Amazing how a little thing like a jungle gym can negate the entire progress we made today."

"Progress?" Angie asked, after Reid explained the project his crew had undertaken without permission. "That sounds promising."

"She told me the truth about Jonah."

"Finally," Jim let out a deep sigh. "When she told you, were you surprised? Or relieved?"

"Neither." Reid took a couple bites of his meal before pushing it aside.

"Are you saying your view of Eva hasn't changed? At all?" Jim's tone was incredulous.

Reid started to protest, but then smiled sheepishly instead. "There's no use in protesting, so I won't. Yes, my attitude toward Miss Eva Marie Conley has changed. Drastically. But not because of what I learned today. I don't think my view of Jonah, or his birth, has changed. Does that sound as confusing to you as it does to me?"

"No," Jim said. "It seemed like you never were overly concerned about how Jonah arrived in her life."

"Oh, I thought about it," Reid said. "But my reaction to the whole situation has been intriguing. When I thought Jonah was hers from a previous unmarried relationship, I didn't feel judgment, and my reaction—or lack of it— bothered me."

"Showing mercy made you uncomfortable?" Angie's brow furrowed.

"It was weird. I couldn't even conjure up a judgmental feeling when I tried to." Reid shrugged. "Must've been a God thing."

"And, then?" Jim pulled Reid's plate closer and started eating the fries.

"When I thought she may have suffered an assault and gotten pregnant, I was furious and amazed at the same time." Reid pulled his tray back and fought off Jim's attack on his fries. "And thankful."

"Thankful?" Angie intervened in the great French fry battle with a hand on her husband's arm. "Eat your salad, Jim." He complied.

155

"Not for what she must have gone through, but gratitude that she kept him."

"He seems like a sweet boy." Jim finished his salad, as his wife had requested, then started in on his dessert.

"You have no idea," Reid said. "He's wormed his way into my heart, the brat!" His grin and obvious affection softened the nickname.

"So how do you feel now, knowing the truth?" Jim leaned back and patted his now full belly.

"Honored. Humbled." Reid swirled the lemon in his water glass with his straw. "I've treated her deplorably, yet she trusts me enough to tell me."

"Well, you'll have to fix the latest detour in your crusade, but I think she'll forgive you." Angie stacked the dishes. "You can start your penance by cleaning up our plates."

***

When she walked into the auditorium for music practice, Reid held up his phone and smiled.

"Would you like to see it? Javier sent me a picture."

"That's impressive," she said as she handed the phone back to him. "I'm sorry I overreacted. Blame it on the heat."

Reid had trouble concentrating on much of anything the rest of the evening. The sight of long golden hair, unbound from its customary hair clip, served as a powerful distraction.

156

35

"Shall I refresh your memory?"

Major problems at another worksite meant the director reassigned Reid the next morning.

"You should be more relieved than you seem," Angie questioned Eva's stoicism as Reid excused himself from the breakfast table. "You've got it easy today. I have to put up Reid instead. Got any advice on staying on his good side?"

"From me?" Eva asked. "That's a joke, right?"

"Is there a special project today that has you concerned?" Angie realized she might have set the conversation in the wrong direction, so she tried to throw Eva a lifeline. Her plan backfired.

"We're putting in the posts for the wheelchair ramp. Quick setting concrete is a bit of an issue between me and Reid." Eva had lost her appetite, a regular occurrence where Reid Jackson was concerned, so she stood and swept up the crumbs left from her breakfast muffin. "I'm going to refill my coffee. Does anyone want more?"

Angie, Jim, and Adam placed their cups on her tray.

"I better get a big tip from you guys." Eva's smile faded as she saw Reid wave her over to join him and Fred. She discarded the trash from the tray and joined the two men, realizing too late that she had thrown away the coffee cups.

157

"I've asked Fred to handle the concrete for the posts. He may need you to supervise his teams at Bravo house while he does, okay?"

"I can do the concrete, Reid." Eva's tight smile let him know she understood exactly what he was doing.

"So, Fred, call me if you need anything," Reid said, ignoring Eva's comment. "I wish you had been put in charge at our site in the first place, so this works out fine. I'll check in with you tonight." As Fred moved away, Eva did also. Reid's hand on her arm stopped her.

"Is there a problem, Miss Conley? I thought you agreed to follow my orders?"

"Orders? How apropos. Should I let the crew know they need to salute you now?"

"Shall I refresh your memory?" Reid held out her arm and rubbed his thumb along the inside of her wrist, outlining the area that had suffered from her foolishness weeks ago.

Fighting to remember how to breathe, Eva tried to pull her arm away, but her brain seemed to fail to send the message to her arm. Reid smiled as he watched her respond to his touch.

"Good, I see we understand each other. Stay away from the concrete." He dropped her arm and leaned over to whisper one last request. "Don't forget your sunscreen. I won't be there to make sure you're covered."

In a daze, she only recovered when she heard Jim as he passed behind her.

"We couldn't wait for your little powwow to end, so I got our coffee." Eva left without hers.

Bravo house was one of the new constructions. Eva helped the team prime the walls so the professional company that was donating their time could spray them overnight. This arrangement meant the work campers could do all the trim work, touch ups, and install all the hardware tomorrow. Although she would rather be setting posts down at Delta house, she enjoyed hanging out with this new group of young people.

Two of the young men, Travis and Kyle, had helped on Monday with the porch demolition and had taken to calling her 'Hammer' after they were observers at the nailing competition. The nickname was one of many Reid threw at her, this one a poorly disguised reference to a famous rapper and the 'M.C.' part of her initials.

"Hammer, they need you down the street," Travis called through the front door. "Fred sent me to get you. We can finish this. I promise I won't let the children make a mess." His comment was ironic, given he was barely a year older than the rest of the crew.

The Delta house crew had finished filling the holes with the concrete. Eva checked each of the crew to make sure they were free of any residue. Fred didn't question her inspections, and Eva realized Reid had explained why he had relegated her to the other house.

"They should set up well enough by the time lunch is over." Fred placed the unused bag in the back of the van. "We can return this partial bag along with the unopened one. There may be another site that can use the opened one."

"I know you can handle the rest of the project today," Fred said, "so I'll head back to Charlie and Bravo after I eat. I'm not going to miss the apple cobbler Miss Edith has promised."

After lunch, the two adults went over the blueprints for the ramp before Fred returned to the houses he had been supervising previously. Eva set the crew to measuring the boards so she could pre-cut them for tomorrow's construction. The ramp was only ten feet long and didn't involve any turns or landings. By the end of the day, a stack of neatly organized planks, rails, and balusters were evidence of their hard work.

"Tomorrow we'll be able to knock this out in a couple of hours, I hope." Eva moved the tools around in the back of the van, having to remove the concrete bags to make room. She waited until everyone was on board before loading the full and partial bags into the side of the van.

"Watch out for these when we unload. I need to return them to the supply shed, so don't step on them when you get out." Together the two bags weighed less than twenty pounds, so she wasn't concerned about being able to carry them from the van to the supply depot. What she didn't anticipate was running into Reid.

"What are you doing, woman?!" He dropped the ladder he was hauling when he saw her halfway across the courtyard.

Bracing herself for his attack as he neared, she tried not to flinch.

"Give them to me, Einstein. Now." He reached for the bags. "What part of 'Stay away from the concrete,' did you not understand?"

"No." She stepped sideways and continued her trek. "What part of 'You're not in charge of me,' do you not understand?"

"Stop, Eva." He lowered his voice, realizing her anxiousness to get away was partially due to the attention his shout had attracted. "My male ego isn't going to survive your continued independence."

"What on earth are you talking about?" Eva stopped suddenly.

"We men are fragile creatures." He followed her as she continued her trek toward the supply room. "You have to let us help otherwise we feel useless, unneeded. It cuts to our very center."

"You're kidding, right?" Eva stopped once more, fascinated by his words. Watching him eye her burden, she pulled the bags closer, fearful he would snatch them out of her arms if she let her guard down.

"We're wired to want to protect those we care about."

"I don't need help."

"Don't need help or don't want to need help? There's a difference, Eva." He watched the battle being warred in her expression. She wanted to let go but didn't want to admit it. Knowing she was embarrassed at his public display, he stepped in front of her, blocking the view of the people in the courtyard. He knew very few, if any, were paying attention to them, but she wasn't happy to have any attention directed her way.

"Overt independence, especially when it can be perceived as stubbornness, makes us feel..." He searched for the best word. "...superfluous."

"Superfluous?"

"Yes, unnecessary, unneeded. Don't you know what superfluous means?" He took the opportunity afforded by her lack of movement to step closer.

"I do. I'm just surprised that you do." Her eyebrow lifted as a smile reached her eyes.

"Funny." Reid visibly relaxed, until he spotted the gray dust on her bare arms. "Hand them over. You have concrete dust all over your skin."

She hesitated.

"I don't have the time or desire to take you to the doctor again." He held out his arms. "Go hit the showers."

"You can't make me." Eva realized her mistake as soon as the words left her lips.

"Try me." He grinned.

"You wouldn't dare," she said. As he took a step closer, Eva heaved the bags at him.

An hour later, Eva headed to dinner. Reid was waiting for her. As she got close, he heard her phone beep. He leaned over her shoulder and saw a name he didn't recognize.

"Who's that?"

"Nobody, Mr. Nosy." She smiled as she checked the text.

"Don't be coy. Who is it?" His hand on her wrist pulled the phone around so he could get a better view.

"It's the doctor from the clinic, not that it's any of your business." She deleted the text with her thumb before he could read it.

"Not my business?" Reid's expression changed from curiosity to concern. "Why is he calling you?"

"To ask me out on a date." Eva met his steely gaze with honesty. "A second date, actually." Her arm dropped to her side as he released her abruptly. Light blue eyes searched her face, their gaze affecting Eva's composure, effectively lulling her into silence.

"Eva?" Reid's gentle shake woke her from her trance. "Wake up. You're zoning out."

"Sorry. You're very distracting." Eva blinked and shook her head to clear her muddled thoughts. "What was the question?"

"When did you go out with Dr. Delicious? And why didn't you tell me?" Reid's interrogation was starting to draw attention, so he pulled her down the hallway past the cafeteria. Eva, embarrassed over the whispered looks they were receiving, followed reluctantly. Keeping several feet between them, Eva leaned against the wall, arms folded.

"It was the evening you visited the library," she said. "That was why I was dressed up."

"So you also lied to me about why you were wearing those gosh-awful heels?" Reid took a small step closer, a wise move since Eva was ready to bolt into the safety of the dining room.

"Not *lied* per se," she said. "Let's call it a slight omission. I do like to dress nicely for work when I'm helping the students with their papers. I didn't tell you about the date because I didn't think you needed to know."

"Slight omission? That's poetic license for sure. Why didn't you tell me later? He didn't use your *private* medical information to find you, did he? How many times has he asked you since then? You're not actually contemplating going out with him now, are you?"

"Are you done, Mr. Prosecutor?" Eva pushed away from the wall and took a tentative step closer. Holding up slender fingers, she ticked off her answers to his questions. "He was a guest speaker at a library function for the Pre-Med students and recognized me. He has called several times. No, I wasn't going to accept his offer. Although I had a wonderful time with him that evening, I didn't encourage him to call me again."

"You didn't? Why?" Reid matched her move with a small step of his own.

"You, Reid," she said. "That's what you want to hear isn't it? That day at the library was fun. I knew that our friendship was changing and it confused me, so I didn't think it was fair to Ethan to say yes to a second date."

"Ethan? You're on a first name basis now?" Reid's mood had moved from concern to irrationality.

"I did go out with him, Reid. I thought it'd be weird to call him 'Dr. Dreamy' all evening." Her teasing didn't help Reid's mood. Hoping he would drop the subject, she reminded him of her earlier defense. "I told you I didn't encourage him."

"But you didn't *discourage* him, obviously," Reid said. "Is the guy dense, or do I need to talk to him?"

"No, he's not an idiot, Reid," Eva said, then bit her lip in hesitation.

"Eva Marie." Reid's voice was low, but not threatening. "I may be good at a lot of things, but I can't read minds. What did you do that has Dr. Determined calling you again?

Tell me!"

"I may have accidentally opened the door slightly right before we left for this trip." Eva smiled and measured her next words carefully. "I was upset with you the night Ethan called to wish me well on the trip. I may have told him exactly when we were returning."

"Upset? With me?" Reid asked. "Why?"

"It was the night of my movie date with Shelley. Remember Daphne?" Eva knew Reid was frustrated as he rubbed the back of his neck in what was becoming a familiar gesture. Knowing her next words would cause a reaction, she widened the distance between them, making sure she had a straight, unblocked path to the cafeteria. "As a matter of fact, I was so upset, if he had proposed over the phone that night, I would've said 'yes,' in a heartbeat."

His grab for her missed its mark. She shot him a grin over her shoulder as she escaped.

Reid surrendered the skirmish and chose a different dinner line, giving Eva some space. He had planned to join another table with his well-stocked plate, but as he neared his usual spot, he remembered Eva's cement issues. Putting down his tray, he requested that Eva hold out her arms for inspection. Satisfied with her cleanliness he patted her on the back. When she winced, he pulled up a chair.

"What did you do?" He reached for the collar of her shirt. The intimacy of his touch outweighed the pain. A very pink swath of sunburn across her neck was evident that she had missed a spot when she applied sunscreen that morning.

"I was right, wasn't I? Without me there you forgot your sunscreen." His finger ran along the offending stripe. She shivered. "Have you put aloe on this yet?"

"Yes, Dr. Jackson, you were right, but I only missed that one spot." She tugged her shirt out of his hands and returned to her dinner.

164

"You three heard that, correct?" Reid turned to the other three adults at the table who had observed the entire interchange. "She admitted I was right in front of witnesses. I need to write this down." Only one person at the table seemed not to find the situation humorous. When Eva and Angie left to get desserts for everyone, he spoke up.

"I see you've made good headway, Jackson." Adam Richter had waited until Jim turned his attention to the older man at the next table before he made his snide remark. "Is the young lady ready and willing, finally?"

A lack of a good steak knife was the only thing that saved Mr. Richter from a possible trip to the emergency room. It also most likely kept Reid Jackson out of jail that night. As Adam felt the cold metal of a dull butter knife pressed firmly against his wrist, he stared into Reid's steel blue eyes.

"If you ever imply anything remotely disparaging about the young lady again, I'll make sure to be more appropriately armed." Reid's voice was low and threatening. "Do I make myself clear?"

"Extremely," Adam said, rubbing his wrist. "My apologies."

36

"Consider it an upgrade."

The concrete was set. Kyle and Travis joined Eva and the girls. Fred had reassigned the young men to make sure the ramp was done today. The less experienced workers could handle the projects in the other homes.

Reid was impressed with Eva's organized project. His compliment was unexpected.

"Who are you and what having you done with Reid Jackson?"

"He's been replaced by a newer, wiser model." He handed her his personal drill to use for the day. "Consider it an upgrade."

"Was it worth the cost?" She checked the bit size she needed, pulled out the correct size, and tightened it into the drill. He watched intently.

"That's still to be determined." He answered over his shoulder as he plugged in the back up battery for the drill.

"The worth? Or the cost?" The crewmembers watched the tennis match of one-liners between the two.

"Yes." Reid pulled her ponytail before he picked up his toolbox and headed to Charlie house. Grinning at their audience, he added, "Get to work, you guys!"

By noon the ramp was almost complete. The spindles

were laid out, ready for the "girls versus boys" competition the crew had planned for their installation. Reid had pre-drilled the holes for the rail supports and the college students were going to see which group could get the top nails in the quickest. Eva and a couple of others would come through later and complete the installation. The guys, certain they were the better skilled, were the ones who had challenged the girls.

Landry had helped all day and wanted to be on the boys' team. Reid had bought a kid-sized hammer at the hardware store and the youngster had shown real promise when Eva let him pound in some of the nails on the ramp's planks.

"That wouldn't be fair to the girls though, buddy," Kyle had said. "They wouldn't have a chance." Satisfied with their flattery, Landry agreed to be the timekeeper.

The other homes were all at critical points in their repairs, otherwise a larger crowd would have gathered for the race. As it was, only Eva and Reid would be joining Miss Edith to observe the race.

"Shall we join the fun?" Reid had come up quietly behind Eva as the competitors argued over which two girls would compete against the pair of boys. The Reid radar she had developed warned her of his approach so she didn't jump.

"Only if you use the correct hand this time." She elbowed him in the stomach. "Don't think I didn't know exactly what you were doing the other day. I'm not clueless, you know."

"Think how much better your lesson went, though, with the girls thinking that you could beat me," Reid said. "As if that would ever happen." She elbowed him again.

Eva was enjoying one of the popsicles that a group of local firefighters had delivered. A drip down the side of her hand took some maneuvering to reach, and in the process, her frozen treat was almost lost.

"Do you need some help, Princess?" His sly look made her wonder exactly what he was offering.

"No, thank you." Eva pointed to the cooler that held the rest of the stash. "Did you get one? When the fire truck pulled up, we were wilting. They arrived with perfect timing. What a delicious treat."

"The popsicles," Reid asked with a frown, "or the firemen?"

"Yes," Eva grinned, batting her eyes as she gazed up at him. "I think it's time."

"Time for what?" Reid lowered his head.

"The race, silly." She waved the frozen treat at him.

"You're playing with fire, Eva."

"Am I?" After finishing off the icy treat, she turned back to the students. "Are you guys ready? Landry, can you count to three?" Eva knelt next to the little boy and helped him count down the start.

The boys won by several seconds. The girls were good sports, and Miss Edith rewarded both groups with fresh lemonade and another batch of cookies. The windfall was that the ramp was almost complete. Thinking she had provided him a gift, Eva turned expectedly to Reid.

"What did you tell them?" He handed her a fresh cookie. "I watched those girls hammer on Monday. I'd hire any of them for my crew at home."

"Are you accusing me of cheating?" After finishing the sweet treat, she leveled each of the last balusters while Reid nailed them in. "What if I simply shared with them your wisdom about the male ego? Perhaps I only hinted that they might not want to worry too much about trying their hardest to outshine the boys. What they did with that information was up to them."

"You rascal!" Reid grabbed the hose Eva had set up at the edge of the porch. He slowly twisted the spray nozzle.

"You wouldn't!" Eva backed up threatening him with a

168

waving hammer. "The children will see us!"

"You should have thought of that before, dearie." Reid satisfied his vendetta by only soaking her legs. She was recovering from her laughter while they sat on the edge of the porch. Thankfully, the students had spent the entire time of the water fight visiting indoors with Miss Edith and Landry.

As she leaned over to dry off her shins, the neck of her shirt slipped to reveal the pink of her sunburn. When she sat up, Reid was holding out the bandana that normally was hanging out of his back pocket.

"Stand up," he ordered. She stood obediently in front of him.

"Is it worse?" She turned around as he tied the red piece of material, adjusting it to cover the skin at the back of her neck.

"No, I'm just making sure it stays covered. Do you have something you can wear tomorrow that covers your neck better?" The front door swung open and Reid stepped away quickly. "Or maybe you can just take your hair down."

"Thank you," Eva said as she fingered the material now tied around her neck. As the boys led Miss Edith down her new ramp, she added, "for finishing the balusters."

"No problem." He spent the rest of the day at the other houses.

***

That evening as the music set ended and the speaker took the stage, Reid led Eva to their seats. He placed her next to Angie and left a spot for Jim on the aisle.

"I know it's been a tough week," the speaker said. "Some of you are probably so sore you're wondering what on earth caused you to volunteer for this torture, right?"

Laughter and cries of agreement rang out.

"We're going to help work out those kinks. Everybody

169

on your feet!" Mild moans of protest spread as they followed his instructions. Turn to your right and place your hands on your neighbor's shoulders.

Reid groaned. Jim swallowed a snicker.

"I'll be gentle," Reid whispered to her. "Let me know if it hurts your sunburn too much, and you'd better warn Angie."

"Thanks, but she already knows, since she helped put lotion on me." Eva answered him over her shoulder as he rubbed them gently. "That feels fine."

"Okay, turn around and return the favor," the director called out the instructions. Eva stood on her tiptoes and teased Reid.

"Let me know if I hurt you too much," she said. "Sometimes I don't know my own strength."

Reid's hands, now on Jim's shoulders tensed. Jim yelped. "Sorry."

"Back to the right and karate chop!" The vibrating giggles filled the auditorium as the college students pounded on their neighbor.

"Last time! Back to the left!"

Eva chopped along Reid's back. "Is that good?" She asked as she smoothed his shirt back into place.

Reid was apparently too exhausted to speak. The pair of men both struggled to maintain their composure. The young pastor seemed unable to stop laughing every time he looked at Reid, who was glaring at his friend in return.

"You okay, buddy?" Jim asked when he finally regained control of his humor. "Did you enjoy that?"

"Shut up." Reid took a deep breath, trying to concentrate on the message and not on the feel of Eva's hands on his shoulders.

It was the next-to-the-last night and the speaker reminded the crews to end well, but not to forget that the relationships they had formed this week—with each other and with their residents—were important.

"Don't leave things unsaid that need to be said," he advised. "One way to do this is through encouragement cards." Participants divided into groups of five or six and wrote short notes giving each person in their group positive feedback. The emcee explained how important it was to tell people when they're doing something right.

"Society spends plenty of time reminding us when we're wrong. As part of God's family, He calls us to bless each other. Just like we've repaired homes this week by building them up in a sense, we need to also do that for each other."

Jim gathered their group of five adults and passed out the index cards. Each person would write a note to the other four. The speaker had also encouraged them to read their notes aloud to the whole group.

"The spoken word is powerful. In this age of technology, we've lost the art of sincere speech, relying too heavily on smiley faces, capital letters, and words on a screen, to express ourselves." Eva knew the importance of this exercise, thinking of the envelope of encouragement cards she kept in her dresser. Still, this time was different. Normally very good at the written word, she struggled over one card in particular. Sooner than expected, Jim called for them to read their messages.

Surprisingly, Adam's message to Reid expressed his admiration for the integrity he exhibited. "It is a goal all men of God should strive for. Thank you for your example this week."

As the sharing moved around the circle, Jim and Angie had them all laughing as they read their notes to each other. After she read only part of her message out loud, Jim tucked the one Angie handed him into his pocket.

"No, can't read that part out loud." Jim read his note to Angie, editing what he chose to share with the group. "I can say, though, that you've made this week, and my life, fuller and more joyful. I can't imagine what miserable shape I'd be in without you."

Reid's comments to everyone were predictably part humor, part inspiration. He praised Adam for his hard work and thanked him for his willingness to give up a week of vacation for this ministry. Eva squirmed as he prepared to read hers.

"Einstein," he said. "You're an awesome mom and not a bad singer." Jim and Angie groaned. "What I've learned this week is that you can also wield a mean hammer. As a contractor, I find that impressive." He folded the card and handed it to her.

Eva's notes to each of the others expressed her appreciation for their acceptance of her into their circle, since it was a last-minute change.

"You've made me feel like family," she said to Angie, then smiled across the circle at Adam. "Mr. Richter, I think you're a much nicer guy than you let people believe, but you haven't fooled me." Seeing that Reid was watching her intently, she decided to get the pain over with, and read his next.

"Mr. Jackson." Hoping he would understand her teasing she donned her most serious voice. "You're very confident and self-assured, which when we first met was annoying, but now I can honestly say that it's, uh..." She hesitated. He sat forward, obviously anticipating the punch line. Looking at the word she had written, Eva made a spontaneous oral edit. "It makes people feel secure."

As the speaker called the group to wrap up their time of sharing, he closed the session in a short prayer. Under the cover of the dimness of the auditorium, Reid reached for Eva's hand. She didn't resist as he held it through the prayer.

"Thank you." Reid rubbed her palm with his thumb before releasing her hand.

"For what?"

"For not pulling away."

Many of the participants were heading to the dining hall. The cafeteria workers, all of them from the community, were showing their appreciation with a late-night ice cream sundae bar.

"I'm exhausted." Eva told Angie she was going back to the room. Before she left the auditorium, she saw that Reid was reading his cards. She knew the moment he was reading hers. A smile broke across his face as he read her words, *"Your arrogance is no longer annoying. I find it comforting."*

When she climbed in bed less than half an hour later, she pulled out Reid's card. Thinking about her own words to him, she was amazed at the change in her perspective. Her feelings for him couldn't be more different than they were less than a week ago.

Miss Edith's wisdom about marriage and parenting haunted her thoughts, though. Eva knew her feelings for Reid weren't about how he treated Jonah. Now, as she read his card, she began to doubt that his admiration of her was anything more than an appreciation for her parenting skills. Their "relationship" was based mainly on his relationship with Jonah. The only part of his card he hadn't shared with the group was a simple postscript. *We need to talk.*

37

"Payback's a bear, isn't it?"

Delta house was done and the crew had been reassigned. Eva was cleaning up around the porch, and checking around the exterior of the home to see if there were any small projects she could do for Miss Edith.

They would only be on site until two this afternoon, to allow time for the landscapers to come in and finish the projects. The small city had attracted some statewide attention, and the community organizers had scheduled a "big reveal" for Saturday morning.

Eva spotted an issue just off the side of the porch. The wires for the phone line had come loose and were caught on the thorny branches of an overgrown shrub. She borrowed a ladder from the Charlie site and grabbed a handful of zip ties. Ignoring the safety warnings in her mind, she settled the ladder as securely as she could against the side of the house. The girls had recruited the boys to finish the last of the heavy lifting work next door and knowing it would only take her a few minutes, she didn't want to steal them away for such a small project.

The oversized white t-shirt she wore was the only clean work shirt she had left. Its baggy sleeves and thin material meant she needed a tank top underneath to preserve some modesty. The neckline didn't cover the troublesome sunburn area, so she followed Reid's advice and left her hair down.

Overcoming her fear of heights alone on a ladder wasn't a wise plan. It was a realization that came too late. As she tugged on the cable, the ladder slipped sideways. Up close, the thorns of the bush were larger than expected and were reluctant to release their prey despite Eva's tug.

Stubbornness prevented her from simply retreating down the ladder and seeking help. Deciding wiggling the cable might work better, she shook it vigorously. The ladder creaked in protest and shifted suddenly.

"Help?" Her weak call for help was pathetic. Not really wanting anyone to see her awkward, self-imposed, dilemma, she took a deep breath. Ready to give up and work her way slowly back down the ladder, the angry shout thwarted her plans.

"What are you doing?!" Reid came around the corner and saw her swaying precariously. He shouted for Travis and Kyle, who appeared within seconds.

"Hold the ladder while I go explain the laws of gravity to Einstein." Reid shouted orders as he climbed up behind her. He wrapped one arm around her waist and balanced his other on the side of the house.

"Of all the idiotic, foolish, stupid things you have ever done, this takes the cake." His scolding did nothing to ease her fear. The shout, her last tug, or the suddenly freed cable—or some combination of the three—had disturbed a wasp nest.

"Stop yelling at me." Her voice shook. "Please, just get me down." The tears on her cheeks silenced him as he untangled her from the thorns that were now grabbing her shirt. He swatted at the angry wasps with his free hand and they retreated temporarily.

"I've got you." Reid spoke quietly now in her ear. "I'm

going to keep my arm around you, okay?"

"I don't know if I can move." The tremble in her voice was so uncharacteristic that Reid pulled her closer.

"The guys are holding the ladder. We're not going to fall. I promise." His calm words took effect and she nodded silently. After pulling the last thorn away from her hair, he brushed the long locks aside. "You're in charge of how fast we descend, okay? Are you ready?"

When they were a safe distance from the ground, Reid asked the boys to let Miss Edith know he'd be bringing Eva in to check her scratches.

"Then go on back next door," he said. "The wasps are still not happy, so keep everybody away." As they disappeared around the corner, Reid stepped off the ladder and pulled her into his arms, holding her as her quiet sobs slowly subsided.

"I'm okay." Eva tried to push away. Reid didn't release her.

"You took ten years off my life." His lips brushed her forehead. At the sound of the screened door, Reid loosened his hold and led her inside. When Miss Edith met them at the door, Reid kept his arm around Eva's waist.

"I can do this young man," Miss Edith said. Reid shook his head.

"You can play chaperone." His smile softened his command as he took the first aid supplies from her.

"I don't need protection from you." Only Reid heard Eva's retort.

"I know." He tilted her chin up. "But someone needs to protect you from yourself." He stripped off Eva's shirt, knowing she had a top underneath. As he treated each scratch, he saw that one of the wasps had managed to sting her. The welt was red and angry.

"Are you allergic to wasps?" He searched through the first aid kit Miss Edith had set on the kitchen counter.

"I don't think so," Eva said as he brushed his fingers across her skin. *Maybe I am since I'm having a hard time breathing right now,* she thought.

"Good." He shoved her outer shirt into her arms before straightening up the first aid kit. "Thank you, Miss Edith. I hope we didn't frighten you."

"No, sonny," the older lady said. "I've got a pitcher of iced tea ready if Miss Eva would like to sit for a while."

"Great idea." Reid handed the first aid kit to Edith and pulled Eva into the front room.

"Now, would you like to explain what the heck you were doing on that ladder?" His previous fear for her safety was now losing the battle with his anger "You almost gave me a heart attack."

The trauma of the last half hour finally caught up to her. Her tears were gone and under the barrage of his sudden attack, her own anger matched his.

"Contrary to what you may think, my world does not revolve around you. I don't wake up every morning and think, 'What can I do to annoy Reid Jackson today?'" Relief that she was safe didn't temper her tone. She opened the front door, determined to escape his condemnation.

The wide eyes of Travis met her. Reid pulled her back inside.

"If you guys will excuse us, I'm having some difficulty convincing Einstein here of the idiocy of her solitary trip up the ladder." He slammed the door in the young man's startled face.

Now embarrassed as well as angry, Eva unsuccessfully tried to wrench her wrist away from his hold.

"Payback's a bear, isn't it?" Not caring that she was throwing a fit in front of Miss Edith, she fought back. "You seem confused. Remember a little boy named Jonah and a fateful trip up a ladder at your bequest?"

Reid dropped her arm.

"Putting yourself in my place may be a little easier now." Eva knew she was out of control, but couldn't stop herself. "You don't even like me and you freaked out when you saw me on the ladder. Picture seeing someone you love precariously perched on a roof. Not very pleasant, is it?"

His silence was infuriating.

"What was it you called me that day?" Her scornful laugh hung between them. "I remember it well. You said, 'hysterical mama bear.'"

In an instant, her outburst ended. She grasped the back of one of the wingback chairs as she struggled to stay upright, her emotional rant having drained her. He took a step toward her, but she held up a shaky hand.

"No. I'm sorry for my outburst," she said. "To answer your original question, I was trying to reattach the telephone cable. I'll leave that to more capable hands and will join the crew at Alpha house to help them finish up the doorknobs, if that's okay with you, Your Majesty."

Not waiting for his answer, she left the house by the back door, stopping in the kitchen to apologize to Miss Edith.

"Don't you worry, dearie." Edith consoled her with a hug. "I understand completely what's going on."

The wise woman let the handsome young man stew in his thoughts for a few minutes. As she watched him from the doorway, she suspected his bowed head meant he was deep in thought, or prayer.

"You know, Mr. Reid, I'm going to give you a piece of advice, whether you want it or not, right?" She handed him a tall glass of tea.

"Yes, ma'am." Reid took a long drink of the cool liquid.

"Tell her soon." She patted his hand. "When you find it, love is something you should hold on to."

Her words haunted him the rest of the shortened workday. Checking in with Fred to make sure the other sites were on track, he returned to Edith's house. Sounds of a chainsaw reached the other houses. One of the boys who had just returned from helping Reid described the scene.

"He's hacking up that bush like it was some sort of super villain and his purpose in life was to rid the world of its presence."

"What did the poor shrub do to make him so mad?" One of the girls asked.

"It attacked Eva."

38

"I think I can control myself."

As she expected, Reid was waiting for her when she pulled into the parking lot. Unloading took longer than usual since all the tools they normally left at the site had to be brought back today. Moving more deliberately than was necessary, she hoped he would run out of patience and leave. No such luck. Instead, he joined the crew and helped them unload all their tools.

Without asking, he grabbed her tools and took them to his truck. Sensing the tension, a few of the young people waited for her reaction. Calling on every ounce of will power she could, she ignored the overt act of provocation.

Seeing that the hoped-for fireworks weren't going to happen, the college students lost interest and headed for their rooms.

"Well?" Reid closed the van doors and grabbed her hand. Pulling her around to the side facing away from the building, he leaned against the van and settled her in front of him.

"Thank you for rescuing me. I was scared, but that doesn't excuse my behavior. I need to apologize."

"Be my guest. I'm just relieved that I'm not doomed to receive the silent treatment the rest of our lives." The implication wasn't lost on Eva, but she ignored it.

"I'm sorry I climbed the ladder without someone there to hold it. I'm sorry I yelled at you in front of Miss Edith."

"Hmmm." He brushed back her hair. "Somewhat half-hearted, but I'll take it."

"You're so maddening."

"Seems to be going around."

"I know I'm not your favorite person, but I know that you're an honorable man and the instinct to protect is strong. For that I'm thankful." Eva blinked away tears as she relived the minutes atop the ladder. "I was really scared, Reid."

"I know, Eva." He pulled her into a loose embrace, knowing someone may interrupt at any moment. "If anything had happened to you, I don't know what I would've done. You may not believe me, but I was terrified, too."

The warmth of his chest was lulling her to sleep. The day's events had drained her energy.

"I'm going to check your sting, okay? Do you want me to find Angie?" He pushed her gently away when he heard her sigh, knowing he needed to guard himself.

"No, I think I can control myself," she said with a shaky laugh. "What do you need that for?" He had pulled a permanent marker out of his pocket.

"It's an old medic trick. I'm going to outline the sting mark so we can check it later to make sure it's not getting any larger. If it does, we'll need to go to a second plan of treatment."

She turned around and let him pull the neck of her shirt down to expose the red mark. His fingers on her skin made her gasp.

"Does that hurt?" He brushed her hair back and touched the sting gently. "It's warm and quite a bit redder than it was earlier. You can stop by the clinic and get an antihistamine, but we'll have to keep an eye on it."

"That tickles." Eva squirmed as he circled the welt with the marker. When he lifted her hair back into place and tilted her chin up, she held her breath.

"I'll see you at dinner, okay?" Reid ran a finger down her jaw. Still holding her breath, Eva could only nod.

After a shower, Reid caught up with Jim and Angie. They had already heard about the day's excitement.

"So, Sir Galahad? How is your lovely damsel in distress?"

"You're so not funny." Reid plopped down in the overstuffed lobby chair and stretched out his legs.

"Seems like rescuing her has become a hobby," Jim said.

"Which isn't easy when the Princess doesn't want to be rescued. I've got the wounds to prove it." He offered the scratches on his arms as proof. "She still thinks I don't like her."

"We know that Eva has no idea what's going on, but the bigger question is do you?"

"Do I what?" Reid leaned his head back, closing his eyes.

"Oh, I don't know," Jim said. "Want to sweep her off her feet? Ride to her rescue on a white horse? Live happily ever after?"

Reid sat up and started to protest, but seeing their expressions, he sheepishly hung his head.

"It's that obvious?"

"Blindingly." Angie was a helpless romantic.

"I think it's been coming for a long time." Reid immediately thought back to Eva defending him when Jonah had misunderstood their water fight. "But when I saw her dangling on that ladder today, I experienced firsthand what the cliché so poignantly expresses. My life did indeed flash before my eyes."

"Well, you'd better don your armor, because here she

comes." Jim stood and pulled his wife up out of her cozy spot on the sofa. "Let's go get in the dinner line. All this drama has left me famished."

"Where are they running off to?" Eva asked as she settled into the spot Angie had vacated before she realized it put her legs inches away from Reid's.

"They said they were going to dinner, but I have a feeling 'dinner' is code for something else." Reid watched her blush. Elbows on his knees, he leaned toward her and claimed her hands. As he did, she caught sight of the scratches on his arms. Earlier at the van, his loose long-sleeved shirt hid them.

"Oh, my!" She rubbed gentle fingers over the red marks. "Does it hurt?"

"You have no idea." Reid forced himself to remain calm. "It's excruciating!"

"Let me put some of the medicine they gave me on them," she said, setting his arm across her knees and rifling through her bag for the tube of ointment. As she dabbed each cut, he winced. "Do you want me to stop?"

"No." He shook his head and bit his lip.

"Are you sure you're okay?" Eva asked as she checked both arms once more. Dark honey brown eyes stared at him.

"Eva, don't look at me like that." He rubbed the palms of her hands with his thumbs. "We could both get in a lot of trouble. I'm going to sit back now, okay?"

"You should have just left me up on that ladder to suffer the consequences of my stupidity." Eva said as he dropped her hands and leaned back, putting some distance between them. "I'm sorry, Reid. I don't really know how to thank you."

"I wish you'd stop saying that. I don't deserve your gratitude." He held up a hand as she started to protest. "No, let me finish. I've been atrocious to you. My behavior toward you from the beginning of our relationship, and my words in particular, have been unforgiveable."

"I've dished out my share of ridicule, too, Reid, and my unwillingness to show you any grace is just as bad or worse." She took a chance and reached for his hand. "If your behavior is unforgiveable, so is mine, but I hope neither is the case, otherwise we're in an unenviable position."

When he didn't respond, Eva thought she had misunderstood his words.

"Did I say something wrong?"

"Absolutely not." He shook his head and raised her hand to his lips. As quickly as the conversation had turned serious, Reid turned it back to teasing. "It's killing you, isn't it?"

"What?" Eva tried to free her hand, but he refused to release it.

"Having to admit you need help."

"Yes." She admitted quietly.

"All this rescuing has made me hungry." Reid pulled her to her feet and pushed her toward the dining room. "Plus, if we don't leave now and join the others, I'm not sure I can resist the temptation."

"Temptation?" Eva asked. Reid ignored her question.

39

"You're clueless sometimes."

As they made their way to the dinner line, Reid's hand rested lightly on the small of her back.

"Why is the swarm looking at me like that?" Reid whispered to her, as they got in line.

"Be nice." She smiled at the group of girls congregated at the door of the dining hall. She waved at the few in the group who had worked on their site.

"I'm serious. It's weird."

"Honestly, Reid. You men are clueless sometimes." Eva tried not to laugh at his discomfort. "They were already vying for your attention, but your act of bravery this morning makes you a true fairy tale hero. A knight in shining armor is very attractive, even if he's rescuing someone else."

"You think I'm a knight in shining armor?" Reid reached around her and grabbed a fork and spoon from the utensil stand. "Why, I'm flattered."

"If you would pay closer attention, you would've heard that I did not claim that as my opinion. I was simply explaining the thinking of your lovely young admirers."

"So, I'm *not* your knight in shining armor?"

"Why do you call them the swarm?" Eva ignored his

question. "That seems a little harsh."

"They're looking at me like I'm the latest unfortunate morsel lying unprotected on the sidewalk."

"You think you're a morsel?"

"You don't?"

They were both laughing as they reached the table, then Reid had to endure additional teasing from Jim and Angie as Eva explained their role reversal.

"He begged me to protect him from the bevy of young ladies whose attention to him has intensified as news of his chivalry has spread through the realm."

"It's not funny." Reid mumbled as he tried to keep his head down, avoiding eye contact with any but his friends at the table.

"No, it's pretty hilarious," Jim said. "Do you need me to run interference for you?"

"Ha, ha." Reid said. "I thought I'd be safe with Princess Albert here, but she seems to be bored with the whole idea."

"Sorry." Eva had tried unsuccessfully to hide a big yawn. "The antihistamine I took for the wasp sting has made me sleepy. I'd just like to curl up in a warm bed right now."

Reid choked on his drink. Both Jim and Angie seemed to find his minor medical emergency a reason for a new round of laughter.

"I'm fine!" He waved Eva off frantically when she tried to come to his rescue.

"Well, okay then." Eva cleared her place and rose to leave. "Can someone come get me out of bed before the evening meeting?" Angie and Jim both seemed to suffer from whatever choking ailment had taken over their area of the cafeteria.

"She's killing me." As she walked away, Reid dropped his head into his hands. As his two friends laughed at his distress, he gathered the remnants of his meal and pushed away from the table.

Angie was still laughing up at Reid as Adam joined their group.

"Who's killing you?" He asked as his slipped his tall frame into the seat Reid had vacated. "Eva? Trouble in paradise again?"

"You'll check on her, Angie?" Reid pointedly ignored Adam. "I marked her back, so we can tell if it's infected."

"You wrote on her back?" Jim stirred the conflict with his question. "What did you write?"

"*Mine.*" Reid glanced from Jim to Adam.

"What?" Jim almost choked once more. "You didn't!"

"No, I didn't," Reid laughed. "I thought about it, but I didn't."

***

Since the evening meeting was moving outdoors around a large campfire, the start time was an hour later. The later time allowed Eva to get a couple hours of needed rest. Angie had awakened her and offered to wait, but Eva had encouraged her to go on ahead. Now feeling refreshed, Eva followed the trail of participants that wound their way toward the scenic lake at the edge of the campus.

Knowing she didn't want a spot close to the bonfire, Eva took her time, enjoying the cooler night air. As she approached the narrowing trail, she switched on the flashlight she had fortunately remembered to grab. The path was uneven and she was still a little wobbly from the antihistamine she had taken for the wasp sting.

A tall, lean form pushed away from one of the trees as she approached. It was Reid.

"My lady?" He offered her his arm. She batted it away, looking around to make sure no one observed his antics.

"You're going to get me in trouble!" She laughed, but when she stumbled within a few steps, she was glad he was there as he steadied her and held her hand the rest of the way.

"What are they going to do? Send us home?"

By the time they reached the circle around the fire, they were relegated to its outer edges. The breeze coming off the lake was chilly and Eva shivered. Reid stepped closer, opened his jacket, and pulled her closer.

"Is that better?" The darkness at the edge of the circle offered them some privacy, so she didn't mind the small gesture.

"Yes, thank you." She stepped back into his warmth.

"We need to finish our talk," he said, his cheek resting just above her ear. "How good an actor are you?"

"Why?" She whispered over her shoulder.

"Just meet me in the cafeteria after the campfire." As the worship time wrapped up, his lips brushed the top of her head before he moved back. Eva blended in with the group as they made their way back toward the campus buildings. In honor of the last evening of the week, the community was sponsoring a pizza party. Some groups were leaving very early in the morning, and had set earlier curfews, so the dining hall cleared out quickly. The groups that remained occupied themselves with noisy card games, plans for their trips home, or quiet conversations.

Reid tossed two clipboards onto the table as he settled across from Eva. She was finishing her single slice of pizza.

"No thanks." She smiled as he offered a slice from his plateful. "I'd hate to deprive you of your necessary sustenance."

"Good answer," he said. "Here." He pushed a clipboard to her side of the table and handed her a pen. "We're going to pretend to be discussing the logistics of our trip home. Feel free to nod, scribble down notes, or do whatever you can think of to sell our act."

"Are we planning something so nefarious that we need

the secrecy?" Eva handed him a napkin as the slice of pepperoni dripped sauce on the table.

"Not tonight." He finished his second slice and pushed the remainder to the end of the table. "I can't make any promises about our next rendezvous, though."

"Do you want some ice cream? I see they just brought out the leftovers from last night?' Eva pushed her chair back and stood. The look Reid was giving her let her know their conversation was going to be important. She wasn't sure she was ready for it.

"Sit," he said. "Please."

"Well, this better be good, Mr. Jackson, if I have to forego ice cream." She mimicked Jonah's best pouty face.

"I've been a fool." Reid chose not to tiptoe into his confession.

"I don't disagree." Eva responded with her standard defense.

"Can you forgive me? Can we start over or at least move forward?" He started to reach for her hand, but paused. He picked up his own pen instead and started to doodle down the side of his pad of paper.

"Perhaps." Eva watched the circles he was making on the legal pad. It was mesmerizing. "What exactly do you mean?"

"I think you know exactly what I mean." Reid wrote "*look at me*" across the page. He turned it around to face her. She complied.

"My respect and admiration for, and my curiosity about you, has grown this week to the point where I need to convey it more directly."

"More directly?" She carefully wrote out her full name, and then some song lyrics in both Spanish and English. If anyone dared look closely at 'her 'notes" they would surely question the validity of this meeting.

"Let me explain it like this." He reached across to her

clipboard and drew a circle in the margin.

"Do you know what that represents?" Eyes wide, she nodded.

"What?" He asked.

"A hug?"

"Yes. I knew you knew what I was talking about." He added several more circles, and then poised the pencil above the paper. "And as much as I'd like to draw an X—or several—I will refrain."

"Thank you."

"Thank you? For refraining?" He tapped the end of her nose with his pencil. "Or for wanting to *not* refrain?"

"Yes." She smiled, glancing up from under lowered lashes. "Oh, and just so you know, 'curiosity' has moved to the top of my list."

"What list?"

"Most romantic words."

Reid's growl was quiet enough that only Eva heard. "You remember that I'll be gone for the next two weeks for Reserve duty, don't you? Do you realize how frustrating that is?"

She bit her lower lip to keep from laughing.

"This isn't funny, missy." He dropped his pencil and pushed away from the table. "I'm going to leave now otherwise this diagramming lesson may become hands-on."

Still holding in her laughter, she simply grinned up at him. He scowled playfully as he leaned closer.

"Goodnight, Eva."

40

"I was just curious."

Jim had asked Eva to pick up the juice and donuts that were to be their contribution to the brunch at the celebration this morning. Knowing the spread at the worksite party would be massive, she planned to only grab a quick cup of coffee.

Reid was on the phone as she rounded the corner of the hallway.

"*Hola*, Javy," she called as she walked by. Reid quickly ended the call and trotted after her. *That was close,* he thought. The man on the other end of his call was Eva's father, not Javier Mendez.

"How did everyone sleep?" Eva asked Jim and Angie as she stirred creamer and sugar into her cup of coffee. Reid had settled in the seat next to her. Adam had been sitting with another group for most meals over the last couple of days.

"Fine," Angie said. "Why do you ask?"

She sipped her coffee as she caught Reid's gaze. "Just curious."

Reid Jackson suffered a sudden fit of choking. Only Angie's intervention, in the form of pounding his back, prevented him from needing medical assistance.

"Are you okay?" Eva asked sweetly as she patted his

arm, which he promptly pulled away.

"Reid's going with you to pick up the food, Eva," Jim said. "You two can take his truck and won't have to come back here to get the rest of us."

"That's not really necessary." Eva caught the furtive look between the two men.

"I disagree. Jim has a specific assignment for me." Reid watched for her blush as he winked at her. "Plus, I need to replace the bush I destroyed yesterday."

When they pulled into the big box store parking lot ten minutes later, Reid stopped her before she opened her door.

"This could be considered our first official date, so please allow me to play the gentleman." After opening the passenger side door, he reached across her and unfastened her seatbelt. When he pulled her around to face him, her position still inside the cab of the truck meant they were effectively eye-to-eye.

"Are you going to tell me about your secret assignment from Jim?" Eva tugged at the brim of his baseball cap, removing it so she could see his expression.

"I'd rather show you." He brushed the strands of hair back from her cheek and trailed his fingers softly along the edge of her jaw. His breath was warm on her neck as he placed a gentle kiss below her ear. "Perhaps this wasn't the most romantic place, but I had orders from the boss."

"Orders?" Her question remained unanswered as he continued his exploration of her neck. When his trek reached her shoulder, bared by her sleeveless top, she tapped his cheek with impatient fingers.

"Reid, are you going to kiss me?" Her free hand found its way into the hair along his collar.

"Yes, dear," he said, but continued his trail down her neck. "Those were the orders."

"This year?" She leaned back in time to see his grin.

"Impatient, are we?" Reid cupped the side of her face, then leaned forward and kissed her gently.

"That was delightful." She slipped her hands around his neck. "Can I have another, please?"

After their "discussion," they knew they were in danger of being late, so they split up inside the store. Eva grabbed the juice before picking up the order of six dozen donuts from the deli. Thankfully, Jim had phoned in the order yesterday. Reid had quickly grabbed a large flowering bush from the garden center. Paying for the purchases and then sprinting to the truck, they were both laughing as they pulled out of the parking lot a half hour later.

"If you don't wipe that silly grin off your face, everyone will know what we've been up to." He had stolen one more kiss when they climbed into the truck.

"I think everyone could see this coming a long time before we did, Mr. Jackson," Eva said. "Not that either of us would've believed them had they told us."

***

The leaders divided the ten-hour trip home into a long drive today so that they could arrive at church close to the end of the morning worship session. Eva, Angie, and Adam took turns driving the van, while Jim and Reid split the time in Reid's truck.

Jim checked them into the hotel and an hour later they loaded up again to go to a local family restaurant for a nicer dinner. After all the passengers were off, Eva climbed to the back of the van. When they had unpacked earlier, she had noticed that the vehicle hadn't been cleaned out since the first of the week. She gathered candy wrappers and empty water bottles.

"I'm waiting, Princess." Reid was admiring the unique view as Eva stretched under the seats. Surprised, she hit her head when he made his presence known. "I'm famished."

"The kids made a mess." She rubbed the back of her head. "I want to clean up back here so it doesn't take so long when we get to the church tomorrow."

"Coward."

"What?"

"Come here."

"Why?"

"Woman, if I have to climb over these seats to get to you, I will."

"That, I would pay to see." She laughed at the mental picture. She inched her way around the van seats toward him. He grabbed her hand when she got close enough and pulled her out of the van.

"That's more like it." He steadied her as she stumbled against him.

"Don't! They'll see us."

"You think they'll be shocked? I don't think so." He pulled her away from the van and closed the doors. "We need to talk."

"This isn't talking," she said as he pulled her around to the driver's side of the van. He opened the door and retrieved her purse. He slipped it over her shoulder and slipped his hands under her hair, lifting it free.

"True. I'll compromise. My preference right now is to kiss you—thoroughly—but I'll settle for you allowing me to hold your hand as we go in to the restaurant."

"No." Eva pulled the keys out of her pocket and locked the van door.

"How about when we come out of the restaurant?"

"Nope." She ducked under the arm he was using to lean against the van.

"Will you at least sit with me in the restaurant?" He followed her across the parking lot. One briefly lifted shoulder indicated her compliance.

"Perfect." He grinned as he opened the restaurant door.

"I knew that's all I could expect anyway." Eva elbowed him as he led her to a large booth in the corner that Jim and Angie had claimed.

Adam started to join them, until Reid's fingering of the steak knife convinced him that joining the college guys would be a better idea.

"I know you don't like Adam, but he's really been avoiding you the last couple of days." Eva delivered her mild reprimand quietly.

"I know, Dewey," Reid said. "I'm working on it, but can we just enjoy dinner tonight? I promise I'll be nicer to him, okay?" Eva rewarded him with a smile, then turned in time to see that Angie and Jim were silently laughing at them. She hid her flaming cheeks behind the menu. Thankfully, the waitress came to take their drink and appetizer orders.

Dinner was uneventful. As they ordered their desserts, a couple of the girls came over and scooted in next to Eva. They were sharing the pictures they had taken during the week. Eva tried to seem interested, but their arrival meant she was now practically sitting in Reid's lap.

Regretting her choice of shorts over jeans, she strained to keep her knee from resting against Reid's. That he was aware of her discomfort was obvious when he scooted his leg closer. She had to resist the urge to kick him.

As Eva leaned over to look at the photos, Reid slipped his arm along the back of the booth behind her.

"Let me see," he said as he leaned across her. Eva jumped at the sound of his voice so close to her ear and turned to find herself nose to nose with his grinning face.

"Stop it!" She growled under her breath.

"Stop what?" His look of innocence was unconvincing.

"Eva, do you want to go to the store with us?" Another pair of young ladies joined the group at the back booth. "We just ordered dessert, so it will be a few minutes. Adam said it would be better if we didn't go by ourselves."

"Sure," Eva said. "Just come get me when you're ready."

Their desserts came and the rest of the group all left to return to their tables. Eva started to scoot away, but Reid's hand on her shoulder prevented her retreat.

"Relax," he said. "The more you resist the more attention you'll draw. You find me irresistible and are fighting the urge to throw your arms around me. Admit it—you want to plant a big one on me, right here in front of everyone." He didn't bother to lower his voice, so Jim and Angie burst out laughing.

As their face-off continued, Reid watched Eva's expression subtly change, thinking how fascinating it was to already be so in tune with her. Effectively ignoring him, Eva picked up her napkin and dabbed the corners of her lips before spreading it back on her lap.

"Do you really want to fight this battle right here, right now?" Eva's expression didn't reveal anything to the couple across the table.

He grinned and nodded, then just as he took a long drink of his coffee, her hand settled on his bare knee.

"Two can play this game, mister," she said.

"I surrender." He finally managed to choke out after he overcame his coughing attack. Before she left to join the girls, he leaned over and whispered. "This 'battle' is far from over, Princess."

After Eva left the restaurant, Angie reached across the table, offering semi-sincere concern for Reid.

"You might need to see a doctor, Reid. That's the second time today you've choked on your coffee."

"You bet he needs a doctor," Jim said. "A *love* doctor!" The ensuing hilarity meant the trio missed Adam Richter slipping out to follow Eva.

"Hey, wait for me!" Adam called after the group heading across the parking lot to the small shopping center. He joined Eva who had slowed, allowing him to catch up.

"Congratulations are in order, I see."

"What do you mean?" Eva could almost hear Reid's warning voice in her head.

"You and Reid," Adam said. "You two looked awfully chummy this evening."

Eva eyed the tall blond man. So many of the young ladies at church seemed to swoon over his good looks and suave manners. Not being prone to easy infatuations, and having been on an actual date with him, Eva was less enamored.

"Does that concern you?" Eva knew that Reid didn't like the man, and she was convinced the feeling was mutual. Since Adam had never seemed mean-spirited to her, Eva decided not to immediately question his motivation. Plus, the idea of a relationship with Reid was so new that even a little jostle was proving dangerous.

"No, just offering my congratulations. He played the game well, but I didn't think he'd be able to pull it off in such style. I suppose I'll have to settle up." Adam let his cryptic remark hang in the air as he left her standing alone at the door of the grocery store.

Eva watched him join the two boys that had offered to escort the girls to the store. She replayed the week, and then chided her foolishness. *What were you thinking? A man who could barely stand to be in the same room with you is now suddenly in love with you? A week like this is not real. You've been living in a bubble that will burst as soon as you get home. Life isn't a fairy tale!*

41

"Maybe she came to her senses."

Reid kept his distance the rest of the evening, knowing Eva was leery of broadcasting their relationship. That something had changed was evident the next morning when she ignored the two messages he sent to her phone. When she joined the girls at their table for breakfast instead of sitting with him and the Baldwins, he was sure something was wrong.

"How are the ladies this morning?" Reid forced lightness into his question. "Everyone sleep well?"

Eva ignored him, letting the girls answer, and didn't look up until after Reid walked away. She dropped her eyes quickly when he turned back with a questioning glance.

"The driving arrangements are going to be different this morning," Jim said as he took Eva's suitcase and set it next to the van. "Reid has reserve duty next week and needs to get some sleep. Adam and I will switch off the driving so Reid can stretch out in the back seat. You and Angie will take turns in the van."

"What on earth happened to change her mind?" Jim wondered aloud as he watched her walk away. He didn't realize he had company until Adam responded.

"Maybe she came to her senses." Adam's comment held

198

a hint of victory, as did his raised eyebrow.

"You know sometimes being a pastor and having to be nice to everyone is difficult. Being pleased with her unhappiness shows a lack of character on your part." Jim slammed the back of the van closed and turned to Adam. "I'm going to leave you with this—rejoice with those who rejoice, mourn with those who mourn. I think you're confused about what it means to be part of a spiritual family."

"Perhaps I'm simply concerned about her," Adam said. "Their relationship seems to have appeared out of nowhere."

"I hope that's your motivation," Jim said, "but somehow I doubt it." Adam stared after the pastor's retreating form, his countenance no longer as confidently arrogant.

Reid slept fitfully for the first couple of hours of the trip. The stop at a rest area allowed for a change of drivers.

"Richter, you can take the napping spot. I'm not going to be able to sleep anymore," Reid said. "Jim can drive and I'll keep him company."

Adam's rising sense of guilt didn't prevent him from falling asleep right away. He had slept little the night before, already doubting his own motivations in what he had told Eva. Now with what Jim had brought up, his sleep was restless at best. Whether his own snoring or hearing his name mentioned, was responsible, Adam awoke half an hour later.

"Something happened last night," Reid was saying. "She wouldn't even look at me this morning. I have a feeling sleepy head in the backseat had something to do with it. I had to warn him off over some comments he made earlier this week, so maybe he was seeking revenge."

"What did he say?" Jim asked.

"I'd rather not repeat it, but let's just say it was no better or worse than the judgments she usually gets. It drives me crazy that she feels the need to let people think the worst, even though I understand why she does. Some judge her for loose morals, assuming she had a child out of wedlock. Even if true, it doesn't give them the right to judge her. Have they never heard of repentance?"

Jim nodded, and glanced into the backseat, where it looked like Adam was still asleep.

"The pity is almost as bad." Reid's quiet tirade continued. "Thinking she was a victim, yet they still judge, and treat Jonah differently, thinking he was the result of some terrible sin. How could they think that? Any couple that has dealt with infertility knows God is the only one who controls who has a child. Who are we to judge the means by which He gave Eva the gift of that marvelous little boy?"

The young pastor hid a smile. The topic wasn't deserving of a smile, but Reid's defense of Eva was. Jim had known Reid for years and had never seen him defend anything, let alone anyone, so passionately.

"What gets me the most steamed is that if they knew the truth, Eva would suddenly be acceptable, or even admired. I completely understand why she lets them think the worse."

"You never treated her any differently," Jim said.

"No, I was atrocious to her from the start, but just because I'm a jerk, not because of Jonah. How she could even consider a relationship with me is amazing." Reid's head plopped back against the headrest. "Or at least it was until this morning. Now I have to disappear for two weeks and let her stew in whatever doubts have crept into that pretty little head of hers. Frustrating gets nowhere close to describing it." The man in the backseat winced at the sound of Reid's bitter laugh.

When they reached the church parking lot, Jim pulled into the far side of the lot, so the noise of their unloading wouldn't disturb the service. Reid waited until Jim had closed the driver's side door before he turned to confront Adam, who was now sitting up gathering his backpack.

"Richter, I need you to do me a favor," he said. He held out a twenty-dollar bill.

"What is that for?" Adam didn't reach for the money.

"Go get a professional portrait done. Head shots should be fine. Let me know if the bill is more than this. I'll pay the difference."

"I don't understand." Adam took the twenty.

"If I find out that you had any part in the sudden cold front that has moved between me and Miss Conley," Reid said as he climbed out of the truck and released the seat for Adam, "I may have to rearrange that handsome face of yours."

***

As the unloading finished, Eva realized her tools and luggage were in the back of Reid's truck. Determined to retrieve them and take them to her dad's car, she scooted around the van, hoping Reid was occupied elsewhere. The service had just let out and she sped up as she heard parents greeting their students.

"Will it kill you to ride with me?" Reid had spotted her attempt before she was halfway across the parking lot. She had climbed onto the back bumper and was trying to pull her luggage over the edge. He reached around her and tugged the suitcase out of her hand. "Jonah can sit between us so there's no chance of accidental contact."

Before she could answer, Reid saw the rest of the congregation flowing out of the building. He stepped behind his truck to observe Eva and Jonah's reunion.

"Reid!" While giving his mom a boy-sized bear hug, Jonah spotted his friend and kicked to be put down. Reid grabbed him mid-leap and swung him up onto his shoulders. Eva's parents joined them as he handed Jonah

201

back to his mom.

"I've got Eva's suitcase and tools in my truck." Reid shook Mr. Conley's hand and gave Mrs. Conley a warm hug. "I'll drive them home, if that's okay. I have to check on my project." Reid pointedly looked at Eva. "Among other things."

"I know she's tired, but Eva looks more strained than I expected." Mr. Conley watched Eva strapping Jonah into Reid's truck. "Is everything all right?"

"No, it's not," Reid said, "but I don't know why."

"Plan to stay for lunch and maybe we can talk," Mr. Conley said. Reid thanked him and then secured the rest of his tools in the bed of the truck. Before getting behind the steering wheel, Reid stopped and leaned into the open passenger's side window.

"I was prepared to put you in the truck myself if you didn't get in on your own." Eva made a face at his retreating back, forgetting her son's presence for a moment.

"Mommy made a silly face at you, Reid." Her traitorous son said as soon as Reid closed the driver's door.

"Of course she did." Unable to broach the subject hanging between them with Jonah sitting between them, Reid let the young man fill the cab with his chatter.

"Thank you for the ride." Eva unbuckled Jonah as soon as the truck came to a stop in her driveway. Reid clenched the steering wheel, then leaned his head back, eyes closed. He took a couple deep breaths before climbing out of his truck.

Eva had unlocked her front door and let her excited son pull her through the house to show her the masterpiece in the backyard. Reid unloaded her tools and opened her garage door, using the code she hadn't yet changed from when he did the renovations. Carefully placing her tools on the bench, he retrieved her suitcase as her parents pulled up.

"We were serious about you staying for lunch." Mrs. Conley held up a bucket of fried chicken.

"She won't like that," Reid said.

"Too bad." Mr. Conley placed a hand on Reid's shoulder. "You need to explain what's happened since you called me. Come show me your handiwork next door."

While the men headed next door, Eva and her mom set out lunch. A shrug of indifference met Christine Conley's announcement that Reid was staying for lunch. Her attempts at small talk and getting any information about the week from her daughter were received with a similar reaction.

"I'm tired, Mom."

"Okay. Go sit down, or unpack if you like, and I'll finish lunch. It'll be ready in a minute. Your dad and Reid should be back by then."

Next door, the two men inspected the nearly completed renovations.

"Impressive, young man," Ron Conley said. "How many homes do you have in process right now?"

"This one is almost ready for market, and I have two others at various stages of renovation. Eva's was only the second one I've done."

"From what I can tell, you did a good job there, too. I'm sure your expertise was helpful this week." The two men had finished their tour and were standing in the dining room.

"At least I was good for something," Reid said.

"That bad, huh?" Eva's dad pulled out one of the kitchen stools and pointed to the other. "Sit. What happened between when we talked on Friday night and this morning?"

"I wish I knew." Reid leaned his elbows on the granite island countertop. "I have a feeling that someone said something to her to make her doubt me." Reid described his concerns about Adam Richter and his frustration over Eva's unwillingness to talk.

"She's probably confused," Ron Conley said. "Especially if what this man may or may not have told her doesn't match your recent change in attitude toward her."

"But it may match my previous behavior," Reid said. "When I think back to the things I said to her, I'm finding it hard to believe she'll ever give me a chance."

"Eva is stubborn. She gets that from me," her dad said, "but she's fair, Reid. If you're sure about pursuing this relationship, you need to make that clear to her before you leave."

***

Lunch was a tense affair. Only Jonah was oblivious. Reid's acting skills outweighed Eva's as he regaled them with tales from the week. He even managed to get Eva to crack a smile, although it disappeared as soon as he caught her eye. As Eva and her mom cleared the dishes, Reid and her dad were discussing the renovations.

"You should go over and see it, Eva," her dad said. "I hear you had a strong opinion about the dining room color."

"I'm sure she has better things to do." Reid's statement was a challenge.

"No, not at all." Eva tossed her dishtowel onto the counter, throwing down her own gauntlet. "You'll be gone for two weeks anyway, correct? I'm sure I would die of curiosity in the meantime."

"After you, Princess." Reid bowed and gestured her out of the house.

"I wanna go!" Jonah jumped down from his stool.

"No." Three of the four adults answered in unison. The five-year-old looked from one to the other in confusion. Only his mother seemed to want him to join the excursion.

Grandpa saved the day. "I need you to help clean up so we can play outside before it rains. Mr. Weatherman said it was going to pour enough to build an ark!"

"Can we build an ark?" Jonah's attention was deftly redirected as his mom and Reid headed out the door.

42

Why are you afraid?

Halfway across the yard, Reid slowed to a stop and turned to watch as Jonah and his grandfather were already on their quest for sticks and branches to build their ship.

"I love that little boy as much as if he were my own flesh and blood," Reid said. Straddling their property lines, he and Eva locked gazes locked in quiet combat.

"I appreciate all you've done for Jonah, but I'm doing fine on my own." Eva was the first to yield as she turned to watch Jonah and her dad. "The idea that you want to be part of our lives is bizarre."

"You say 'bizarre,' but seem to mean 'unwelcome.' Which is it?" Reid crossed his arms and watched her avoid eye contact.

"I don't know." Eva finally met his steely blue gaze. "Are you going to show me the house or not? I'd like to get this over with."

"I'll pretend you mean getting the tour 'over with' but we both know that's not completely true." Reid shook his head and resumed his path to the house next door. "I'll make this quick, since I have a couple hours of work to do at the office before I can leave tomorrow." Reid had given her parents all the details over lunch, while she pretended not to listen. Javy had handled all major work issues well over the past week, but some legal papers and proposals needed Reid's attention since he'd be gone for another two weeks. His flight left very early and he would have to be at the airport by four in the morning.

When she followed him without complaint, Reid stopped at the front door and faced her once more with a crossed-armed battle stance.

"I know something happened overnight to change your mind, but my choice remains clear. Until God convinces me otherwise, I'm committed to convincing you that this relationship is going to work."

"Maybe I don't want to be convinced." Eva's chin rose as Reid moved closer.

"Why are you afraid? Yesterday you were flirting with me and now you've shut me out." Hoping humor would thaw the chill Reid leaned closer and ran a finger slowly down her cheek. He smiled as he watched her eyes widen in response. "Can we get back to flirting? I was just beginning to enjoy myself."

"Well, that makes one of us." Eva leaned back and scrunched her nose in distaste.

Reid's jaw clenched as he let his hand drop. When he continued to stare at her, Eva resorted to the safety of sarcasm once again.

"Do you need help unlocking the door? Time is ticking away, and you have things to do, remember?"

"I'll concede this battle but not the war," he said as he turned away and unlocked the door. He quietly continued his self-defense. "Eva, you seem to think I'm using Jonah against you. That's not true. How I feel about you is totally independent of my friendship with your son. Although I'll admit that I'm willing to use any weapon in my arsenal to fight for this. That includes Jonah, your parents, Shelley, the Baldwins, and anybody else I can think of."

"War analogies seem perfect," Eva said. "Which is precisely why I'm not willing to continue this farce. A battle isn't a good foundation for a relationship."

"At least you're willing to admit that we're in a relationship." He laughed as he ushered her into the newly finished house. "We're in a battle all right, but we're on the same side. We're both fighting your doubts and fears."

He stopped and turned just inside the door. She had no time to react as he slipped one hand around her waist and cradled her face with the other. Despite the suddenness, his embrace was gentle. As he slid her hands up around his neck and his lips claimed hers, his fingers brushed against the skin of her back. Eva's response was instinctive. Clinging to him, she let him deepen the kiss. His lips moved to her neck and she tensed.

"No! This is not real!" She pushed against his chest.

"What we just shared was very real." Reid didn't let her move away, holding her gently by the wrists.

"I'm so glad you think this is funny."

"I don't think this is funny, my dear. Frankly, I'm terrified," Reid said, "but kissing you makes me smile. I think you should admit that you enjoyed it, too."

"Shall I congratulate you for playing the game well? You've discovered that I'm attracted to you, just like every other single, warm-blooded woman in a thirty-mile radius." Her protests were less effective as she stayed wrapped in his arms.

"This isn't a game. As flattering as it is to have you respond so passionately to my kisses, that's not all I want for us. I want to capture your heart and your mind." Reid pulled her closer against her half-hearted resistance. His breath was warm against her temple. "Not just the beautiful, tempting, and enticing outer part, perfect as it is."

Eva made another meager attempt to escape.

"Wait. I'm not done." Reid took her face in both hands,

forcing her to give her full attention. "If you think I have any interest in any other woman in the universe, much less a thirty-mile radius, then I may have to rethink your nickname." After a quick kiss on her cheek, Reid released her and flipped on the lights.

It had been several weeks since she had seen the interior renovations. Moving slowly through the living room and into the dining area, she took in all the changes that had been made to the room since she had seen it last. She ran gentle fingers across the dining room wall. The pale yellow brightened up the space and picked up the accents from the kitchen countertops and cabinets.

"I told you this was the best color," she said as Reid came up behind her.

"I know. I should've learned my lesson by now." His voice was quiet as he leaned over her shoulder. "You're always right, Einstein."

Eva's sharp intake of breath should have warned him, but Reid had to catch himself to keep from falling as she wheeled around suddenly. Her forced indifference finally gave way.

"That's it! My name is Eva. *Eee-vah*. Not Einstein, not Dewey, Hammer, Missy, or Al. And it's definitely not Princess." She punctuated each word, poking his chest with a shaking finger. The intimacy of being alone with him had renewed her reservations, not strengthened her feelings as Reid had apparently planned.

The blood drained from Reid's face as she backed away.

"Eva." He reached for her.

"Don't touch me!" She spun out of his grasp.

"Please, Eva. I'm leaving in a few hours. Do you know how frustrating that is? I'll be gone for two weeks and will have no way to combat whatever nonsense has been planted in that beautiful brain of yours."

"Nonsense?" Eva asked. "Just the opposite. I finally

came to my senses."

"There's got to be more to it." Reid took her hand in his. "In the last twelve hours, you've gone from flirting with me to freezing me out. I have strong suspicions about what happened, but I need to hear it from you."

"Do you mind?" Eva stared at his hand on her wrist.

"Tell me, Eva." He released her but didn't move away. As he brushed back a stray strand of hair from her cheek, she leaned away from his touch.

"Should I offer my congratulations or just console you?"

"What the h—," he began, "—heck are you talking about?" He searched her face for clues.

"I hear you won the challenge," she said. "He was right. You certainly do play the game well." The echo of her words faded as she watched Reid process her accusation.

"Richter!" Reid said in disgust, stepping away from her. "I knew it! I'm definitely going to rearrange his smirking face now. What did he say to you?"

"Are you denying that you accepted the gauntlet he threw down?" Eva's chin rose in defiance.

"Is that what he said?"

"Not exactly," she said, a slight hesitation in her voice, "but that's what he implied."

Uncertainty crossed her face, but she remained silent as he paced the length of the living and dining room. The clenched jaw and fists were telltale signs of his frustration. Eva's brow furrowed.

"I don't know if I'm more upset with him or with you. That you would take his word as truth is unbelievable. Don't you know me well enough by now to trust me?"

"You're mad at me? That's rich!" Her statement brought Reid to an abrupt stop. One arm on each side of her effectively trapped her against the wall. Her eyes widened as he leaned closer.

"Don't worry, as much as you may want me to, I'm not

going to kiss you again," he said as she stared up at him. His voice softened. "Yes, I'm angry—and frustrated—that you believe his lies, but that doesn't change the facts."

"I don't want to do this, Reid," she said quietly. "Please, just let it go."

"Too late. I've already surrendered. You've captivated me. I can't let you go. I love you, Eva Marie Conley." He watched her eyes widen. "I think you feel the same." Touching the spot just above the edge of her blouse with one warm finger, he added, "We simply need to get your heart and your head to agree."

Eva pushed his hand away. "I don't want to love you, Reid." Her lowered eyes meant she missed the devastated look that crossed his face. "You confuse me and I can't trust my heart. Too much depends on it. We should've known our initial animosity would be too much to overcome."

Silence met her words as Reid started to reach for her once again, but instead he let his hand drop to his side. Purposefully not touching her, Reid led Eva through the door, locking it behind them. They walked back to her front porch, emptiness hanging between them.

Reid glanced at his watch, knowing he had to leave soon or risk being up all night finishing paperwork. He took a deep breath and made one last plea.

"As drastic as the change in your outlook has been, I have to admit I'm not surprised. The idea of letting me love you goes against your super-independence and I should've realized that." Reid raised her hand to his lips, and then held it against his chest. "I'm not giving up that easily. I'm going to fight for this. If that means I have to battle your fear and insecurities, so be it. My certainty outweighs your doubts."

When Eva started to protest his assessment, he shook his head. "Don't argue with me. Not right now, please. I'm too angry to react properly."

"Have a good time on duty." She jerked her hand away and turned her back on him in dismissal. A steady, but gentle, hand on her arm stopped her before she escaped through her front door.

"Don't speak to Adam Richter while I'm gone. I've already warned him, rather strongly, to stay away from you."

"Is that an order?" Eva started to peel his fingers off her arm. "You're taking this military duty a little too far, don't you think? What right do you have to forbid me to do anything?"

"Forbid, order, request, or plea," he said. "Call it whatever you want. Please. Stay away from him while I'm gone." He kissed the top of her head before releasing her.

"Sir, yes, sir!" Eva saluted before closing the door, admittedly a little more forcefully than necessary. Out of the corner of her eye she saw her dad walk Reid to his truck. As she leaned against the back of her door, his words haunted her. *Yes, I'm angry.* The sound of his slamming truck door a few moments later woke her from her trance.

"She doesn't want to talk about it," Christine Conley informed her husband when he came back inside. Eva had retreated to her room.

"Oh, I'm sure she doesn't," Eva's dad replied. "She made her choice very clear. I just hope she hasn't done something so foolish that it can't be undone." His words drifted into the bedroom where the forlorn figure sank against the wall.

43

"Sounds like a plan to me."

Eva watched her son swinging his legs, tongue between his lips, concentrating on his masterpiece.

"What are you drawing?" Christine Conley admired her grandson's work over his shoulder.

"A picture for Reid. He gave me his address at Army camp and said I could send him one to put in his locker."

Eva's silence didn't go unnoticed. At her mom's questioning look, Eva shook her head.

"Just because he's good for my son is not a reason to be in a relationship." Eva explained. Miss Edith's words came to mind as she tried to rationalize putting Reid out of her life. *Jonah will be devastated.*

"It's also not a reason *not* to be," her mom said. "What are you afraid of? Loving someone, or the vulnerability of having them love you? Daring to depend on someone is a bit like riding a roller coaster. If you don't take the chance, you'll miss out on the adventure."

An hour later, the Conleys were preparing to leave. Eva hadn't slept well and her parents seemed to be using her weakness to play some strange tag-team advice game.

"What are you afraid of?" Her dad repeated her mom's earlier question.

"It feels like I'm on a ladder and I don't like heights and someone's kicking it out from under me. I know that sounds like romantic gibberish."

"Well, you know I've always believed that God is the author of romance, so I'm not sure your so-called 'romantic gibberish' is a bad thing."

"What if the ladder shakes so much that I fall?"

"I think you're simply afraid of who's holding the ladder."

"Reid? You think I should let myself fall off the ladder and tumble into Reid's arms?"

"Sounds like a plan to me." Her dad ruffled her hair as her mom took over the role of interrogator.

"Whatever that Adam fellow told you that made you think poorly of Reid has to be wrong. I think you know that. You should confront him."

"Adam?" Eva laughed as she pictured Reid's reaction. "Reid told me I wasn't allowed to talk to him."

"The fact that you're inclined to do as Reid asked is an indication that you don't believe this Adam's story." Her mother and father shared a secret smile.

"Maybe." Eva nursed her cup of coffee. "I don't disbelieve it either, though."

Her parents had been gone for a couple of hours when the doorbell rang. It was close to lunchtime, and Eva was still rehashing her mom's words while she made a batch of cookies. Thinking it was Javy, or perhaps the mail carrier was delivering the week's mail now that she'd returned, she didn't bother to look through the window before opening the door.

As if her thoughts had conjured him up, Adam Richter stood on her threshold, extending a bouquet of flowers.

"Oh! I'm not supposed to talk to you." Eva started to close the door.

"Orders from Jackson?" Adam laughed when she

nodded. "May I come in? I brought chaperones." He pointed to Jim, Angie, and Kendra. "We brought ice cream, too."

As the adults sat at the dining room table, finishing coffee, cookies and ice cream, Adam explained his reasons for stopping by.

"A simple apology will in no way fix what I've done. My eavesdropping yesterday in the truck—which Reid doesn't yet know about—made me see how disastrous my interference could be."

"Eavesdropping?" Eva looked from Adam to Jim. "You all were talking about me?"

"Reid and I were," Jim said. "We thought Adam was asleep. Reid made a good case for the sincerity of his feelings. It was very convincing, am I correct, Adam?"

"Yes, it was," Adam said. "Eva, I'm sorry. There was no challenge of any kind. I knew I was never in the running for your affections and frankly, I was jealous. Although Reid and I aren't friends, he doesn't deserve my disrespect. Except for the passionate promises he's made to defend your honor at the expense of my physical well-being, he's never been less than cordial to me."

"He threatened you?" Eva hid her smile behind her drink.

"Just a little." Adam ventured a slight smile of his own. "I also need to apologize for how I treated you. I'm ashamed to admit it, but I made assumptions about you and Jonah. Realizing how ungracious I was being was hard to hear, but a tough night of self-reflection has humbled me." Relief at finally confessing his guilt was evident in his voice. "I hope you can forgive me, and more importantly, forgive Reid. He did nothing wrong."

Eva sat quietly as the importance of Adam's words sank in. He fidgeted slightly and she squeezed his hand.

"Thank you, Adam. I forgive you," Eva said. She

finished her coffee and set her cup back in its saucer. They talked quietly for a few more minutes and she confirmed her forgiveness with a quick hug as he said his goodbyes.

"Eva." Jim had refrained from comment until Adam left, but now leaned over and took Eva's hand. "We all know that forgiving Adam is only part of the issue here."

Eva pulled her hand away and stacked the plates. Taking them to the kitchen let her avoid answering him. Jim followed.

"Adam's allegation only added to my reasons I'm hesitant to let this quasi-relationship continue, but I appreciate your willingness to come by." Eva rinsed the dishes and finally answered her patiently waiting interrogator.

"Avoiding the issue doesn't make it go away," Jim said.

"The *issue* has already gone away, remember?" Eva loaded their plates and mugs into the dishwasher, refusing to make eye contact with her concerned pastor and friend. Jim let her stew and returned to the living room, shaking his head at his wife's questioning look. As the visitors prepared to leave a few minutes later, Angie pulled Eva aside.

"This doesn't mean I'm ready for a deeper relationship with Reid Jackson," Eva said before Angie could launch into her case, "so don't get your hopes up."

"He loves you, Eva," Angie said. "Give him a chance to show you."

The next morning, Eva sat on the back porch while Jonah enjoyed his new play set. The house next door was complete so Javy and the crew hadn't made an appearance. Jonah was anxious to show them the tricks he was already perfecting on his new jungle gym, especially since Bryce and his family were on vacation.

Shelley and Troy were away for a week, which meant Eva wouldn't have to face the interrogation she was sure Reid's sister would level at her. It also meant her friend couldn't help with the regret and confusion Eva felt.

Shaking off the recurring melancholy, Eva turned on the sprinkler and let Jonah point it toward the swings so he could enjoy both activities at once. When Javy arrived a few minutes later, Jonah begged him to join in the fun.

"I'd love to, Jonah, but I have to work today." The foreman was beaming as he watched his young friend enjoy the present the crew had constructed. "You keep playing while I talk to your mom, okay?"

"You guys finished up early." Eva invited the foreman to sit with her on the porch "It looks great. Jonah will be sad, though, not to see all his friends every day. Please let Manuel and the other guys know how much Jonah is enjoying his present. Tell them I appreciate it, too. We don't deserve such kindness."

"I'm sure there are many, including me, senorita, who would disagree. That is why I am here. I have something for you." Javy held out an envelope. "Reid wanted me to give this to you and also to ask you a favor."

"A favor?" Eva stared at the envelope then dropped it on the table.

"Reid and I were very impressed with the landscaping you've done at your house. He wanted me to ask you if you'd be willing to do some work next door." Javy handed Eva a note with a check attached. "We need to get the house ready to go on the market."

"Me? Reid wants me to landscape his house?" She blinked at the check for two hundred dollars attached to a note that reiterated what Javy had said.

"Is that enough?" Javy asked. "He said you have free rein, and I can give you more money if you need it."

"What if he doesn't like it?" She looked at the yard. Most of the construction debris was gone, save for a pile of unused bricks and some lumber. The back of the property was already clear so she would be planting flowers and shrubs to improve the curb appeal.

"That's not likely," Javy said. "Will you do it?"

"Yes," she heard herself say.

***

The letter sat unopened on the table next to her recliner. The night at camp when they had written encouragement cards, Jim had handed her a stack of extra cards. Apparently, he had done the same for Reid.

"I'm sure you have more to say than will fit on a three by five card."

Reid had transferred his thoughts to paper. Eva took a deep breath and ripped open the envelope. That night was a turning point in her view of Reid, although she hadn't realized it at the time.

There were two pages in the envelope. The first had a hastily written note. *I was hoping to give this to you under better circumstances, but it expresses my thoughts and hopes as well now as when I first wrote it. All I can add now is that I love you.*

Reid's handwritten note was not quite a page long:

> *You've forgiven me. I don't deserve it. My attitude toward you, and the way I treated you from the beginning was atrocious. My only excuse? I think I knew, subconsciously, that when you walked around the corner of your house that morning, my life had changed. My "I've got this, God. No need for You to interfere," kind of life. Beauty captivated the Beast, the plot was set, the end of the story already decided. Now I can't wait for the next chapter. All I need is for you to give me hope of a happy ending. Sounds corny, I know. Blame it on the heat and lack of sleep.*

218

She folded the letter carefully and called Jonah in for dinner. Eva thought of her own letter, still sitting in her dresser drawer. Before she fell asleep, she re-read what she had written that night.

> *You'll notice that I wrote "comforting" and not "secure" as I shared with the group. I hope that by now that doesn't shock you. This week has been transformative. (Yes, I know that you know what that means). This evening's lesson on being needy has reminded me that I ought to be more needy, not less. I have become very self-sufficient in an effort to make Jonah (and me) safe and secure. But all my efforts and independence have made me less secure. I didn't realize how insecure until you showed up. All the contention, complaining, and criticizing was unsettling. But that was God's way of showing me that I had built this facade of security based completely on my own efforts. You challenged my independence— shook my foundation. That vulnerability didn't make me feel lost or unsure, though. It was, and is, strangely comforting.*

Regret joined doubt as she struggled to fall asleep. Because of her recurring uncertainty, the letter containing Jonah's artwork—and only his artwork—had left in this morning's mail. Eva offered up a simple prayer. *Lord, please let me know I haven't ruined everything by sending Reid away with no hope. If You are in this, please let me know.*

44

"I'm protecting my investment."

The storm brewing in the Gulf of Mexico matched the turmoil in Eva's thoughts. In Florida for barely six months and they were facing their first hurricane. Being inland meant the brunt of the winds would miss them but forecasters still expected the category one storm to cause damage when it reached them. Her parents were in the middle of a visit to the Keys, and had turned around when the storm formed. Knowing Eva's parents would come in to ride out the storm with their daughter, Reid had sent word through Javy offering space in the garage next door for the extra car. The storm's rapid development had surprised many. Eva struggled to keep Jonah from sensing her fear, so when her parents arrived it was a welcome relief. Although she had successfully hidden her concerns from Jonah, her parents were more perceptive.

"What has you so on edge, dear?" While he interrogated her, Ron Conley moved boxes around in the garage so he could fit her car inside. "I know that you know we're not going to get hit by a devastating storm. Does this have anything to do with your refusal to talk about Reid?"

When Eva didn't respond, her dad stopped his work. Eva stood, a basket of laundry poised on her hip. She blinked away tears, and then slowly sank against the wall. Ron reached her side and pulled her into a tight hug.

"What have I done, Dad?" Her tears alternated with nervous laughter. "A godly man shows interest in me, loves my son, and the first chance I get, I choose to believe the worst."

Ron held his distraught daughter as she gave into the emotions she had kept under tight control for the last two weeks. Christine Conley stuck her head into the garage to check on what was taking so long.

"Reid?" Her husband nodded when she mouthed her question.

"Eva, you need to trust what he told you when he left." When Eva's tears settled into shaky breaths, her dad settled her onto the stool in front of her tool bench.

"His last words were that he was angry." Eva had replayed the scene hundreds of times. "I think I was fooling myself. I know now that I didn't really believe Adam's claims, but I let Reid think I did."

"Did he honestly leave you with no hope?" Her dad suspected there was more to the story. Reaching out to Eva, even though it was through Javy and not directly, was the action of a man who intended to return, and who was ready to work on a relationship. Ron made this point to Eva.

"I don't want to talk about it. I have three days before he gets back, and he probably won't even stop by here anyway." Donning false sentiments, she hopped off the stool and retrieved the laundry. "Not that it matters to me anymore."

"How does the saying go?" Her dad laughed as she pushed past him. "Methinks the lady doth protest too much."

Knowing they were in for a night of heavy storms, Mr. Conley had Jonah help him secure the swing set and move the lawn furniture onto the back porch. The promised winds hadn't arrived yet and the day was blazing hot. Eva checked on the newly planted landscape next door and removed any potential missiles.

The leftover bricks were safely stacked inside the shed and the pile of unused lumber stowed on the back porch. Eva had showered and changed into a clean tank top and cutoff jean shorts, but noticed that the breeze had finally begun to pick up, so the heat was more bearable than it had been this morning. She was planting the last two shrubs in her landscape project, deciding at the last minute that it would be better to get them in the ground before the big storm.

Although several inches of rain were in the forecast for this evening, Eva knew the young plants would need to recover from the shock of transplanting, so she was giving them a light watering. Her dad had offered to finish the task, but Eva insisted on completing the project, since Reid was paying her. The time alone allowed her to wallow once again in self-pity, a habit she had perfected over the last twelve days.

As she sprayed the new bushes and flowers, she marveled at the bright blue skies and puffy white clouds. She laughed to herself, thinking that her mood was more like the huge storm brewing just off the coast.

"He'll be home on Sunday and will have to stop by to check on the house. Maybe the storm will take a sudden jog and move back out to sea. Then there won't be a need for him to come by." Her muttering was a poor attempt to mentally prepare for the inevitable. "Serves you right, Princess." Using one of Reid's ridiculous nicknames deepened her sadness. She had realized too late that she was in love with Reid Jackson.

Eva removed her gloves, rinsed her arms, and then bent to wash off the small smudge on her shin, thankful she was relatively clean since she had already showered. *Clean hands, clean start.* She mumbled to herself, then laughed at her self-indulgence. *C'mon, Eva! Get a handle on yourself. You sent him away. Get over it and move on!*

Busy with her self-reflection and self-pity, she didn't hear the truck.

"Should I have you arrested for trespassing?" Reid had been watching her for several minutes, battling his own nerves and the longing that the simple sight of her created.

Eva swayed, hose still in hand, as her thoughts seemed to take physical form.

"Hey, I'm unarmed!" He had to move quickly to avoid a soaking.

"What are you doing?" Eva froze as he approached and took the hose from her hands.

"Disarming you." Reid twisted the nozzle shut and grabbed the hand towel from her back pocket. Eva stood unmoving as he dried off her legs and then motioned for her hands.

"Manicure?" He examined her delicately painted nails.

"Mom insisted. She thought I deserved it after work camp." Eva jerked her hand away. "Not that it's any of your business."

"Ah, Miss Prickly Pear is back. I've missed her." Reid tapped the end of her nose. Before he could reach for her, she moved to wind up the hose. "I agree with your mom, but it makes me a little nervous. I don't want any competition."

Reid's teasing didn't tame Eva's discomfort as she tried to ignore him and catch her breath at the same time.

"What are you doing here?" Reid asked as he skirted behind her and turned off the spigot. "Besides trespassing?"

"I asked you first." Eva met his grin with an inelegant sniff. "What are you doing here?"

"The Army sent us home early. In case you hadn't heard, there's a hurricane coming." Reid took the hose from her hand and finished securing it against the wall. "You know, big storm, lots of wind. I'm protecting my investment."

"Your *investment* will be fine—no thanks to you. I've removed all the loose debris from the yard. It's in your shed so at least it won't create missiles to attack my house now."

"That's not the investment I meant."

Reid grinned as Eva's brow furrowed in confusion. One dark eyebrow rose over the blue eyes that had haunted her dreams for so many months.

"What do you mean?" Eva took a tentative step backward, an outstretched hand behind her as she sought the security of the brick wall.

His explanation was interrupted as Jonah spotted him.

"Reid!" Jonah ran across both yards, delight on his face. "We're getting a hurricane!"

"I heard," Reid said as he knelt to intercept Jonah's full out attack, taking his eyes off Eva only briefly.

"Welcome back, Reid. C'mon back, Jonah." Mr. Conley came across the yard, sensing the boy's timing was inconvenient at best. "We need to get inside to help your grandma with dinner."

"But I want to stay with Reid." The boy's pout was ineffective. Reid's attention was on Eva who was slowly retreating toward the corner of the house.

"Go with your granddad, Jonah," Reid said.

"Why?" The defiance broke Reid's temporary inattention. He lifted the boy up to face him eye to eye.

"Two reasons, son. One, because you should obey your granddad," he said, then pointed toward Eva before adding, "and two, because I'm going to kiss your mom."

Reid returned the boy to solid ground and shook Ron Conley's hand. Reid picked up the towel and Eva's gloves and handed them to Jonah.

"Take these home. Tell your grandma that we'll be there

in a few minutes, okay?"

"Good luck." Eva's dad grinned over his shoulder.

"What are you doing?" Eva continued to inch her way along the brick wall as Reid advanced on her tenuous position.

"Have you lost your ability to understand English while I've been away?" Reid had her trapped between him and the house. Perhaps Spanish would be better. *¿Cómo se dice*, 'I'm going to kiss you?'"

"Te voy a besar." Eva answered without thinking. Realizing her mistake, she ducked under his arm and escaped around the corner, forgetting his agility. He caught her easily.

"Are you crying?" Reid slipped one arm around her waist from behind, leaning his cheek against her hair. Eva shook her head.

"Are you lying?" He leaned back when Eva's shrug was noncommittal. "You *are* crying, aren't you?" His triumphant tone earned him a swift response.

"Yes, I'm crying." She twisted around and faced him defiantly. "There! You win! You've succeeded in turning me into a weak, vulnerable, weepy female. That was your goal all along, wasn't it? Congratulations."

His laughter didn't soothe her but she didn't struggle for release.

"You're not weak, but I'm glad you're finally willing to be vulnerable. You've spent too much time trying to do everything on your own." He ran the back of his hand down the side of her cheek, and then slipped it along the back of her neck. Pulling her closer, he kissed the top of her head. "And I'm definitely glad you're female!"

"You're insufferable," Eva said, biting her lip to prevent an involuntary smile as she started to relax.

"Why were you crying, Eva?" Reid's lips moved to a spot just behind her ear. "I'm hoping it's not because you're upset that I came back."

"No, Reid. Stop. That tickles." Eva squirmed as his lips resumed their trip, now settling on her neck. "I can't concentrate when you're doing that."

"Very well." Reid sighed and straightened up but didn't move away. He captured her chin and met her eyes. "Tell me, so I can get back to what I was doing."

"I'm sorry, Reid." Eva's eyes filled with tears again. Reid wiped a lone escapee from her cheek. "I shouldn't have let you think I believed Adam's story. I knew it wasn't true, but I used it as an excuse to push you away. I was afraid I had ruined everything. I won't blame you if you don't forgive me."

She was crying in earnest now. Reid pulled her close once more and waited. As she relaxed, the wind began to pick up.

"The storm is getting closer, Eva, and I want to get back to our previous discussion. You were saying something about kissing me." Reid leaned his forehead against hers. "I missed you, Eva."

"Jonah missed you, too."

"You're funny. As much as I care about your son, that's not why I'm here. The best thing I can do for Jonah is to love his mother well. You, my dear, are my priority." His voice was more serious as he gently lifted her face, forcing her to meet his gaze. "Now, let's try this again. I missed you, Eva."

"I missed you, too, Reid." She rested her hands on his shoulders, and then ventured a tentative caress on his neck.

"So, are you surrendering the field?" His hands tightened on her waist. "If you continue to fight me and my desire to protect you, my shiny armor will be all dinged up."

"Well, I wouldn't want that." She smiled and drew a finger along his jaw. "I like your shiny armor."

"Do you, now?" Reid mumbled around her fingers that

were now over his lips.

"Uh-huh." She smiled dreamily. Reid leaned closer, but stopped, his lips just inches away from hers.

"What changed your mind?" His eyes searched hers.

"Adam." She laughed at Reid's expression.

"I thought I told you not to talk to him," Reid said, trying to sound angry but failing as her fingers ran through his hair.

"It was hard not to when he showed up with ice cream and flowers."

"You let him inside your home?" Reid's hands tightened once again on her waist. "I'm going to throttle him and send you to time out."

"Calm down, dear. We had a lovely evening. I made cookies. We talked. He confessed that he had made everything up. Oh, and he gave me a twenty-dollar bill to give you. He said you'd understand," Eva patted his cheek. "He was very sweet."

"Sweet?" Reid backed her up against the side of the house and placed his hands on the wall, one on each side of her. "You mean to tell me I have Mr. Adam Richter to thank for you standing here looking at me like that?"

"Absolutely," she said. "All of us had a wonderful visit."

"All of us?"

"Didn't I say that Jim and Angie were here?"

"No, dear lady, you didn't." His lips on her cheek caused her to shiver. "Ice cream and flowers are the magic ingredients? I wish I had known that earlier."

"I like ice cream and flowers." She sighed. "And kisses."

"You had better mean *my* kisses or the whole scenario of the visit you just described is going to land me in jail."

Eva answered by fulfilling his request for a kiss that managed to leave them both breathless.

"I love you, Eva." He whispered into her hair that was coming loose from its clip.

"I know." She pulled him closer and kissed him again. "I love you, too, Reid. I know I said I didn't *want* to love you, but I do. I realized over the last two weeks that I've begun to view the world, life, my decisions—everything—with you in mind. It's very disconcerting, almost dizzying. It's time to let go of the tight control I had on my life and trust that God can take care of everything. I knew that meant letting you in my life. Completely."

Her speech was the most words she had ever spoken calmly to him. Their lengthiest conversations to date had consisted of her railing at him and his loudly defending himself. He grinned.

"Was that funny?"

"No, I'm just enjoying this new side of our relationship. It bodes well. Realizing I loved you, wanted to love you, committed to loving you, was the most freeing thing I've ever done. To have you voice that you're willing to do the same is an answer to prayer." They shared a few moments alone before the first hints of the storm began. It was only a slight shift in the breeze, but was enough to get their attention.

"We need to go inside." Reid tugged her hair the rest of the way out of its clip and ran his fingers through the long strands.

"If you insist." She didn't move.

"I'm staying here tonight." His breath on her neck sent shivers along her neck. "Troy and Shelley got back into town last night. They'll be able to protect the house without me."

"I know the electricity is on here, but did Javy get the water turned on, too?" Eva finally pulled away enough to look at him. "What are you going to sleep on?"

"Not here," he said, nodding toward the house behind her. "At your house. Don't look so shocked. Your dad already okayed it."

"Are you sure that's a good idea?" She ran her hands down his arms and laced her fingers with his.

"Why?" He let her lead the way back to her house. "Don't you trust me?"

"You, yes." She squeezed his hand before she let it go. "Me, I'm not so sure." She eluded his grasp with a laugh.

45

"It's a gift."

Jonah had willingly given up his bed to his mom, since he was getting to sleep in the pup tent Reid had set up. The Conleys settled into Eva's room while she helped Reid open the futon in the living room.

"Are you sure this will be okay for you?" Eva asked as she tucked in the sheets. "I think it's comfortable, but I can sleep just about anywhere."

"Eva, I'm a big boy, and believe me, compared to some of the places I've had to sleep on duty, this will be delightful." He pulled her down onto his lap in the recliner next to his makeshift bed. A few minutes later, he moved her to the edge of the futon. "You can't stay here, you know."

"I know. I'm just trying to get used to this idea still." She made no move to leave. "Plus, I *do* like you. Quite a lot."

"What are you finding so difficult to get used to?" He ran his fingers along her cheek.

"Stop. I can't think when you do that." She stilled his hand and leaned her forehead against his. "I've been miserable for the last two weeks. I was terrified that I had ruined everything and that you wouldn't come back. I'm sorry I doubted you."

"The fact that I love you past the point of total distraction means I'm going to fight for you. Even if I have to chase you up a ladder so I can rescue you again." He treated himself to another brief kiss. "You do realize I'm a stubborn, impatient man and I'm used to getting my way?"

"Oh, no! I think I've changed my mind." She stood quickly before he could react.

"Get back here, ma'am." He hauled her back onto the arm of the recliner. "I am impatient, and this relationship," Reid said as he captured her hand and kissed the palm, "is going to be official soon, do you understand?"

Eva's silence hung between them.

"I sense hesitation. Am I correct?" Reid tilted her chin up when she still didn't answer. "We'll talk about this tomorrow. Go to bed, now."

A small pout turned to a teasing smile. Reid was relieved that the playfulness had replaced her doubts, if only briefly.

Indulging in one more kiss, he gently placed her back on her feet. "Please, Eva. You need to go now otherwise all this talk about sleeping will be pointless. This is far too tempting for me to maintain any level of self-control."

"I hope Jonah will sleep through the noise if the storm is worse than predicted." Eva let Reid push her gently toward her son's room. She turned at the door and slipped her arms around his neck. "I love you. Thank you for coming back to me."

"There was never another option," he said and kissed her once more. "Go, now, Eva. Please." He repeated his plea and heard her chuckle as she closed the door.

The futon turned out to be surprisingly comfortable, so Reid was surprised to be awake a couple of hours later. Surprise turned to delight as he opened his eyes to see Eva bent over him.

"Reid, wake up!" Her frantic whispers and gentle nudges were finally penetrating his sleepy fog. The last two weeks

231

had been physically and emotionally exhausting. His body resisted the interruption. "The shutter outside Jonah's window is banging. I'm afraid it's going to break the window."

"I'm awake!" Reid slipped his t-shirt back on, grinning at Eva's wide eyes and thinking back to a similar look at work camp. He couldn't resist reminding her. "See anything you like?"

"Yes." Eva was glad the darkened room hid her red cheeks. She resorted to teasing and rolled her eyes. "But that discussion will have to wait."

"It sounds like the rain has died down," Reid said as he slipped on his shoes and grabbed an umbrella from her hall closet. "We must be between bands of the storm. Maybe we won't get too soaked." They made short work of the repair. Eva held the umbrella and flashlight as Reid re-anchored the shutter. They moved quietly around the outside of the house so he could check the others.

"I hope the noise wasn't loud enough to wake my mom and dad," Eva said as they quietly slipped off their wet shoes on the back porch. They had avoided getting too wet and were content with wrapping up in big beach towels to dry off. "What time did the power go out?"

"A couple hours ago, I think." Reid said. "The sun should be up soon, not that we'll be able to see it." He watched Eva rub the ends of her hair with the edge of the towel. As she began to wrap it around her waist, he grabbed the end and pulled her onto the futon. They fell backwards.

"Reid." His kiss silenced her plea. When her fingers touched his hair, he sat up quickly.

"Jonah's awake." He stood and nodded toward the boy's room. "Go get him."

She returned a couple of minutes later to find that Reid had returned the futon to sofa stance, and had set up his pillows for her to place Jonah on. The little boy settled back to sleep, leaning against Reid. As Eva lit a couple emergency candles, Reid lifted the boy gently, moving him to make room for Eva to sit between them.

"He's back asleep." Reid whispered as he brushed her damp hair back from her cheek.

"So am I." Eva snuggled deeper into his warmth.

"To be asleep, you're awfully lucid," Reid replied.

"It's a gift." Eva felt Reid's quiet laughter as he pulled her closer to his chest.

"I love you," Reid said. "Beyond all reason and rhyme. To the moon and back. So much it hurts."

"You're talking awfully crazy for being awake, mister." Eva tilted her face up to his.

"It's a gift," he said, then kissed her deeply before carrying Jonah back to bed.

46

"Get used to it."

The hurricane was long gone, but the electricity had only come back on mid-morning. The boys—Reid, Jonah, and Eva's dad—had occupied themselves with a massive construction project as they waited for the trailing rain to pass, surpassing the castle fort Bryce and Jonah had made weeks ago. Mr. Conley helped clean up the few limbs that had fallen as Reid ascertained that neither house had sustained any significant damage. Eva's parent left early the next day, anxious to get to Derek's since Mariella was due any day.

A week later, Reid and Jonah were diligently unloading the dishwasher. As they completed the task, an onerous one if their complaining was any indication, Reid suggested they go outside to enjoy the sunset. A spectacular display of pinks and purples spread across the evening sky as Jonah climbed up onto the play set and Eva joined Reid on the bench under the live oak.

"Do you remember this spot?" Reid gently twisted a strand of her hair around one of his fingers. "It's where I first saw you. Fiery hair, even fiercer temper."

"I can dye my hair if you like."

"Don't you dare!"

"I know you don't like redheads. You prefer brunettes. You said so the day I threw the nails at you."

"You didn't throw the nails at me—although you wanted to." Reid had now buried his hands in her long locks. "Did I really say that?"

"Yes, you did." Eva's head rested on his chest as she relaxed under his skillful hands.

"Just shows how crazy you make me." Reid pulled back and lifted her face. "When I first saw you come around the corner of your house, the light caught your hair. It was dazzling."

"I don't recall that being the term you used. I think you called it flaming," she said, "like my temper."

"Don't remind me." He kissed her in belated apology. "By the time we had our nail fight it had been several days and I realized that I was having a hard time keeping my eyes off you. I only said that I didn't like redheads because I hadn't yet realized that they were actually my favorite."

"You're silly."

"It's all your fault." Reid leaned back, one arm along the top of the bench, his fingers tracing circles on her bare arm. "I'm beyond fixing, but I wouldn't mind if you tried."

"To fix you?" She wrapped her arms around his waist, and nestled her head under his chin.

"Herculean feat, I admit." Reid untangled her arms and put a few inches of space between them. "Are you up for the challenge?" He watched her expression as she paled and pulled away, just as she did each time Reid ventured into this topic.

"Don't, Reid."

"Eva, talk to me. You know where this is going, and you've done nothing to convince me you don't feel the same. Both your brother and your parents said they knew this was inevitable within minutes of meeting me. Surely you trust them, so why the hesitation?" Reid tugged her

235

gently back into his arms.

"Why can't we just agree that we're a couple?"

"That's not good enough for me. I want to spend my life with you, to make it our life. If I recall correctly, you said something very similar the day of the hurricane. Where are these doubts coming from?" He felt her tremble.

"There's something I haven't told you." Eva took a shaky breath. "I'm afraid when I do, you'll change your mind. I don't want to mess this up."

"Not a chance," Reid said. "I love you. Unless you have a secret husband stashed somewhere, you're not getting out of this, so go ahead and tell me." His humor earned a watery giggle.

"It's about Jonah," she said.

"I know you're still concerned about the adoption," Reid said, aware of the legal issues that were still being resolved. Candy's recollections of those weeks were vague. She never claimed unwillingness in the liaisons, but was unable to narrow down the list of men who could be Jonah's biological father. The lawyers were working to satisfy the notification requirements before the adoption could be finalized.

"Not that part," Eva said. "This is more about me and the events before he was born."

"Eva, nothing you can tell me is going to change my intentions." Reid adjusted his position so he could see her face. "Tell me. You've carried this burden long enough, let me help."

Eva fiddled nervously with the hem of her shorts, fingering the embroidery along the edge. Teary eyes finally lifted to meet Reid's.

"I've given you the wrong impression about my life at the time that Candy got pregnant. Her situation could've easily been mine." Over the next few minutes, Eva shared more honestly with Reid than she had with anyone in the last six years. A popular roommate her freshman year led Eva on a wild round of parties almost every weekend. Candy, who had been frequenting parties since she was a teenager, would often join them. The scenes were completely out of Eva's comfort zone, but the temptations were fierce. A young man befriended her at a party one weekend and then made a point of pursuing her romantically over the next couple of weeks. At the time, her only experiences with men were casual dates and a couple youthful romances in high school.

"One Friday night we hit several parties, and I had a few more drinks than normal." Eva stared past Reid, the memories obviously painful. "I don't remember much until he was opening the door to his room." Reid sat quietly as she finished her story. Someone down the hall recognized Eva from church. Knowing her date's reputation, the young man intervened. He was one of the college's star basketball players and his size alone made the offender's decision to relinquish her an easy one. Eva found out later that the whole deal was part of a bet.

"A bet?" Reid tensed. "I'm going to resist asking for his name and current location. That also explains why you were so upset by Richter's accusation."

"I realized that, and should've told you then, but I'm still ashamed of how naive I was," Eva said. "He had wooed me well and I was so ashamed. I requested a new roommate and switched dorms mid-semester. Candy made it clear she thought my embarrassment was childish. Her pettiness led me to do something I've regretted ever since. She was making bad choices and, although I did try to warn her once, I didn't try hard enough. She basically told me to mind my own business."

"Obviously, Candy knew you cared, though, since she reached out to you for help when she needed someone."

"I'm sorry I didn't tell you before. You've been so

honest with me about your journey, and your relationships, but I just couldn't face you with the truth."

"I love you, Eva Marie." Reid pulled her close and whispered quietly. "You're precious to me. All of you. Your past, present, and future. My mistakes, your missteps, my successes, and yours, all come together to make us who we are. Please don't ever think you can't share your deepest thoughts and feelings."

Eva relaxed in his arms and they sat quietly for a few minutes, enjoying the cool evening. "You know what I miss, Reid?" She fingered the buttons on his shirt. "The nicknames."

"Really?" Reid leaned away so he could see her expression. "I thought you made your feelings quite clear."

"I'm a girl, remember? I can change my mind," she said. "Why so many choices, though? I never could understand why you kept adding new ones."

"The plethora of names was merely a reflection of the complexity of your character." Reid delivered his defense with a serious, scholarly tone. When Eva stopped laughing, he continued. "Every nuance of your personality seemed to demand a new name. I couldn't help myself. I will gladly resume their use, Princess." He punctuated his announcement with a kiss.

Pulling out his phone as their conversation waned, Reid brought up the adoption issues again. "I have an idea." Eva sat in disbelief as she listened to his call.

"Richter? I've got a favor to ask," Reid said. "Your sister's a family lawyer, isn't she?"

47

"Always, my fair lady."

The pink slip was actually printed on standard white paper. Even though Eva had been warned about the letter—and been assured that it was simply routine—it was still a shock. The university's new president was taking a radical move to deal with a public relations fiasco that had arisen at the end of the semester. Allegations of nepotism and favoritism had monopolized the news for several days. The former president took early retirement at the request of the Trustees.

All clerical positions and support staff had to re-apply for their positions. The letter in her hand served as her official notice. The head librarian, as well as the trustee in charge of the library oversight, had assured the entire staff that none were in danger of permanently losing their positions.

Still, it was enough to cause Eva to be unusually quiet during dinner. Reid had arranged for a babysitter so his sister and Troy could join them for a date night. Shelley's talkative personality covered most of Eva's quiet, but Reid was aware something was wrong.

"Dewey, are you going to tell me or am I going to have to drag it out of you?" Reid tended to reserve the silliest of her nicknames for when she was most pensive.

"I got a pink slip in the mail today." Eva had glanced across the table to make sure the other couple was still looking at the dessert menu before she whispered quietly to Reid. Despite the dimness of the restaurant, she saw his surprise.

"A pink *slip*?" His voice cracked. "Oh, a *pink* slip. I was picturing something entirely different."

"What's so funny?" Shelley asked as Eva wiped tears from her eyes and struggled to regain her composure. Eva simply waved as another round of giggles overtook her.

"Just a slight misunderstanding. Go back to your menus," Reid said. When Eva finally caught her breath, she returned to her explanation.

"I know it's just a formality, but it was disconcerting nonetheless," she said with a sigh.

"You know you could always work for me," Reid said. The waitress appeared at that point and he ordered coffee and a piece of cake for them to share. "Your landscaping skills are superb. Besides, family-owned enterprises survive economic downturns better than other small businesses."

"Family-owned businesses?" Eva blinked up at his grinning face.

"Now whose turn is it to be obtuse?" He leaned his forehead against hers and whispered. "You know exactly what I mean, Princess."

Their desserts arrived so Eva didn't have to respond. Shelley couldn't resist commenting on Reid's teasing.

"Leave Eva alone, little brother," she said. "You're making her blush."

***

The promised reprieve from the university came three days later. Eva was officially re-hired and Reid came over for dinner to celebrate. A day of rain meant his work had

240

wrapped up early, so he and Jonah spent the extra time building another fortress.

"Jonah," Eva called from the kitchen while she took the last pan of cookies out of the oven. Before he could tunnel out of their makeshift castle, Reid shook his head.

"There's no Jonah here, milady." Reid winked as he put a finger over Jonah's grinning lips.

"Who's going to eat these cookies then?" Eva stuck her head around the corner and observed the hurried movement under the blanket that now hung from the ceiling fan. "Are you sure there's no Jonah in there?"

"No Jonah in here, but there is a hungry dragon."

"Oh no," Eva leaned against the kitchen doorway. "That's too bad. I'm afraid of dragons. Is it a big scary one?"

"Come see for yourself if you dare!" Reid stuck his head out from under the blanket and gestured with one finger and a wink.

"Are you the brave knight guarding the dragon's lair?" Eva knelt at the entrance of the castle. "Will you protect me?"

"Always, my fair lady," Reid said in a whisper. For Jonah-the-dragon's benefit, he offered a slightly louder response. "Only those pure in heart, and beautiful ladies, are safe."

The dragon offered up a vicious roar.

"Oh, and he says, those bearing gifts of cookies are safe, too." Reid tugged Eva's hand, causing her to stumble onto the pillows forming the wall of the fortress. "Are you brave enough?"

"Reid, you're not supposed to kiss the enemy!" Jonah protested as the two adults seemed to forget about his fierce hunger. "Mommy, you're not playing fair!"

"That's Princess Mommy to you, son!" Reid said as he lifted the dragon out of the castle. Jonah's green sweatpants and long-sleeved t-shirt were paired with a bright green baseball cap with a dragon logo on it. It was an unconventional, but effective, costume.

After the ferocious beast consumed the Princess's offering, the brave knight volunteered to settle him in front of the television with a half hour cartoon while she cleaned the kitchen. As the show was beginning, Jonah climbed onto Reid's lap.

"Reid, when are you going to suppose?"

"Suppose?" Reid paused the show and turned his attention to the sleepy boy.

"Yeah, you know when you say, 'Will you marry me?' and she says, 'I suppose.' Grandpa says you're probably going to."

Reid fought to hide his laughter.

"So, it'd be okay with you if I marry your mom? That will make me your Daddy, you know." Reid and Eva had just received word from Adam's sister, Becca, that the adoption legalities were finally settled. Still, typically the adoption wouldn't be official for three or four months.

"I know. I wanted to call you Daddy already but Mommy said I couldn't yet."

"Do you think she's okay with marrying me?"

"Oh, I know she is. She's got a big ol' fat magazine with a bunch of wedding pictures in it next to her bed." Jonah's opinion of his mom's reading selection was evident.

"Yucky girl stuff, huh?"

"I guess it's okay," Jonah said with a shrug. "For a girl. She says I'll have to dress up too, probably."

"I know, son, but you'd better get used to it." Reid clicked the cartoon back to play. "You'd be surprised at what we men have to do to make our women happy."

242

48

"I suppose I must."

The stacks of periodicals were neat and Eva was now re-shelving the encyclopedias that students had left on tables or shelved incorrectly. She struggled with some of the heavy tomes and finally set a large edition on the shelf behind her while she climbed on the step stool to reach the upper shelf.

"How many times do I have to tell you to stay off ladders?" Reid's voice caused Eva to wobble slightly. Only his hands reaching through the shelf and grabbing her waist prevented her from falling.

"Reid!" She batted his hands away and leaned down to see his grinning face in the next aisle. "What are you doing here?"

"Never mind what I'm doing here, woman," Reid said. "You didn't answer my question. Why are you practicing acrobatics without my presence?"

"Hoping some gallant knight will come by and save me. Climbing on ladders has served me well in the past." She let him claim her hand between the books.

"It took me forever to find you back here." He kissed her palm gently. "I was told there was a gorgeous red head wandering the library. I'm glad it wasn't an urban legend."

"Well, if I see her, I'll tell her you're looking for her." Eva grabbed her previous burden and pointed to the end of the row. "You may be disappointed, though."

"Disappointed?" They walked down separate aisles, but continued their flirtation at each available opening.

"Yes, I hear she's madly in love and the lucky man is fiercely protective of her affections."

"Lucky man, indeed." Reid pulled her into an alcove at the end of the row and kissed her.

"Stop!" Eva's protest was not convincing as she responded to his kiss.

"Meet me in the Ancient History section," Reid said in an exaggerated whisper. "We can make out."

"Tempting, but I don't want to lose my job." She handed him the large book and led the way to the correct shelf. After he slipped it back into its spot, she thanked him with a quick kiss.

"Now, why are you really here?" They were making their way slowly through the aisles as she looked for stray books. "It's not often I see you dressed up like this during the day."

Eva allowed him to seat her in a secluded corner. There were only a handful of students and faculty currently in the library guaranteeing a level of privacy.

"This one's my favorite, you know." One slender finger outlined the buttons on the front of his shirt.

"Oh, I know," he said as she traced the stripes of blue and dark purple. "I'm here to deliver a proposal." She had given his business cards to several college professors and staff members. Her efforts had netted him several projects.

"That's nice," she said. "What kind of job is it?"

"Part repair, part new construction," he said, his lips against her ear.

"Um, that's nice." Preoccupied by the kisses he was sneaking onto her neck, she missed his grin at her distracted repetition.

"I'm not sure you understand, Eva." Reid untangled her arms and put a few inches of space between them.

"Do you remember the conversation we had on the bench a while ago about my pitiful state? You expressed some interest in the task of fixing me. Are you still up for the challenge?"

"Most definitely." She grinned.

"It may take you a while," Reid said. "A long while. Like a lifetime."

Eva's grin faded and she blinked away sudden tears as he slipped off the bench and knelt in front of her.

"Will you, Eva Marie Conley, save me from myself, and make my life complete?" Reid kissed the palm of her hand. "Marry me?"

She stared at the blueness of his eyes, enhanced by the hint of his own tears. Then her grin returned and she sighed dramatically.

"I *suppose* I have to." One dark eyebrow rose and he growled playfully. "Since I love you beyond all reason." She pulled him to her and kissed him.

49

"Good news comes in threes."

Eva answered the fourth phone call from her husband with a sigh. "This is going to be a long nine months if you call every hour to check on me."

"Sorry," Reid's words did not match his tone. "I've never done this before."

"Neither have I, remember?" Eva laughed. "But I hear that women have been doing this successfully for thousands of years."

"True, but none of them were my wife."

"Well, as excited as you are about this, I should warn you that Jonah has news, too." The kindergarten teacher's aide had called Eva during Jonah's snack time.

"I can't wait. Now if you tell me we have chocolate cake for dessert, I can officially say that good news comes in threes."

"Ugh," Eva said. "Chocolate cake doesn't sound very appealing right now, but we'll see."

As they stared at the large pink plus symbol on the home pregnancy test that morning, they knew Eva's recent queasiness now had an explanation

"Is it bad?" Reid asked, concern evident in his voice. "What can I do?"

"I'll be fine, Reid. Go back to work. I love you." Eva hung up the phone, grabbed a handful of crackers from her lunch bag, and settled down to browse the book she had found in the prenatal section. It would make for some not so light, but highly informative reading during her afternoon break. An unexpected call ten minutes later let her know their evening would be delightful.

The sight of Adam Richter enjoying a glass of iced tea at his kitchen island didn't surprise Reid. Although Adam's sister had worked diligently since they had first contacted her—and her assurances had cleared away Eva's objection to setting a wedding date—they were still dealing with papers that needed attention six months later.

"Coach Richter's here, Daddy," Jonah informed Reid unnecessarily. Adam and the couple had become good friends. His colorful reputation, or most of it, was a fabrication that he had never bothered to squelch, having enjoyed the 'bad boy' attention it earned him. The last few months he had not only mended the mess he had made but with the help of the newlyweds, he had worked hard to get people to see the real Adam. In the fall he had volunteered to help Reid with Jonah's soccer team and this season he was the basketball coach for the group of five- and six-year-old boys.

Eva greeted her husband with a quick kiss before pouring him a glass of tea.

"How are you, Princess? I love you." Reid whispered, ignoring their guest, before he took her drink offering. Setting the glass on the counter, he kissed her, his embrace unexpectedly passionate, given that they had an audience.

"C'mon, Jackson!" Adam covered his eyes with widespread fingers, ineffectively blocking his view of the kiss. "You already stole the only girl worth pursuing from right under my nose. There's no need to rub it in!"

"Why are you here, Adam?" Reid took a drink of the tea.

"Show your dad your surprise, Jonah." Knowing the whole truth behind Adam's errand, Eva interrupted before the realtor could respond.

"I lost a tooth, Daddy!"

"Awesome, son. After dinner, I'll show you how to squirt water through that cool gap."

"Mommy already did." Jonah grabbed his cup off the counter.

"She did, did she?" Both Adam and Reid looked in awe at Eva who had moved out of Reid's embrace and was feigning interest in the spaghetti sauce on the stove.

"I can show you!" Jonah took a large sip of water.

"No, Jonah, not now." Eva turned him toward the porch. "Go back out and pick up your toys. Dinner will be ready in a few minutes."

"Adam? Your turn," Eva said. She slipped her arms around Reid's waist and whispered in his ear. "Remember what you said about good news coming in threes?"

Councilman and realtor, Adam Richter, pulled an envelope out of his expensive Italian-made business suit.

"My sister is a formidable foe, but an even better friend," he said. "She asked me to deliver this personally."

Eva felt Reid tense.

"As Eva has apparently already guessed," Adam continued, "it *is* good news. Congratulations, Mr. and Mrs. Jackson. You are now officially parents." Reid stared at the notarized, signed, official birth certificate listing Reid Byron Jackson and Eva Marie Jackson as the parents of Jonah Conley Jackson.

***

With his sleepy wife's hair spread across his chest later that evening, Reid brushed her forehead with his lips.

"Do you think we were wrong to tell Adam about the baby before we told Jonah, or our parents?"

"No, dearest," Eva smiled against the warmth of his shoulder. "He deserved to be rewarded for being the bearer of such good news."

"Speaking of good news," Reid said, pulling her chin up for another quick kiss, "The tooth, the baby, the adoption. Good news did come in threes today."

"Yes, it did." Eva wrinkled her nose as Reid brushed the hair back from her face. "I love you, Reid Jackson."

"I know," he said as he kissed her brow. "You can't help yourself."

"Silly boy." Eva poked him in the ribs. He settled next to her, propped on an elbow, and smiled down at her.

"I have an issue to discuss with you, Mrs. Jackson." Reid kissed the end of her nose. "I think you owe me a proper kiss to make up for my disappointment."

"Disappointment?" Eva ran warm fingers down his cheek.

"I was really looking forward to chocolate cake."

A Note from the Author

I hope you enjoyed Reid and Eva's story. Their banter always makes me laugh.

The inspiration for this story came from the opportunities I've had to participate in home repair and service projects through my church. The students and youth leaders that serve on these trips experience the joy of giving without expecting anything in return. One of the most often repeated statements is, "They blessed me much more than I did them."

I would encourage you to seek out opportunities through your local church, food banks, and volunteer service organizations, as well as national groups such as Habitat for Humanity and Group Mission Trips.

My dear friends, stand firm and don't be shaken.
Always keep busy working for the Lord.
You know that everything you do for him is worthwhile.
I Corinthians 15:58

~Lyn

P.S. I *love* to hear from my readers. Let me know your favorite characters, if you're inspired, and how God uses humor and romance in your life! Find me on my Facebook page: Lyn Ellerbe Books